ED McBAIN

ROMANCE

WARNER BOOKS

A Time Warner Company

WARNER BOOKS EDITION

Copyright © 1995 by Hui Corporation
All rights reserved.

Cover design by Jackie Merri Meyer
Hand lettering by Carl Dellacroce

Warner Books, Inc.
1271 Avenue of the Americas
New York, NY 10020

W A Time Warner Company

Printed in the United States of America

Originally published in hardcover by Warner Books.
First Printed in Paperback: March, 1996

10 9 8 7 6 5 4 3 2 1

"Ed McBain owns this turf."
—*New York Times Book Review*

*

"The best crime writer in the business."
—*Houston Post*

*

"It's easier by far to set aside popcorn after two bites than to put down one of McBain's novels."
—*Washington Post*

*

"Good, solid McBain for the legions of his fans."
—*Cosmopolitan*

*

"The hot wire style has kept McBain ahead of the competition for three decades."
—*Philadelphia Inquirer*

*

"A master storyteller."

—*Washington Times*

*

"No living mystery writer creates more suspenseful scenes or builds plots better than McBain."
—*Greensboro News & Record*

*

"McBain remains fresh and inventive. . . . The faithful reader will not be disappointed."
—*San Antonio Express-News*

*

"You'll be engrossed by McBain's fast, lean prose."
—*Chicago Tribune*

more . . .

"McBain has fun in this 48th 87th Precinct tale, weaving romantic dialogue into the investigation and taking shots at various dramatic personae. . . . When McBain has fun, so do his readers."

—Publishers Weekly

*

"The McBain stamp: sharp dialogue and crisp plotting."

—Miami Herald

*

"McBain redefines the American police novel. . . . He can stop you dead in your tracks with a line of dialogue."

—Cleveland Plain Dealer

*

"He keeps getting better. . . . His plots have become more complicated, and he juggles his subplots, his sidebar stories, with practiced—and improved—skill and surety. . . . McBain remains a literary boss on his chosen turf."

—Tulsa World

*This is for
my son and daughter-in-law,
Mark Hunter
and
Lise Bloch-Mohrange Hunter*

The city in these pages is imaginary.
The people, the places are all fictitious.
Only the police routine is based on established
investigatory technique.

ROMANCE

1

KLING MADE HIS CALL FROM AN OUTSIDE PHONE BECAUSE HE didn't want to be turned down in a place as public as the squadroom. He didn't want to risk possible derision from the men with whom he worked day and night, the men to whom he often entrusted his life. Nor did he want to make the call from anyplace at *all* in the station house. There were pay phones on every floor, but a police station was like a small town, and gossip traveled fast. He did not want anyone to overhear him fumbling for words in the event of a rejection. He felt that rejection was a very definite possibility.

So he stood in the pouring rain a block from the station house, at a blue plastic shell with a pay phone inside it, dialing the number he'd got from the police directory operator, and which he'd scribbled on a scrap of paper that was now getting soggy in the rain. He waited while the phone rang, once, twice, three times, four, five, and he thought She isn't home, six, sev . . .

"Hello?"

Her voice startled him.

"Hello, uh, Sharon?" he said. "Chief Cooke?"

"Who's this, please?"

Her voice impatient and sharp. Rain pelting down everywhere around him. Hang up, he thought.

"This is Bert Kling?" he said.

"Who?"

The sharpness still in her voice. But edged with puzzlement now.

"Detective Bert Kling," he said. "We . . . uh . . . met at the hospital."

"The hospital?"

"Earlier this week. The hostage cop shooting. Georgia Mowbry."

"Yes?"

Trying to remember who he was. Unforgettable encounter, he guessed. Lasting impression.

"I was with Detective Burke," he said, ready to give up. "The redheaded hostage cop. She was with Georgia when . . ."

"Oh, yes, I remember now. How are you?"

"Fine," he said, and then very quickly, "I'm calling to tell you how sorry I am you lost her."

"That's very kind of you."

"I know I should have called earlier . . ."

"No, no, it's appreciated."

"But we were working a difficult case . . ."

"I quite understand."

Georgia Mowbry had died on Wednesday night. This was now Sunday. She suddenly wondered what this was all about. She'd been reading the papers when her phone rang. Reading all about yesterday's riot in the park. Blacks and whites rioting. Black and whites shooting each other, killing each other.

"So . . . uh . . . I know how difficult something like that must be," he said. "And I . . . uh . . . just thought I'd offer my . . . uh . . . sympathy."

"Thank you," she said.

There was a silence.

Then:

"Uh . . . Sharon . . ."

"By the way, it's Sharyn," she said.

"Isn't that what I'm saying?"

"You're saying Sharon."

"Right," he said.

"But it's *Sharyn*."

"I know," he said, thoroughly confused now.

"With a 'y,' " she said.

"Oh," he said. "Right. Thank you. I'm sorry. *Sharyn,* right."

"What's that I hear?" she asked.

"What do you mean?"

"That sound."

"Sound? Oh. It must be the rain."

"The rain? Where are you?"

"I'm calling from outside."

"From a phone booth?"

"No, not really, it's just one of these little shell things. What you're hearing is the rain hitting the plastic."

"You're standing in the rain?"

"Well, sort of."

"Isn't there a phone in the squadroom?"

"Well, yes. But . . ."

She waited.

"I . . . uh . . . didn't want anyone to hear me."

"Why not?"

"Because I . . . I didn't know how you'd feel about . . . something like this."

"Something like what?"

"My . . . asking you to have dinner with me."

Silence.

"Sharyn?"

"Yes?"

"Your being a chief and all," he said. "A deputy chief."

She blinked.

"I thought it might make a difference. That I'm just a detective/third."

"I see."

No mention of his blond hair or her black skin.

Silence.

"Does it?" he asked.

She had never dated a white man in her life.

"Does what?" she said.

"*Does* it make a difference? Your rank?"

"No."

But what about the other? she wondered. What about whites and blacks killing each other in public places? What about *that,* Detective Kling?

"Rainy day like today," he said, "I thought it'd be nice to have dinner and go to a movie."

With a white man, she thought.

Tell my mother I'm going on a date with a white man. My mother who scrubbed white men's offices on her knees.

"I'm off at four," he said. "I can go home, shower and shave, pick you up at six."

You hear this, Mom? A white man wants to pick me up at six. Take me out to dinner and a movie.

"Unless you have other plans," he said.

"Are you *really* standing in the rain?" she asked.

"Well, yes," he said. "*Do* you?"

"Do I what?"

"Have other plans?"

"No. But . . ."

Bring the subject up, she thought. Face it head-on. Ask him if he knows I'm black. Tell him I've never done anything like this before. Tell him my mother'll jump off the roof. Tell him I don't need this kind of complication in my life, tell him . . .

"Well . . . uh . . . do you think you might *like* to?" he asked. "Go to a movie and have dinner?"

"Why do you want to do this?" she asked.

He hesitated a moment. She visualized him standing there in the rain, pondering the question.

"Well," he said, "I think we might enjoy each other's company, is all."

She could just see him shrugging, standing there in the rain. Calling from outside the station house because he didn't want anyone to hear him being turned down by *rank*. Never mind black, never mind white, this was detective/third and deputy chief. As simple as that. She almost smiled.

"Excuse me," he said, "but do you think you could give me some kind of answer? Cause it's sort of wet out here."

"Six o'clock is fine," she said.

"Good," he said.

"Call me when you're out of the rain, I'll give you my address."

"Good," he said again. "Good. That's good. Thank you, Sharyn. I'll call you when I get back to the squadroom. What kind of food do you like? I know a great Italian . . ."

"Get out of the rain," she said, and quickly put the phone back on the cradle.

Her heart was pounding.

God, she thought, what am I starting here?

The redheaded woman was telling him that she'd been receiving threatening phone calls. He listened intently. Six phone calls in the past week, she told him. The same man each time, speaking in a low voice, almost a whisper, telling her he was going to kill her. At a table against one wall of the room, a short man in shirtsleeves was fingerprinting a bearded man in a black T-shirt.

"When did these calls start?"

"Last week," the woman said. "Monday morning was the first one."

"Okay, let's take down some more information," the man said, and rolled an NYPD Detective Division complaint form into his typewriter. He was wearing a .38-caliber pistol in a shoulder holster. Like the man taking fingerprints at the table against the wall, he too was in shirtsleeves. "May I have your address, please?"

"314 East Seventy-first Street."

"Here in Manhattan?"

"Yes."

"Apartment number?"

"6B."

"Are you married? Single? Div . . . ?"

"Single."

"Are you employed?"

"I'm an actress."

"Oh?" Eyebrows going up in sudden interest. "Have I seen you in anything?"

"Well . . . I've done a lot of television work. I did a *Law &
Order* last month."

"Really? That's a good show. I watch that show all the
time. Which one were you in?"

"The one about abortion."

"No kidding? *I* saw that. That was just last *month*!"

"Yes, it was. Excuse me, Detective, but . . ."

"That's my *favorite* show on television. They shoot that
right here in New York, did you know that? Will you be doing
any more of them?"

"Well . . . right now I'm rehearsing a Broadway play."

"No kidding? What play? What's it called?"

"*Romance.* Uh, Detective . . ."

"What's it about?"

"Well, it's sort of complicated to explain. The thing is, I
have to get back to the theater . . ."

"Oh, sure."

"And I'd like to . . ."

"Hey, sure." All business again. Fingers on the typewriter
keys again. "You say these calls started last Monday, right?
That would've been . . ." A glance at the calendar on his desk.
"December . . ."

"December ninth."

"Right, December ninth." Typing as he spoke. "Can you
tell me exactly what this man said?"

"He said, 'I'm going to kill you, miss.'"

"Then what?"

"That's all."

"He calls you 'miss'? No name?"

"No name. Just 'I'm going to kill you, miss.' Then he hangs
up."

"Have there been any threatening letters?"

"No."

"Have you seen anyone suspicious lurking around the building or . . . ?"

"No."

". . . following you to the theater or . . ."

"No."

"Well, I'll tell you the truth, miss . . ."

"This may be a good place to pause," Kendall said.

Both actors shaded their eyes and peered out into the darkened theater. The woman playing the actress said, "Ashley, I'm uncomfortable with . . ." but Kendall interrupted at once.

"Take fifteen," he said. "We'll do notes later."

"I just want to ask Freddie about one of the lines."

"Later, Michelle," Kendall said, dismissing her.

Michelle let out a short, exasperated sigh, exchanged a long glance with Mark Riganti, the actor playing the detective who adored *Law & Order,* and then walked off into the wings with him. The actor playing the other detective stood chatting at the fingerprint table with the bearded actor playing his prisoner.

Sitting sixth row center, Freddie Corbin turned immediately to Kendall and said, "They wouldn't be wearing guns anywhere *near* a thief being printed."

"I can change that," Kendall said. "What we've *really* got to talk about, Freddie . . ."

"It spoils the entire sense of reality," Corbin said.

His full and honorable name was Frederick Peter Corbin III, but all of his friends called him Fred. Kendall, however, had started calling him Freddie the moment they'd been introduced, which of course the cast had picked up on, and now everybody *associated* with this project called him Freddie. Corbin, who had written two novels about New York City cops, knew that this was an old cop trick. Using the familiar diminutive to denigrate a prisoner's sense of self-worth or self-respect. So you think you're *Mr.* Corbin, hah? Well, *Freddie,* where were you on the night of June thirteenth, huh?

"Also," he said, "I think he's overreacting when he discovers she's an actress. It'd be funnier if he *contained* his excitement."

"Yes," Kendall said. "Which brings us to the scene *itself.*" *Kendall's* full name was Ashley Kendall, which wasn't the name he was born with, but which had been his legal name for thirty years, so Corbin guessed that made it his real name, more or less. Frederick Peter Corbin III really *was* Corbin's *real* real name, thank you. This was his first experience with a director. He was beginning to learn that directors didn't think their job was *directing* the script, they thought their job was *changing* it. He was beginning to hate directors. Or at least to hate Kendall. He was beginning to learn that all directors were shitheads.

"What *about* the scene?" he asked.

"Well . . . doesn't it seem a bit *familiar* to you?"

"It's *supposed* to be familiar. This is police routine. This is what happens when a person comes in to report a . . ."

"Yes, but we've *witnessed* this particular scene a hundred times already, haven't we?" Kendall said. "A *thousand* times. Even the detective reacting to the fact that she's an *actress* is a cliché. Asking her if he's seen her in anything. I mean, Freddie, I have a great deal of respect for what you've done here, the intricacy of the plot, the painstaking devotion to detail. But . . ."

"But what?"

"But I think there might be a more exciting way to set up the fact that her life has been threatened. Theatrically, I mean."

"Yes, this *is* a play," Corbin said. "I would assume we'd want to do it theatrically."

"I know you're a *wonderful* novelist," Kendall said, "but . . ."

"Thank you."

"But in a *play* . . ."

"A dramatic line is a dramatic line," Corbin said. "This is the story of an actress surviving . . ."

"Yes, I know what it . . ."

". . . a brutal murder attempt, and then going on to achieve a tremendous personal triumph."

"Yes, that's what it's *supposed* to be about."

"No, that's what it *is* about."

"No, this is a play about some New York cops solving a goddamn *mystery*."

"No, that's not what it's . . ."

"Which you do very well, by the way. In your novels. There's nothing wrong with stories about cops . . ."

"Even if they *are* crap," Corbin said.

"I wasn't about to say that," Kendall said. "I wasn't even *thinking* it. All I'm suggesting is that this shouldn't be a *play* about cops."

"It isn't a play about cops."

"I see. Then what is it?"

"A play about a triumph of will."

"I see."

"A play about a woman surviving a *knife* attack, and then finding in herself the courage to . . ."

"Yes, *that* part of it's fine."

"What part of it *isn't* fine?"

"The cop stuff."

"The cop stuff is what makes it real."

"No, the cop stuff makes it a play about cops."

"When a woman gets stabbed . . ."

"Yes, yes."

". . . she goes to the *cops*, Ashley. She doesn't go to her chiropractor. Would you like her to go to her *chiropractor* after she's stabbed?"

"No, I . . ."

"Because then it wouldn't be a play about *cops* anymore, it'd be a play about *chiropractors*. Would that suit you better?"

"Why does she have to go to the cops *before* she's stabbed?"

"That's known as suspense, Ashley."

"I see."

"By the way, that's a terrible verbal tic you have."

"What is?"

"Saying 'I see' all the time. Somewhat sarcastically, in fact. It's almost as bad as 'You know.'"

"I see."

"Exactly."

"But tell me, Freddie, do you actually *like* cops?"

"I do, yes."

"Well, nobody else does."

"I don't believe that."

"Nobody else in the whole wide world."

"Please."

"Believe it. No one wants to sit in a theater for three hours watching a play about *cops*."

"Good. Because this *isn't* a play about cops."

"*Whatever* the fuck it's about, I think we can effectively lose a third of the first act by cutting to the chase."

"Lose all the suspense . . ."

"I don't find a woman talking to cops suspenseful."

"Lose all the character develop . . ."

"That can be done more theatrically . . ."

"Lose all . . ."

". . . more dramatically."

Both men fell silent. Sitting in the darkness beside his director, Corbin felt a sudden urge to strangle him.

"Tell me something," he said at last.

"Yes, what's that, Freddie?"

"And please don't call me Freddie."

"I beg your pardon."

"It's Fred, I prefer Fred. I have a thing about names. I like being called by the name I prefer."

"So do I."

"Okay, so tell me, Ashley . . . why'd you agree to direct this play in the first place?"

"I felt . . . I *still* feel it has tremendous potential."

"I see. Potential."

"Must be contagious," Kendall said.

"Because *I* feel it has more than just *potential,* you see. *I* feel it's a fully realized, highly dramatic theater piece that speaks to the human heart about survival and triumph. I happen to . . ."

"You sound like a press release."

"I happen to *love* this fucking play, Ashley, and if you *don't* love it . . ."

"I do not love it, no."

"Then you shouldn't have agreed to direct it."

"I agreed to direct it because I think I can *come* to love it."

"If I make it *your* play instead of mine."

"I didn't say that."

"Ashley, are you familiar with the Dramatists Guild contract?"

"This is *not* my first play, Freddie."

"*Fred,* please. And, yes, I admit it, this *is* my first play, which is why I read the contract very carefully. Once a play goes into rehearsal, Ashley, the contract says not a line, not a *word,* not a *comma* can be changed without the playwright's approval. That's in the contract. We've been in rehearsal for two weeks now . . ."

"Yes, I know that."

"And you're suggesting . . ."

"Cutting some scenes, yes."

"And I'm telling you no."

"Freddie . . . Fred . . . do you ever want this fucking play you love so much to move downtown? Or do you want it to die up here in the boonies? Because I'm telling you, *Fred,* Freddie *baby,* that the way it stands now, your fully realized, highly dramatic theater piece that speaks to the human heart about survival and triumph is going to fall flat on its ass when it opens three weeks from now."

Corbin blinked at him.

"Think about it," Kendall said. "Downtown or here in the asshole of the city."

Detective Bertram Kling lived in a studio apartment in Isola, from which he could look out his window and see the twinkling lights of the Calm's Point Bridge. He could have driven over that bridge if he'd owned a car, but there was no point owning a car in the big bad city, where the subway was always faster if not particularly safer. The problem was that Deputy Chief Surgeon Sharyn Everard Cooke lived at the very end of the Calm's Point line, which gave her a nice view of the bay, true enough, but which took a good forty minutes to reach from where Kling boarded the train three blocks from his apartment.

This was Sunday, the fifth day of April, exactly two weeks before Easter, but you wouldn't have known it from the cold rain that drilled the windows of the subway car as it came up out of the ground onto the overhead tracks. A grizzled old man sitting opposite Kling kept winking at him and licking his lips. A black woman sitting next to Kling found this disgusting. So did he. But she kept clucking her tongue in disapproval, until finally she moved away from Kling to the farthest end of the car. A panhandler came through telling everyone she had three children and no place to sleep. Another panhandler came through telling everyone he was a Vietnam War veteran with no place to sleep.

The rain kept pouring down.

Kling's umbrella turned inside out as he came down the steps from the train platform onto Farmers Boulevard, which Sharyn had told him he should stay on for three blocks before making a left onto Portman, which would take him straight to her building. He broke several of the umbrella ribs trying to get it right side out again, and tossed it into a trash can on the corner of Farmers and Knowles. He was wearing a black raincoat, no hat. He walked as fast as he could to the address Sharyn had given him, which turned out to be a nice garden apartment a block or so from the ocean. In the near distance, he could see the lights of a cargo ship pushing its way through the downpour.

He was thinking he'd never do this again in his life. Date a girl from Calm's Point. A woman. He wondered how old she was. He was guessing early to mid-thirties. His age, more or less. Thirtysomething. In there. But who was counting? She would tell him later that night that she had just turned

forty on October the fifteenth. "Birth date of great men," she
would say. "And women, too," she would say, but would not
amplify.

He was wringing wet when he rang her doorbell.

Never again, he was thinking.

She looked radiantly beautiful. He lost all resolve.

Her skin was the color of burnt almond, her eyes the color
of loam, shadowed now with a smoky blue over the lids. She
wore her black hair in a modified Afro that gave her the look
of a proud Masai woman, her high cheekbones and generous
mouth tinted the color of burgundy wine. Her casual suit was
the color of her eye shadow, fashioned of a nubby fabric with
tiny bright brass buttons. A short skirt and high-heeled pumps
collaborated to showcase her legs. She did not look like a
deputy chief surgeon. He almost caught his breath.

"Oh, dear," she said, "you're soaked again."

"My umbrella quit," he said, and shrugged helplessly.

"Come in, come in," she said, and stepped back and let
him into the apartment. "Give me your coat, we have time
for a drink, I made the reservation for six-thirty, I could've
met you in the city, you know, you didn't have to come all
the way out here, you said Italian, there's a nice place just a
few blocks from here, we could have walked it, but I'll take
the car, oh dear, this *is* wet, isn't it?"

It occurred to her that she was rattling on.

It occurred to her that he looked cute as hell with his blond
hair all plastered to his forehead that way.

She took his coat, debated hanging it in the closet with all
the *dry* clothes there, said, "I'd better put this in the bathroom,"
started to leave the foyer, stopped, said, "I'll be right back,
make yourself comfortable," gestured vaguely toward a large
living room, and vanished like a breeze over the savanna.

He stepped tentatively into the living room, checking it from the open door frame the way a detective might, the way a detective actually *was,* quick takes around the room, camera eye picking up impressions rather than details. Upright piano against one wall, did she play? Windows facing south to what had to be the bay, rainsnakes slithering down the wide expanse of glass. Sofa upholstered in leather the color of a camel hair coat he'd once owned. Throw pillows in earth shades scattered hither and yon around the room. A rug the color of cork. A large painting over the sofa, a street scene populated with black people. He remembered that she was black.

"Okay," she said from the door frame, "what would you like to drink?" and came striding into the room, long-legged stride, he liked that about her, the fact that she was almost as tall as he was, just a few inches shorter, he guessed, five-nine, five-ten, in there. "I've got Scotch and I've got Scotch," she said.

"I'll take the Scotch," he said.

"Water, soda, neat?"

"Little soda."

"Rocks?"

"Please. You look beautiful," he said, not expecting to say what he was thinking, and surprised when he heard the words leaving his mouth.

She looked surprised, too.

He immediately thought he'd said the wrong thing.

"Thank you," she said softly, and lowered her eyes and went swiftly to a wall unit that looked like a bookcase with a built-in television and stereo but that turned out to have a drop-leaf front that revealed a bar behind it. He watched as she poured the Scotch—Johnnie Red—over ice cubes in two shortish glasses, added a little soda to each, and then carried the glasses, one in each hand, to where he was standing uncertainly near the sofa.

"Please sit," she said. "I should have brought you a towel."

"No, that's okay," he said, and immediately touched his wet hair, and then—seemingly embarrassed by the gesture—sat at once. He waited for her to sit opposite him, in a plum-colored easy chair that complemented her suit, and then raised his glass to her. She raised her own glass.

"Here's to golden days," he said, "and . . ."

". . . and purple nights," she finished for him.

They both looked surprised.

"How do you happen to know that?" he asked.

"How do you?"

"Someone I used to know."

"Someone *I* used to know," she said.

"Good toast," he said. "Whoever."

"So here's to golden days and purple nights," she said, and grinned.

"Amen," he said.

Her smile was like sudden moonlight.

They drank.

"Good," she said. "It's been a long day."

"Long *week*," he said.

"I hope you like Northern Italian," she said.

"I do."

"You know, I really wish you hadn't insisted on coming all the way . . ."

"First date," he said.

She looked at him. For a moment, she thought he might be putting her on. But, no, he was serious, she could see that in his eyes. This was a first date, and on a first date, you went to a girl's house to pick her up. There was something so old-fashioned about the notion that it touched her to the core. She suddenly wondered how old he was. All at once, he seemed so very young.

"I also checked movie schedules out here," she said. "Do you like cop movies? The one about the bank heist is playing near the restaurant, the last show starts at ten after ten. What time do you have to be in tomorrow?"

"Eight."

"Me, too."

"Where?"

"Majesta. Rankin Plaza. That's where . . ."

"I know. I've been there a lot."

"What for?"

"Well, once I got shot, and another time I got beat up. You have to check in at Rankin if you're applying for sick leave. Well, I guess you know that."

"Yes."

"Eight's early."

"I'll be okay if I get six hours sleep."

"Really. Just six hours?"

"Habit I developed in medical school."

"Where was that?"

"Georgetown U."

"Good school."

"Yes. Who shot you?"

"Oh, one of the bad guys. That was a long time ago."

"Who beat you up?"

"Some more bad guys."

"Do you enjoy dealing with bad guys?"

"I enjoy locking them up. That's why I'm in the job. Do you enjoy being a doctor?"

"I love it."

"I love being a cop," he said.

She looked at him again. He had a way of saying things so directly that they seemed somehow artfully designed. Again, she wondered if he was putting her on. But no, he seemed entirely guileless, a person who simply said whatever was on his mind whenever it occurred to him. She wasn't sure she liked that. Or maybe she did. She realized she was studying his eyes. A greenish brown, she guessed they were, what you might call hazel, she guessed. He caught her steady gaze, looked puzzled for a moment. Swiftly, she looked down into her glass.

"What time do you leave for work?" he asked.

"I can make it in half an hour," she said, and looked up again. This time, he was studying her. She almost looked away again. But she didn't. Their eyes met, locked, held.

"That'd be seven-thirty," he said.

"Yes."

"So if the movie breaks at midnight . . ."

"It should, don't you think?"

"Oh, sure. You'll easily get your six hours."

"Yes," she said.

They both fell silent.

He was wondering if she thought he was dumb, staring at her this way.

She was wondering if he thought she was dumb, staring at him this way.

They both kept staring.

At last she said, "We'd better get going."

"Right," he said, and got immediately to his feet.

"Let me get your coat," she said.

"I'll put these in the sink," he said.

"Okay," she said, and started out of the room.

"Uh . . . Sharyn?" he said.

"Yes, Bert?"

Turning to him.

God, she was beautiful.

"Where's the kitchen?" he said.

Michelle Cassidy was telling her agent all about the dumb lines she had to say in this stupid damn play. Johnny was listening with great interest. The last really good part he'd got for her was in the touring company of *Annie,* when she was ten years old. She was now twenty-three, which made it a long time between drinks. Johnny had landed her the leading role in the musical because she had a strong singing voice for a ten-year-old—the producer said she sounded like a pre-pubescent Ethel Merman—and also because the natural color of her hair was the same as the little orphan's, a sort of reddish orange that matched the adorable darling's dress with its white bib collar. Johnny knew the natural color of Michelle's hair because he'd begun sleeping with her when she was just sixteen.

What happened was Michelle had toured the *Annie* role until she began developing tits at the age of twelve years and eight months, a despairing turn of events for all concerned, especially Johnny, who at the time represented only two other clients, one of whom was a dog act. Johnny figured that suddenly blossoming into a dumb curvaceous teenybopper was the end of Michelle's career as a waif. But the red hair still shone like a traffic light, and it certainly didn't hurt that he could tout her as the former star of *Annie,* even though her voice was beginning to sound a bit strident—wasn't it only *boys* whose voices changed during adolescence? He auditioned her for a dinner theater production of *Oliver!*, figuring she'd had experience as an orphan and maybe they could bind her chest, but the director said she looked too much like a girl, no kidding. So Johnny got her an orange juice commercial on the strength of the fiery red hair, and then a string of other commercials where she played a variety of bratty budding thirteen-year-olds in training bras and braces. When she was fourteen, he got her into an L.A. revival of *The King and I* as one of the children, even though by that time she was truly beginning to look a trifle voluptuous in those flimsy Siamese tops and pantaloons.

Truth was, Michelle's voice had changed to something that now resembled the bleat of a sacrificial lamb—which she was soon to become, in a manner of speaking, although as yet unbeknownst to herself. She'd never been a very good actress, even when she was Tomorrow-ing it all over the stage, but during her television years she had picked up a barrelful of mannerisms that now made her look hopelessly amateurish. Too old for kiddy roles, too young for bimbo roles although she certainly looked the part, Johnny figured she would have to mature into her body, so to speak, before he could get her any decent adult roles. Meanwhile, so it shouldn't be a total loss, he seduced her when she was sixteen, in a motel room in the town of Altoona, Pennsylvania, three miles from the dinner theater where she was playing one of the older children in *Sound of Music*.

Johnny Milton—his entire name was John Milton Hicks, but he had shortened it to just plain Johnny Milton, which he thought sounded snappier for an agent—was lying naked in bed beside Michelle on this rainy Sunday night, listening intently to her plight because he was almost a hundred percent certain that the first starring role he'd landed for her since the orphan gig was in a play that would be heading south the night after it opened. The theatrical doomsayers here in this city had already mutated the title from *Romance* to *No Chance,* a certain harbinger of failure. Johnny was worried. He became even more worried as Michelle recited some of the lines she had to say in the scene where the squadroom detective gets all excited about having seen her on *Law & Order.*

"I mean," Michelle said, "this is supposed to be a precinct in New York's *theater* district, Midtown North, Midtown South, what*ever* the hell they call it. So why is he wetting his pants over meeting a person had a bit part on *Law & Order*? Also, suppose *Law & Order* goes off by the time the play opens? *If* it opens. We make a reference to a TV show isn't even *on* anymore, it'll make us look like ancient history. If you want my honest opinion, Johnny, I think this play stinks on ice. You want to know what this play is? This play is something Freddie should've written for television, is what this play is. A movie of the week is what this play is. A piece of *shit* is what this play is, excuse my French."

Johnny tended to agree with her.

"I open in this play," Michelle went on, gathering steam, "I'll be back doing dinner theater two weeks later. Make it two *days* later. If you can even *book* me ever again. I mean, really, John, who *cares* about the girl in this play, who *cares* if she gets to perform on opening night? Because you want to know something? The *other* play stinks, too, the play *within* the play, whatever the hell Freddie calls it, the play they're supposed to be rehearsing. It's even worse than the *real* play. He'll get *two* Tonys for worst play of the year, the one *he* wrote and the one the playwright in his *play* wrote. How did I manage to get stuck in *two* lousy plays is what I'd like to know?"

Johnny was wondering what they could do to salvage this deplorable situation.

"Also, I think you should know Mark's been playing a little grab-ass backstage," Michelle said.

Mark Riganti. The actor playing a character named the Detective, who nearly faints with joy when the character named the Actress tells him she's been on *Law & Order*. Mark was not a very good actor. Take a lousy play—*two* lousy plays, as Michelle had pointed out—add a lousy actor and a lousy actress in the leading roles, and what you've got is trouble. Though Johnny couldn't fault Mark for groping Michelle backstage, which he himself was beginning to do at this very moment, albeit in bed.

"I'll ask Morgenstern to talk to him," he said.

"Lot of good that'll do," Michelle said. "He was there first."

Johnny sighed heavily.

The trouble with Michelle—aside from her being a not very good actress who never could dance and who no longer possessed a very good singing voice—was that men could not keep their hands off her. Women, too, to hear her tell it. At least in Ohio, one time. The trouble was her looks were too damn distracting. People, men *and* women, tended to forget that someone who *looked* the way Michelle did could possibly be a good actress, which she wasn't, anyway. Being so sumptuously endowed would have been a failing at any time, unless a girl wanted to play bimbos or hookers for the rest of her life, a not insignificant ambition for many actresses Johnny had known and incidentally slept with. But coming out of your dress in a role that called for the actress to recite lines like "This is the world's noblest calling" could be something of an impediment in a play where the girl's extraordinary talent is rewarded with stardom due to her courage, dedication and perseverance.

After getting stabbed, that is.

The plot of Freddie's play revolved around the Actress getting stabbed by some crazy person whose identity is never made entirely clear because Freddie felt that resolving the mystery would cheapen the play. Freddie had more exalted interests in mind. Like exploring the concept of giving one's all for one's art, for example. The dedication of the Actress in his play was intended as a sly reference to the play's title, in that her true *romance* is with the theater, which she loves from "the very depths of her soul," as she puts it in a memorable soliloquy premised on the corniest scene in *Chorus Line*. In his play, Freddie loved to ponder the significance of even the tiniest creative act as opposed to the worthlessness of mundane matters like earning a living or feeding a family. Freddie's *Romance* was a "play of ideas," as he was fond of telling Kendall. Contrarily, Kendall felt the play was far *too* "mysterious" and not quite "serious" enough.

Neither of them seemed to understand something Johnny had known from the first time he'd ever read a crime novel: there *ain't* no way you can turn a murder mystery into a silk purse. That's because the minute somebody sticks a knife in somebody else, all attention focuses on the victim, and all you want to know is whodunit.

Which isn't such a bad idea, he thought.

Focusing attention on the victim.

2

BECAUSE SHE DID A LITTLE DOPE EVERY NOW AND THEN, SHE WAS never comfortable around cops anyhow. She knew this had to be done, coming here this afternoon, but just *approaching* a police station made her nervous. Gave her the willies just *seeing* those big green globes with the numerals 87 on them, one hanging on each side of the tall wooden entrance doors, each one screaming "Cop! Cop!" And sure enough, a real *live* cop in a blue uniform was standing at the top of the steps just to the right of the doors, looking her over as she climbed the steps, and fumbled with the brass knob, and opened the door. She smiled at him as if she'd just killed her mother with a hatchet.

Where she was when she stepped through the door was inside a big, noisy, high-ceilinged room with a lot of uniformed cops milling around, and a high wooden desk on her right, with a brass rail in front of it about waist high, and a sign on the counter stating ALL VISITORS MUST STATE BUSINESS. There were two more uniformed cops behind the desk, one of them drinking coffee from a cardboard container. A clock behind the desk read ten minutes past four. The rain had stopped, but it was still pretty brisk for April, and the room seemed chillier somehow than it did outside, maybe because there were no windows in it or maybe because it was full of cops. She stepped up to the desk, cleared her throat, and said to the one drinking coffee, "My name is Michelle Cassidy, I'd like to talk to a detective, please."

Kling wondered if Deputy Chief Surgeon Sharyn Everard Cooke had ever been inside a detective squadroom. You worked here at the Eight-Seven long enough, you began believing everybody in the entire *city* had been here before, everybody knew *precisely* what it looked like, down to the tiniest fingernail scraping. But he couldn't imagine Sharyn's job taking her anywhere near the outer reaches of the solar system here, which he sometimes felt the 87th Precinct was. A planet devoid of anything but the basest form of animal life, an airless, sunless, apple-green void where nothing ever changed, everything remained always and ever exactly the same.

He wondered if her office at Rankin Plaza was painted the same bilious green as the squadroom here. If so, was it as soiled as the paint on the walls of this room that was used and abused twenty-four hours a day, three hundred and sixty-five days a year, *six* in leap year, which this happened to be? He could remember the squadroom being painted only once in all the time he'd worked here. He was not looking forward to *that* experience again anytime soon, thank you. He supposed *apple green* and *shoddy* were the operative interplanetary words that best described the squadroom, or in fact the entire station house. Well, maybe *shoddy* was too mild a word, perhaps a better description would have been *seedy* or even *shabby,* although to tell the truth the only valid description was *shitty,* a word he had not yet used in the deputy chief's presence, and might never find an opportunity to use with her ever in his lifetime if last night's date was any indication.

The Italian restaurant she'd chosen was called La Traviata, which might have led one to believe they'd be piping operatic music into the place, but instead they seemed to favor Frank Sinatra's Hundred Greatest Hits. Which was okay with Kling. He was a Sinatra fan, and he really didn't mind hearing him sing "Kiss" over and over again, even if by the fifth time around he knew all the lyrics by heart.

Kiss . . .
It all begins with a kiss . . .
But kisses wither
And die
Unless
The first caress . . .
And so on.
But then "One for My Baby" came on for the third time.

The conversation had hit one of those unexpected road-blocks by then, although Kling couldn't figure out what he'd said or done to cause her sudden silence. Being a detective, he knew that people sometimes reacted belatedly to something that'd been said or done minutes or even hours ago—sometimes *years* ago, as was the case with a lady they'd arrested recently for poisoning her husband twelve years *after* he'd called her a whore in front of their entire bowling team. So he was sitting there across from her, trying to figure out why all at once she looked so thoughtfully sullen, when, gee whiz, what a surprise, here came "One for My Baby" again. Hoping to yank her out of whatever the hell was bugging her, and thinking he was making a brilliant observation besides, he remarked that here was a song that merely *threatened* to tell a story, but never got around to actually *telling* the story.

"Guy's had a disastrous love affair," he said, "and he keeps promising the bartender he'll tell him all about it, but all he ever does is *tell* him he's going to tell him."

Blank expression on her face.

As if she were ten thousand miles away.

He wondered suddenly if she herself was trying to recover from a disastrous love affair. If so, was she thinking about whoever the guy might have been? And if so, when had the ill-fated romance ended? Twelve years ago? Twelve days ago? Last night?

He let it go.

Concentrated instead on the linguini with white clam sauce.

"Is it because I'm black?" she asked suddenly.

"Is what because you're black?" he asked.

"That you asked me out."

"No," he said. "I don't think so."

Is it? he wondered.

Before now, he'd never dated a black woman in his life.

But what the hell had brought *that* on?

"Is it because *I'm* white?" he asked lightly, and smiled. "That you accepted?"

"Maybe," she said.

And did not return his smile, he noticed.

"Well . . . do you want to talk about it?" he asked.

"No. Not now."

"When?"

"Maybe never."

"Okay," he said, and went back to the linguini.

He figured that was the end of the story. So long, Whitey, nice to've known you, but hey, this ain' gon work, man.

When she told him after dinner that she'd really rather not go to a movie, they both had to get up so early, and it was already close to ten, he was certain this meant so long and goodbye, bro, see you roun the pool hall one of these days. They shook hands outside her apartment. She thanked him for a nice time. He told her he'd had a nice time, too. It was still raining, but only lightly. He walked through the drizzle from her building to the train station five blocks away.

Three black teenagers came into the car while the train was still on the overhead tracks in Calm's Point. They seemed to be considering him as they approached. He gave them a look that said *Don't even* think *it,* and they went right on by.

The phone on his desk was ringing.

What Michelle saw when she reached the top of the second-floor landing was another sign nailed to the wall, indicating that the DETECTIVE DIVISION was either just down the corridor past several doors respectively labeled LOCKER ROOM and MEN'S LAVATORY and CLERICAL OFFICE, or else right there on the landing itself, since the sign merely announced itself in black letters on a smudged white field, but gave no other directions. She followed her instincts, and—being right-handed—turned naturally to the right and walked down the hall past the smell of stale sweat seeping from the locker room, and the stench of urine floating from behind the men's room door, and the wafting aroma of coffee brewing in the clerical office, a regular potpourri here in this "little old cop shop," as the Detective called it in the play they were rehearsing. At the end of the hall, she saw first a slatted wooden rail divider and beyond that several dark green metal desks and telephones and a bulletin board with various photographs and notices on it, and a hanging light globe, and further into the room some more green metal desks and finally a bank of windows covered with metal grilles. A good-looking blond man sat at one of the desks. She stopped at the railing, cleared her throat again the way she had downstairs, and said—remembering to project—"Detective Kling?"

Kling looked up.

The woman had hair the color of a fire truck dipped in orange juice. Eyes the color of periwinkles. Wearing a tight blue sweater that matched the eyes. Peacoat open over it. Navy-blue skirt to match the coat. Big gold-buckled belt. Blue high-heeled pumps.

"The desk sergeant said I should see you," she said.

"Yes, he called me a minute ago," he said. "Come on in."

She found the latch on the inside of the railing gate, looked surprised when the gate actually opened to her touch, and came tentatively into the room. Kling stood as she approached his desk, and indicated the chair opposite him. She sat, crossing her legs, the blue skirt riding high on her thighs. She lifted her behind, tugged at the skirt, made herself comfortable in the hard-backed chair. Kling sat, too.

"I'm Michelle Cassidy," she said. "I spoke to someone up here earlier this morning, he said I should come in."

"Would you remember who that was?"

"He had an Italian name."

"Carella?"

"I think so. Anyway, he said to come in. He said someone would help me."

Kling nodded.

"Let me get some information," he said, and rolled a DD form into the typewriter. He spaced down to the slot calling for the date of the complaint, typed in today's date, April 6, spaced down some more to the NAME slot, typed in C-A-S-S, stopped and looked up. "Is that A-D-Y or I-D-Y?" he asked.

"I," she said.

"Cassidy," he said, typing. "Michelle like in the Beatles?"

"Yes. A double L."

"May I have your address, please?"

She gave him her address and the apartment number and her phone number there, and also a work number where she could be reached.

"Are you married?" he asked. "Single? Divorced?"

"Single."

"Are you employed, Miss Cassidy?"

"I'm an actress."

"Have I seen you in anything?" he asked.

"Well . . . I played the lead in *Annie,*" she said. "And I've been doing a lot of dinner theater work in recent years."

"I saw the movie," he said. "*Annie.*"

"I wasn't in the movie," she said.

"Good movie, though," he said. "Are you in anything right now?"

"I'm rehearsing a play."

"Would it be a play I know?"

"I don't think so. It's a new play, it's called *Romance.* We're opening it uptown here, but we hope to move downtown later. If it's a hit."

"What's it about?"

"Well, that's the funny part of it."

"What is?"

"It's about an actress getting phone calls from somebody who says he's going to kill her."

"What's funny about that?"

"Well . . . that's why I'm here, you see."

"I'm sorry, Miss Cassidy, I'm not foll . . ."

"I've been getting the same kind of calls."

"Threatening calls, do you mean?"

"Yes. A man who says he's going to kill me. Just like in the play. Well, not the same language."

"What *does* he say? Exactly?"

"That he's going to kill me with a knife."

"With a knife."

"Yes."

"He specifies the weapon."

"Yes. A knife."

"These are the *real* calls we're talking about, is that right?"

"Yes."

"Not the ones in the play."

"No. These are the calls I've been getting for the past week now."

"A man saying he's going to kill you with a knife."

"Yes."

"Which of these numbers does he call?"

"My home number. The other one is the backstage phone. At the theater."

"He hasn't called you there?"

"No. Not yet, anyway. I'm very frightened, Detective Kling."

"I can imagine. When did these calls start?"

"Last Sunday night."

"That would've been . . ." He looked at his desk calendar. "March twenty-ninth," he said.

"Whenever."

"Does he seem to know you?"

"He calls me Miss Cassidy."

"What does he . . . ?"

"Sort of sarcastically. Miss *Cassidy*. Like that. With a sort of *sneer* in his voice."

"Tell me again exactly what he . . ."

"He says, 'I'm going to kill you, Miss Cassidy. With a knife.' "

"Have there been any threatening letters?"

"No."

"Have you seen any strangers lurking about your building . . ."

"No."

". . . or the theater?"

"No."

"Which theater is it, by the way?"

"The Susan Granger. On North Eleventh."

"No one hanging around the stage door . . ."

"No."

". . . or following you . . . ?"

"No."

". . . or watching you? For example, has anyone in a restaurant or any other public place . . . ?"

"No, nothing like that."

"Just the phone calls."

"Yes."

"Do you owe money to anyone?"

"No."

"Have you had any recent arguments or altercations with . . ."

"No."

"I don't suppose you *fired* anyone in recent . . ."

"No."

"Any boyfriends in your past who might . . ."

"No. I've been living with the same man for seven years now."

"Get along okay with him?"

"Oh, yes."

"I have to ask."

"That's okay. I know you're doing your job. We have the same thing in the play."

"Sorry?" Kling said.

"There's a scene where she goes to the police, and they ask her all these questions."

"I see. What's his name, by the way? The man you've been living with."

"John Milton."

"Like the poet."

"Yes. Well, actually, he's an agent."

"Would anyone have reason to be jealous of him?"

"I don't think so."

"Or want to get back at him for something? Through you?"

"Gee, I don't think so."

"Do you get along with all the people involved in this play?"

"Oh, sure. Well, you know, there are little . . ."

"Sure."

". . . tiffs and such. But for the most part, we get along fine."

"How many people *are* there?"

"In the cast? Just four of us, really. Speaking roles, anyway. The rest of the people are sort of extras. Four actors do all the other parts."

"So that's eight altogether."

"Plus all the technical people. I mean, this is a *play*. It takes lots of people to put on a play."

"And you say you get along with all of them."

"Yes."

"This man who calls you ... do you recognize his voice, by any chance?"

"No."

"Doesn't sound at all familiar, hm?"

"No."

"Yeah, well, I didn't think it would. But sometimes . . ."

"Well, he doesn't sound like anyone I *know*, if that's what you mean. *Personally*, I mean. If that's what you mean."

"Yes, that's what I . . ."

"But he *does* sound familiar."

"Oh?"

"He sounds like Jack Nicholson."

"Jack . . . ?"

"The actor."

"Oh."

"That same sort of voice."

"I see. But you don't *know* Jack Nicholson personally, is what you're . . ."

"I *wish* I knew him," she said, and rolled her eyes.

"But you don't."

"No, I don't."

"The caller just *sounds* like Jack Nicholson."

"Or somebody trying to *imitate* Jack Nicholson."

"I don't suppose you know anyone who does Jack Nicholson imitations, do you?"

"Yes, I do," she said.

"You do?" he said, and leaned across the desk toward her. "Who?"

"Everybody."

"I meant *personally*. Anyone in your circle of friends or . . . ?"

"No."

"Can you think of anyone at *all* who might want to harm you, Miss Cassidy?"

"No, I can't. I'm sorry."

"I don't suppose you have caller ID, do you?"

"I sure don't," she said.

"Well," he said, "let me talk this over with some of the other detectives, get their opinion, run it by the lieutenant, see if he thinks we can get a court order for a trap-and-trace. I'll get back to you as soon as I can."

"I wish you would," she said. "I think he's serious."

There were three deputy chiefs working under the police department's chief surgeon. One of these was an elderly shrink, another was an administrative executive, and the third was Sharyn herself. Sharyn was a board-certified surgeon with four years of medical school behind her, plus five years of residency as a surgeon, plus four years as chief resident at the hospital. The shingle on the door to her office read:

SHARYN EVERARD COOKE, M.D.
DEPUTY CHIEF SURGEON

She had worked here at 24 Rankin Plaza for the past five years, competing for the job against a hundred applicants, some of whom now served elsewhere in the police department's medical system; there were twenty-five district sur-

geons employed in five police clinics throughout the city.
Each of them earned $62,500 a year. As one of the deputy
chief surgeons, Sharyn earned $68,000 a year, for which she
had to put in some fifteen to eighteen hours a week here in
the Majesta office. During the rest of the week, she maintained
her own private practice in an office not far from Mount
Pleasant Hospital in Diamondback. In a good year, Deputy
Chief Cooke earned about five times what Detective/Third
Grade Kling earned.

Which had nothing to do with the price of fish, as her
mother was fond of saying.

She had not yet told her mother she'd dated a white man
last night.

Probably never *would* tell her.

The man in her office at four-thirty that Monday afternoon
was a black man. There were some thirty-one thousand police
officers in this city, and whenever one of them got sick, he
or she—fourteen percent of the force was female—reported
to one of the district police surgeons who worked for two and
a half hours every day of the week at staggered times specified
by the department and familiar to every member of the force.
The district surgeon conducted a thorough physical examina-
tion, and then determined whether the officer should be
allowed to stay out sick—with full pay, of course—or be put
on limited-capacity duty for ninety days, after which the officer was expected to return to active duty unless he was *still*
sick. It was up to the district surgeons and ultimately the
deputy chief surgeon to determine whether a cop was really
ill or simply malingering. Any cop who was out sick for more
than a year was brought before the Retirement Board under
Article IV, and requested either to return to full duty or else

leave the job. There was no alternative. It was all or nothing at all.

The black man sitting in a straight-backed metal chair alongside Sharyn's desk had been out sick for a hundred and twenty-two days now. Part of that time, he'd been flat on his back in bed at home. The rest of the time, he'd worked on and off at restricted-duty desk jobs in precincts here and there throughout the city. His name was Randall Garrod. He was thirty-four years old and had been a member of the force for thirteen years. Before he began developing severe chest pains, he had worked as an undercover out of a narcotics unit in Riverhead.

"How are the pains now?" Sharyn asked.

"Same," he said.

"I see you've had an electrocardiogram . . ."

"Yeah."

". . . and a stress test . . ."

"Yeah."

". . . *and* a thallium stress test, all of them normal."

"That's what they say. But I still have the pains."

"Gastroenterologist took X rays, did an endoscopy, found nothing."

"Mm."

"I see you've even had an echocardiogram. No indication of a mitral valve prolapse, everything normal. So what's wrong with you, Detective Garrod?"

"You're the doctor," he said.

"Take off your shirt for me, will you?"

He was a bit shorter than she was, five-seven or -eight, Sharyn guessed, a small wiry man who stood now and unbuttoned his shirt and then draped it neatly over the back of the metal chair. His chest, arms, and abdomen were well-muscled,

he obviously worked out regularly. His skin was the color of
a coconut shell.

She thought suddenly of Bert Kling. Stethoscope to Garrod's chest, she listened.

——That color is good for you.

Referring to her suit. The blue of her suit. The smoky blue
that matched her eye shadow.

"Deep breath," she said. "And hold it."

Listening.

Sinatra was singing "Kiss" for the ten thousand, two hundred and twenty-eighth time.

——So hold me tight and whisper

——Words of

——Love against my eyes.

——And kiss me sweet and promise

——Me your

——Kisses won't be lies . . .

"Another one, please. And hold it."

——That color is good for you.

But what had he *really* been saying, this blond, hazel-eyed
honkie sitting opposite her, twirling linguini on a fork, what
had he *really* been saying about color? Or *trying* to say. How
come he hadn't until that very moment noticed or remarked
upon the very obvious fact that she was black and he was
white? *That color is good for you, sistuh,* and then moving
on fast to comment pithily on a dumb song featuring a drunk
in a saloon pouring out his heart to a jaded bartender who
kept setting them up, Joe, when all *she* wanted to know . . .

——Is it because I'm black?

——Is what because you're black?

——That you asked me out.

———No, I don't think so. Is it because I'm *white?* That you accepted?

———Maybe.

———Well . . . do you want to talk about it?

———No. Not now.

———When?

———Maybe never.

———Okay.

Which, of course, had been the end of all conversation until it came time to say Gee, you know, Bert, I don't think we have time to catch that movie, really, and besides we've both got to be up early tomorrow morning, and anyway do you *really* like cop movies, maybe we ought to call it a night, huh?

———Thank you, I had a very nice time.

———No, hey, thank *you.* I had a nice time, too.

Palpating the chest wall now, pushing along the sternum . . .

"Feel any pain here?"

"No."

"How about here?"

"No."

Ruling out any inflammation of the carti . . .

"What's this?" she asked suddenly.

"What's *what?*" Garrod said.

"This scar on your shoulder."

"Yeah."

"Looks like a healed bullet wound."

"Yeah."

"Is that what it is?"

"Yeah."

"I didn't see anything in your file about . . ."

"It's in there, all right."

"A gunshot wound? How'd I miss a gunshot wound?"

"Maybe you didn't go back far enough."

"When did you get shot?"

"Six, seven months ago."

"Before the chest pains started?"

"Yeah."

She looked at him.

"The scar's got nothin to do with those pains," he said. "The scar don't hurt at all."

"But the pains started after you got shot."

"Yeah."

"You keep testing normal . . ."

"Yeah, but . . ."

"EKGs, stress tests, GI tests, everything normal, no muscular problems . . ."

"One thing's got nothing to do with . . ."

"How soon after the shooting did you go back to work?"

"Few weeks after rehab."

"Where was that?"

"Buenavista."

"Good program there."

"Yeah."

"Went back to undercover?"

"Yeah."

"Were you doing undercover when the chest pains started?"

"Yeah, but . . ."

"Who'd you work with at Buenavista?"

"Oh, the physical therapists. Getting the shoulder working again. I'm in good shape, you know . . ."

"Yes."

"So it didn't take long."

"Did you talk to anyone about getting shot?"

"Oh, sure."

"About the psychological aftereffects of getting shot?"

"Sure."

"About post-trauma syndrome?"

"Lots of cops in this city get shot, you know. I'm not anybody special."

"But you *did* talk to someone at Buenavista about . . ."

"Well, it didn't apply, you see. I had no problem with it."

Sharyn looked at him again.

"There's someone I'd like you to see," she said. "I want you to stop at the sick-call desk on your way out, and make an appointment with him. His name is Simon Waggenstein," she said, writing it on one of her cards. "He's one of the deputy chief surgeons here."

"Why do I have to see another doctor? All I've done so far is go from one doctor to . . ."

"This one's a psychiatrist."

"No way," Garrod said at once, and stood up, and yanked his shirt from where he had draped it over the chair. "Send me back to active duty, fuck it, I ain't seeing no psychiatrist."

"He may be able to help you."

"I got *chest* pains and you want me to see a *head* doctor? Come on, willya?"

Angrily pulling on the shirt, buttoning it swiftly, not looking at her.

"Why haven't you applied for a pension?" she asked.

"I don't want a pension."

"You want to stay on the force, is that it?"

"I'm a good cop," he said flatly. "Getting shot don't make me no less a good cop."

"But you can quit with a pension anytime you want . . ."

"I don't want to quit."

"You don't have to invent imaginary chest pains to keep you off the street . . ."

"They're *not* imaginary!"

"You're *entitled* to the pension . . ."

"I don't *want* the . . ."

"You can claim . . ."

"I want *back* on the street!"

". . . federal disability insur . . ."

"I wasn't afraid to go *back*!"

"But if you didn't want to risk it again, nobody would blame . . ."

"They *already* blame me!" he said. "They think I got shot because I wasn't doing the job right. I must've been doing something wrong or I wouldn'ta got shot in the first place, you understand? To them, I'm some kinda failure. They don't even want to be *around* me, man, they're afraid *they're* liable'a get shot if they're even *around* me. I take that disability pension . . ."

He stopped, shook his head.

"I'm a good cop," he said again.

"You go another eight months with chest pains nobody can find, you'll be looking at an Article Four . . ."

"Yeah, but if I *quit* . . ."

"Yeah?"

"If I grab the pension and run . . ."

"Yeah?"

"They'll say the nigguh's got no balls."

"Neither have I," Sharyn said.

They stood looking at each other. The phone rang, startling them both. She picked up the receiver.

"Chief Cooke," she said.

"Sharyn? It's me."

Bert Kling?

Now what the hell?

"Just a second," she said, and covered the mouthpiece. "Promise me you'll make that appointment," she said.

"Give me the fuckin card," he said, and snatched it from her hand.

The rehearsal had resumed at five P.M. that Monday and it was now a little past six. All four actors in the leading roles had been on the stage together for the past hour in three of the play's most difficult scenes. Tempers were beginning to fray.

Freddie Corbin had named his four major characters the Actress, the Understudy, the Detective, and the Director. Michelle found this pretentious, but then again she found the whole damn *play* pretentious. The other four actors in it played about ten thousand people, half of them black, half of them white, none of them with speaking roles, all of them intended to convey "a sense of time and place," as Freddie himself had written in one of his interminably long stage directions.

The two male extras played detectives, thieves, doormen, restaurant patrons, ushers, librarians, cabdrivers, waiters, politicians, hot dog vendors, salesmen, newspaper reporters and television journalists. The two female extras played prostitutes, police officers, telephone operators, secretaries, waitresses, cashiers, saleswomen, token takers, newspaper reporters and television journalists. All four, male or female, were also responsible for quickly moving furniture and props during the brief blackouts between scenes.

There were two acts in the play and forty-seven scenes. The sets for each scene were "suggestive rather than literal," as Freddie had also written in one of his stage directions. A

table and two chairs, for example, represented a restaurant.
A bench and a section of railing represented the boardwalk
in Atlantic City, where the Actress wins the Miss America
beauty pageant that is the true start of her career.

The scene they were rehearsing this afternoon was the one
in which someone stabs . . .

"Do we ever find out for *sure* who stabbed her?" Michelle
called to the sixth row, where she knew their esteemed director
was sitting with Marvin Morgenstern, the show's producer,
affectionately called either "Mr. Morningstar" after the Her-
man Wouk character, or else "Mr. Moneybags" after his occupation. Michelle had shaded her eyes with one hand and was
peering past the lights into the darkness. She felt this was a
key question. How the hell was an actress supposed to portray
a *stabbing* victim if she didn't know who the hell had stabbed
her?

"That's not germane to the scene," Kendall called from
somewhere in the dark, she wished she could *see* where, she'd
go out there and stab *him*.

"It's germane to *me,* Ash," she called, whatever the hell
germane meant, still shading her eyes, still seeing nothing but
the glare of the lights and the blackened theater beyond.

"Can we just get on with the scene?" he said. "We'll go
over who done what to whom when we do notes."

"Excuse me, Ash," she said, "but the *scene* happens to be
what I'm talking about. And the *whom* who gets the *what*
done to her happens to be *meem*. I come out of the restaurant
and I'm walking toward the bus stop, and this *person* steps
out of the shadows . . ."

"Oh, for Christ's sake, Meesh, let's just *do* the fucking
thing, okay?"

Mark Riganti, the actor playing the Detective. Tall and lean and dark-haired and wearing jeans, sneakers, and a purple Ralph Lauren sweater.

"We've *been* doing the fucking thing," Michelle said, "over and over *again,* and I *still* don't know who it is that steps out of the shadows and stabs me."

"That's not important," Andrea said.

Andrea Packer, the *All About Eve* twit who was playing the Understudy. Andrea was nineteen years old, with long blond hair, dark brown eyes and a lean, coltish figure. In real life, she had a waspish tongue and a cool manner that perfectly suited the character of the Understudy; sometimes, Michelle felt she wasn't acting at all. Her rehearsal outfit this afternoon consisted of a short blue wraparound skirt over black leotard and tights.

Michelle hated her guts.

"Maybe it's not important to *you,*" she said, "but then again *you're* not the one getting stabbed. *I'm* the one getting stabbed by this unidentifiable *person* who steps out of the shadows wearing a long black coat and a black hat pulled down over his or her head, who is really Jerry . . ."

"Hi," Jerry said, popping his head out from behind the teaser, where he'd been waiting for his cue.

". . . who was the waiter with the mustache in the scene just before this one. I don't think it's the waiter with the *mustache* who's stabbing me, is it? Because then it becomes just plain ridiculous. And it can't be the *Detective* who's stabbing me because *he's* the one who leads me back to finding myself again and all that. So it's got to be either the Understudy or the Director because they're the only other important characters in the play, so which one is it? Is it Andrea or is it Coop, I just want to know who it *is.*"

"Well, I don't think it's *me*," Cooper Haynes said apologetically. He was forty-three years old, a dignified-looking gentleman who'd done years and years of soap opera—daytime serial, as it was known in the trade—usually playing one or another sympathetic doctor. In *Romance,* he was playing the Director. Actually, he was much nicer than any director Michelle had ever met in her life, even the ones who *didn't* try to get in her pants. "I haven't been playing the part as if I'm the one who stabs her," he said, and shaded his eyes and looked out into the darkness. "Ash, if I *am* the stabber, I think I should know it, don't you? It would change my entire approach."

"I think we're *all* entitled to know who stabs me," Michelle said.

"I truly don't *care* who stabs you," Andrea said.

"Neither do I," Mark said.

"Ashley's right, it's not germane to the scene."

"Or even to the play."

"Maybe the butler stabs you," Jerry whispered from the wings.

"If a person gets stabbed, people want to know who stabbed her," Michelle insisted. "You can't just leave it hanging there."

"This isn't a play about a person getting stabbed," Andrea said. "*Or* hanged."

"Oh? What's it about then? An understudy who can't act?"

"Oh-*ho!*" Andrea said, and turned away angrily.

"Freddie, are you out there?" Michelle shouted to the theater. "Can *you* tell me who stabs . . . ?"

"He's not here, Michelle," Kendall said wearily.

He was uncomfortably aware that Morgenstern was sitting beside him here in the sixth row and he didn't want his producer to get the impression that he was losing control of his actors, especially when he actually was. The moment an actor started screaming for clarification from the playwright was the moment to come down hard, star or no star. Which, by the way, Michelle Cassidy wasn't, *Annie* or no *Annie,* which was a hundred years ago, anyway.

Using his best Otto Preminger voice, seething with controlled rage, he said, "Michelle, you're holding up rehearsal. I want to do this scene, and I want to do it right, and I want to do it *now.* If you have any questions, save them for notes. Meanwhile, I would like you to get stabbed *now,* by *whoever* the hell stabs you, as called for in the script at this point in the play's time. You have a costume fitting at six-thirty, Michelle, and I would like to break for dinner at that time, so if we're all ready, let's begin again. Please. From where Michelle pays her check, and comes out of the restaurant, and walks into the darkness . . ."

From where he stood in the shadowed side doorway of the delicatessen that shared the alleyway with the theater, he saw her coming out of the stage door at the far end, tight blue sweater and open peacoat, short navy-blue mini, gold-buckled belt, blue high-heeled shoes. He backed deeper into the doorway, almost banging into one of the garbage cans stacked alongside it. She checked her watch, and then stepped out briskly in that long-legged stride of hers, high heels clicking, red hair glowing under the hanging stage door light.

He wanted to catch her while she was still in the alley, before she reached the lighted sidewalk. The delicatessen's service doorway was just deep enough in from the street to prevent his being seen by any pedestrians, just far enough away from the stage door light, too. Clickety-click-click, long legs flashing, she came gliding closer to where he was standing. He stepped into her path.

"Miss Cassidy?" he said.

And plunged the knife into her.

3

STANDING AT THE SQUADROOM WATER COOLER, DETECTIVE/ Second Grade Stephen Louis Carella could not help overhearing Kling's conversation at the desk not four feet away. He filled his paper cup and turned away, standing with his back to Kling, looking through the wire-grilled window at the street below—but he could still hear the conversation. Deliberately, he tossed the empty cup at the wastebasket, and headed back across the room toward his own desk.

Carella was close to six feet tall, with the wide shoulders, narrow hips and gliding walk of a natural athlete—which he was not. Sitting behind his desk, he sighed and looked up at the wall clock, marveling at how the time did fly when you were having a good time. They were only three hours into the shift, but for some reason he was enormously weary tonight. Whenever he was this tired, his brown eyes took on a duller hue, seeming to slant more emphatically downward than they normally did, giving his face an exaggerated Oriental cast.

Four detectives had relieved the day shift at a quarter to four that Monday afternoon. Mayer and Hawes caught a liquor store holdup even before they took off their topcoats, and were out of the squadroom almost before they'd officially arrived. At around four-fifteen, a redheaded woman came up and told Kling somebody was trying to kill her, and he took down all the information and then discussed the possibility of a trap-and-trace with Carella, who said they wouldn't have a chance of getting one. Kling said he'd talk it over with the boss soon as he came in. Lieutenant Byrnes *still* wasn't here and Kling was *still* on the phone with someone named Sharon, whom he kept asking to meet him for coffee when the shift was relieved at midnight. From the snatches of conversation Carella could still overhear, Sharon wasn't being too receptive. Kling kept trying. Told her he'd be happy to take a cab to Calm's Point, just wanted to talk to her awhile. By the time he hung up, Carella *still* didn't know if it had worked out. He only knew there were five long hard hours ahead before they'd be relieved.

They caught the theater squeal at eight minutes past seven. The Susan Granger, a small theater on North Eleventh, near Mapes Avenue. Woman stabbed in the alley there. By the time Carella and Kling arrived, the woman had already been carted off to the hospital. One of the blues at the scene told them the victim's name was Michelle Cassidy and that she'd been taken to Morehouse General. Kling recognized the name. He told Carella she was the redhead who'd come to see him only three, three and a half *hours* ago, whenever the hell it was.

"Told me somebody was threatening to stab her," he said.

The uniformed cop shrugged and said, "So now he did."

They decided it was more important to talk to the victim than to do the neighborhood canvass just now. They got to

Morehouse at about seven-thirty and talked to the ER intern
who'd admitted Michelle Cassidy. He told them that two
inches lower and a bit to the right and Miss Cassidy would
at this very moment be playing first harp in the celestial
philharmonic. Instead, she was in room two thirty-seven, her
vital signs normal, her condition stable. He understood she
was an actress.

"Is she someone famous?" he asked.

"She played Annie," Kling said.

"Who's Annie?" the doctor asked. His name was Raman-
than Mehrota. It said so on the little plastic tag on his tunic.
Carella guessed he was Indian. In this city, the odds on finding
a doctor from Bombay in any hospital emergency room were
extraordinarily good. Almost as good as finding a Pakistani
cabdriver.

"They've got TV cameras up there," Mehrota said. "I
thought she might be someone famous."

"She is now," Carella said.

The TV reporter was doing their job for them. All they had
to do was stand at the back of the room and listen.

"When did this happen, Miss Cassidy?"

Carella recognized the woman as one of Channel 4's roving
reporters. Good-looking woman with curly black hair and
dark brown eyes, reminded him of his wife, except for the
curls; Teddy's hair was straight, but just as black.

"Everybody else had already gone to dinner," she said, "but
I had a costume fitting, so I was a little late leaving. I was
just coming out of the theater when . . ."

"What time was this?"

"A little after seven. We'd been rehearsing all day long . . ."

"Rehearsing what, Miss Cassidy?"

"A new play called *Romance*."

"What happened when you left the theater?"

"A man stepped out of a doorway there in the alley. He said, 'Miss Cassidy?' And then he stabbed me."

The camera came in on the reporter.

"Michelle Cassidy, stabbed tonight outside the Susan Granger Theater, where she is rehearsing—ironically—a play about a man who stabs an actress. This is Monica Mann, Channel 4 News, live at Morehouse General Hospital."

She stared into the camera for a moment until the operator gave her the signal that she was clear. She turned to the bed then, said, "Terrific, Miss Cassidy. Good luck with the show," and then turned again to her crew and said, "We're out of here."

The hot lights went out. The TV people cleared the room, and the nurse went outside to let in the newspaper people. The two city tabloids had each sent a reporter and a photographer. Carella could just see tomorrow's headlines:

ANNIE
STAR
STABBED

Or:

ACTRESS
SURVIVES
STABBING

The stately morning paper hadn't deigned to send anyone to the hospital; maybe the editor didn't realize a former child actress was the victim. Or maybe he simply didn't care. Cheap stabbings were a dime a dozen in this town. Besides, there'd been a riot in Grover Park this past Saturday, and the paper was still running postmortem studies on the causes of racial conflict and the possible remedies for it.

Again, all Carella and Kling had to do was listen. They realized at once that this was to be a more in-depth interview than television, with its limited time, had been able to grant.

"Miss Cassidy, did you *see* the man who attacked you?"

"Yes, I did."

"What'd he look like?"

"A tall slender man wearing a long black coat and a black hat pulled down over his head."

"What kind of hat?"

"A fedora. Whatever you call them."

"A brimmed hat?"

"Yes. Black."

"Wide-brimmed? Narrow-brimmed?"

"Wide. He had it pulled down over his eyes."

"Was he wearing gloves?"

"Yes. Black gloves."

"Did you see the knife?"

"No. Not really. I sure *felt* it, though."

Nervous laughter.

"You wouldn't know what *kind* of knife it was, would you?"

"A sharp one."

More laughter. Not as nervous this time. The kid was being a good sport. She'd just been stabbed in the shoulder, inches away from the heart, but she was able to joke about the weapon. The reporters liked that. It made good copy. Good-looking woman besides. Sitting up in bed in a hospital gown that kept slipping off one shoulder. As the reporters asked their questions, the photographers' cameras kept clicking.

Kling noticed that neither of the two reporters had yet

asked her what *color* the man was. Maybe journalists weren't allowed to. As cops, he and Carella would ask that question the minute the others cleared the room. Then again, they were looking to find whoever had just attempted murder. The reporters were only looking for a good story.

"Did he say anything to you?" one of the reporters asked.

"Yes. He said, 'Miss Cassidy?' Same thing he calls me on the phone."

"Wait a minute," the other reporter said. "What do you mean?"

"He's been calling me for the past week. Threatening to kill me. With a knife."

"This same *man*? The one who *stabbed* you tonight?"

"It sounded like the same man."

"Are you saying his voice sounded the same? As the man on the phone?"

"Exactly the same. Just like Jack Nicholson's voice."

Both reporters were scribbling furiously now. Jack Nicholson stabbing a young actress in the alley outside a rehearsal theater? Jesus, this was made in heaven!

"It *wasn't* Jack Nicholson, of course," Michelle said.

"Of course not," one of the reporters said, but he sounded disappointed.

"Who *was* he?" the other one asked. "Do you have any idea who he was?"

"Someone familiar with *Romance*," she said.

"Someone familiar with *romance*, did you say?"

"*Romance*. The play we're rehearsing."

"Why do you say that?"

"Because what happened in that alley *also* happens in the play.

Carella could now see the subhead on the story:

ALLEY ROMANCE STABBING

Now they wanted to know all about the scene in the play, and who else was in the play, and who had written it, and who was directing it, and when it would be opening here, and whether there were plans for moving it downtown, the cameras clicking, the reporters tirelessly questioning her while a black nurse fluttered about the bed telling them they mustn't exhaust her, didn't they realize the poor woman had been *stabbed*?

A man wearing a maroon sports shirt open at the throat, a gray sports jacket, and darker gray trousers rushed into the room, went immediately to the bed, took Michelle's hands in his own and said, "Michelle, my *God*, what *happened*? I just heard the news! Who *did* this to you? My *God*, why *you*?"

The reporters asked him who he was, and he introduced himself as Johnny Milton, Michelle's theatrical agent, and handed cards to both of them, and said he'd heard the news a few minutes ago, and rushed right over. Somewhat imperiously, he asked who the two men in the suits at the back of the room were, didn't they realize a woman had been *stabbed* here?

"We're the police," Carella said quietly, and showed the agent his shield.

"Hello, Detective Kling," Michelle said from the bed, waggling her fingers at him.

And suddenly all reportorial attention was on Kling, the two journalists wanting to know how he happened to know the victim, and then soliciting from Michelle herself the fact that she'd reported the threatening calls to Kling at approximately four-fifteen that afternoon, before she went back to rehearsal.

"Got any leads yet, Detective Kling?" one of the reporters asked.

"None," Carella said. "In fact, if you've got everything you need, we'd like to talk to Miss Cassidy now, if you don't mind."

"He's right, boys," her agent said. "Thanks for coming up, but she needs some rest now."

One of the photographers asked Michelle if she would mind one last picture, and when she said, "Okay, but I'm really very tired," he asked if she would mind lowering the gown off her left shoulder to show the bandaged wound, which she did in a demure and ladylike manner, while simultaneously managing to show a little bit of cleavage.

The moment everyone was gone, Kling asked, "Was the man who stabbed you white, black, Hispanic or Asian?"

The black nurse seemed about to take offense, but then Michelle said, "White."

At nine that night, Ashley Kendall was still rehearsing his cast, but instead of Michelle up there playing the Actress, her understudy was filling in for her. Kendall hated Corbin's pretentious naming—or *non*-naming—of the characters in his play. Right now, he was rehearsing the Actress's understudy, who happened to be an actress named Josie Beales, but on the same stage with her was an actress named Andrea Packer, who was playing the *character* named the Understudy, although *her* understudy was an actress named Helen Frears. It could get confusing if you weren't paying attention.

Josie was twenty-one, with strawberry-blond hair that was only a timid echo of Michelle's fiercer tresses. But she was taller than Michelle, and less cumbersomely endowed, and therefore moved more elegantly. In Kendall's opinion, she was also a far better actress than Michelle. In fact, he'd wanted to cast *her* as the Actress, but had been outvoted by Mr. Frederick Peter Corbin III. So now Miss Tits had the leading role, and Josie was a mere understudy who moved furniture and props and played a variety of non-speaking roles. Such was the tyranny of playwrights. Josie hadn't expected to be here tonight. She'd been interrupted at home, eating dinner— actually a container of yogurt and a banana—and watching *Love Connection* in her bathrobe, when the stage manager called to say, "You're on, babe." She'd thrown on a pair of jeans and a sweatshirt and rushed right over. Now she waited with the other actors for the rehearsal to resume.

Kendall supposed he could have called off the rehearsal, but Michelle's earlier behavior and stormy departure had left the other actors feeling confused and miserable. Besides, he was grateful for the opportunity to run through the scenes with an accomplished and disciplined young woman like Josie standing in, and without Mr. Moneybags Morgenstern sitting by witnessing a tantrum. The producer was gone now. In his stead in the sixth row center sat the exalted playwright himself, who had been home earlier today rewriting some *lines* that were troubling him, when he should have been rewriting three or four *scenes* that were troubling Kendall. Or maybe even the whole damn *play,* for that matter.

Everyone in the theater already knew that their "shtar" had been stabbed in the alley outside and taken to Morehouse General. Chuck Madden, the show's stage manager, had called there a few minutes ago. Now he leaned into the sixth row, and informed Kendall and Corbin that some blue-haired volunteer had told him Miss Cassidy's condition was stable and that she'd be released from the hospital sometime later tonight.

"Thank you, Chuck," Kendall said, and rose and said, "People?"

The actors chatting onstage, waiting for things to start, turned and squinted out into the darkened theater.

"I know you'll all be delighted to learn that Michelle's okay," Kendall said. "She'll be going home tonight, in fact."

"Terrific," someone said without enthusiasm.

"Who did it, do they know?" someone else asked.

"I have no information on that," Kendall said.

"Not germane, anyway," someone else said.

"I heard that, Jerry!"

"Sorry, boss!"

"Chuck? Are you back there yet?"

"Yes, sir!"

Chuck Madden sprang out onto the stage as if he'd almost missed a cue. He was wearing high-topped workman's boots, a rolled, blue woolen watch cap, and painter's coveralls that partially showed his bare chest and muscular arms. He was twenty-six years old, some six feet tall, with chestnut-colored hair and brown eyes. He shielded those eyes now and peered out toward the sixth row of the theater.

"Do you think you can do something with the lights when she comes out of the restaurant?" Kendall asked.

"Like what'd you have in mind?"

"It's supposed to be dark, the stabber is supposed to come out of the shadows. We've got Jerry popping out with the lights up full . . ."

"Yeah, give me some atmosphere," Jerry said.

"I know this is far too early to be discussing lighting . . ."

"No, no, what'd you want?"

"Can you give me a slow fade as she makes her cross? So that the stage is almost black when Jerry comes at her?"

"I like it, I like it," Jerry said.

"Let me talk to Kurt, see what he . . ."

"I heard it," the electrician called. "You've got it."

"Start the fade just as she comes through the door," Kendall said.

"Got it."

"People? Shall we try it?"

"*Uno más,*" Chuck said. "From the scene at the table."

Corbin had constructed his play in an entirely predictable manner. Once you recognized that there'd be a short quiet scene followed by a yet shorter scene intended to shock, and then a lengthy discourse on the shocker, you pretty much had the pattern of the play. As a result, there were no surprises at all; Corbin had given birth to a succession of triplets, most of them malformed.

The triplet they were now about to rehearse yet another time . . .

It was Kendall's conviction that this particular stretch would *never* play . . .

. . . consisted of a scene between the Actress and the Director sitting at a table in a restaurant, followed by a scene in which someone non-germane *stabs* the Actress, which is then followed by a scene in which the Detective interrogates ad infinitum the other two principals. There was simply no *way* to make this drivel come alive. The writing in the restaurant scene was *so* foreboding, *so* portentous, so *fraught* with foreshadowing, that any intelligent member of the audience would *know* the girl was going to get stabbed the minute she *left* the place.

"Why haven't you told me this before?"

The Director speaking.

The one onstage. Not Kendall himself sitting out here in the sixth row.

"I . . . I was afraid you were the one making the calls."

"Me? *Me?*"

This from Cooper Haynes, the dignified gentleman doctor of soap opera fame, looking thoroughly astonished by the mere *idea* of being the person making threatening phone calls to the actress he was directing. His stupefaction looked so genuine that it almost evoked a laugh from Kendall, exactly the *wrong* sort of response at this point in the play's time.

"I'm sorry, I know that's ridiculous. Why would you want to kill me?"

"Or anyone."

Another line which—when delivered in Cooper's wide-eyed bewildered way—could result in a bad laugh. In the dark, Kendall was furiously scribbling notes.

"You must go to the police."

"I've been."

"And?"

"They said they can't do anything until he actually *tries* to kill me."

"That's absurd."

"Yes."

"With whom did you speak?"

"A detective."

"And he said they could do nothing?"

"That's right."

"Impossible! Why . . . do you know what this means?"

"I'm so frightened."

"It means you can be sleeping in your bed . . ."

"I know."

". . . and someone could attack you."

"I'm terrified."

"It means you can leave this restaurant tonight . . ."

"I know."

"This very moment . . ."

"I know . . ."

"And someone can come at you with a knife."

"What shall I do? Oh dear God, what shall I do?"

"I'm going home right this minute to make some calls. I know a few people downtown who'll get on this *detective* of yours and see that he *does* something about this. Finish your coffee, I'll drop you off on my way."

"That's all right, go ahead. I thought I'd walk, anyway. It's just a few blocks."

"Are you sure?"

"Yes, go ahead."

"I worry about you, darling."

"No, don't."

"I worry."

"Good scene," Corbin whispered.

Kendall said nothing.

He watched as Cooper walked over to Helen Frears, who was playing the cashier, and settled his check, and then pushed his way through the imaginary revolving doors to the street outside. As he walked off into the wings, Josie sat finishing her coffee at the table.

"*Here's* where the fade should start," Kendall said, and made a note to cue the fade earlier. Josie finished her coffee, picked up a napkin, delicately wiped at her mouth with it, milking the moment, rose, put on her coat, still milking it— God, she was *so* good—pushed her chair back under the table, walked to the cashier, settled her bill, and then pushed through the same imaginary revolving doors.

The fade began.

As Josie began crossing the stage, the restaurant behind her—the table and chairs first, and then the cashier's stand—slowly went to black. Clutching her coat collar to her throat as if protecting herself against a fierce wind, she moved out boldly, the light continuing to vanish behind her with each step she took. And then, ominously, the light *ahead* of her began to grow dim as well, so that now she was moving into deeper and deeper shadows beyond which lay only blackness.

Out of that blackness there suddenly appeared a tall man in a long black coat and slouch hat, Jerry Greenbaum himself, no jokes this time, Jerry Greenbaum playing it for real in a costume he had salvaged someplace and was wearing for the first time. Where in earlier rehearsals he had used a wooden stick to simulate the knife, now—and possibly inspired by the lighting—he was wielding a bona fide bread knife he'd picked up backstage someplace, holding it high above his head like Tony Perkins coming at Marty Balsam in *Psycho,* coming at Josie with the same stiff-legged long-skirted stride Perkins had used, enough to chill the blood from memory of the scene alone, if not exactly what Kendall himself had directed in *this* scene.

The knife descended viciously, its blade glinting with pinpoint pricks of light as Josie turned to shield the fake thrust from the audience. The stabber ran off into the blackness. Josie fell to the stage, lay there motionless.

And now the other actors materialized like mourners at an Irish wake, surrounding the stricken Actress, the Detective firing questions at each of them as if she were really dead, asking the Director what they had talked about at dinner, asking the Understudy whether they had argued recently, and finally turning to the Actress herself, who—surprise of all surprises!—wasn't dead at all, but who rose from the stage now and fell back into a chair doubling as a hospital bed, and weakly answered the Detective's questions along with the rest of them in a scene outstanding only for its sheer boredom and longevity.

"Thank you, people, it's beginning to come together," Kendall said. "Take ten and I'll give you my notes."

As the actors began moving off, Jerry popped onstage, still wearing the long coat and the wide-brimmed hat.

"How was that, boss?" he shouted to the theater. "Scary enough?"

"Very nice, Jerry," Corbin said, and Kendall gave him a look.

"Little Hitchcock there, huh?" Jerry said.

"Very nice," Corbin said again, and Kendall gave him another look.

The two men sat silently for a moment.

"She's very good, isn't she?" Corbin said at last.

"Josie? Yes. She's wonderful."

"Made it come alive for the first time," Corbin said.

Kendall said nothing. The play was a long way from coming alive. Josie's performance had given it a good boost tonight, but unless Corbin sat down and rewrote the damn thing from top to bottom . . .

"Almost a shame," Corbin said.

"What is?"

"That he missed."

The two men came into the theater while Kendall was giving the cast his notes. Both were wearing topcoats. No hats. In the light that silhouetted them from the lobby as they came through the doors at the rear of the theater, he could see that one was blond and the other had dark hair. They were both tall, wide-shouldered men of about the same height and weight, both in their thirties somewhere, he guessed. The blond had hazel-colored eyes. The one with the dark hair had slanted brown eyes.

"Mr. Kendall?" the blond one called, inadvertently interrupting him in the middle of a sentence, which Kendall didn't appreciate one damn bit.

"Sorry to bother you, I'm Detective Kling, 87th Squad, this is Detective Carella, my partner."

He was showing a shield now.

Kendall was unimpressed.

"Miss Cassidy told us you might still be rehearsing here," Kling said. "We thought we'd save some trouble if we caught you all in the same place."

"I see," Kendall said dryly. "And just what sort of trouble were you hoping to save?"

"Few questions we'd like to ask," Kling said.

"Tell you what," Kendall said saccharinely. "Why don't you and your partner here go out to the lobby together, and have a seat on one of the red plush velvet benches out there, and when I'm finished giving the cast my notes—which I was *attempting* to do when you interrupted—we'll all come out there and play cops and robbers with you, okay? How does that sound?"

The theater went suddenly as still as a tomb.

"Sounds fine to me," Kling said pleasantly. "How does that sound to you, Steve?"

"Sounds fine to me, too, Bert."

"So what we'll do," Kling said, "is go find that red plush velvet bench in the lobby, and sit out there hoping the person who stabbed Michelle Cassidy won't make California by the time you finish giving the cast your notes. How does *that* sound to you?"

Kendall blinked at him.

"See you when you're done," Kling said, and turned and began walking toward the back of the theater again.

"Just a minute," Corbin said.

Kendall blinked again.

"The notes can wait," Corbin said. "What did you want to know?"

Which cued a scene outstanding only for its sheer boredom and longevity.

"You look tired," Sharyn said.

"So do you," Kling said.

"I am," she said.

It was almost midnight. Sharyn had called the squadroom at eleven to say she was in the city . . .

To any native of this town, there was Calm's Point, Majesta, Riverhead, Bethtown—and the City. Isola was the City, even though without the other four, it was only one-*fifth* of the city. Sharyn had called the squadroom to say . . .

. . . she was in the city and if he still wanted to have a cup of coffee she could meet him someplace uptown, which is where she happened to be. At St. Sebastian's Hospital, as a matter of fact. As an afterword, she mentioned that she was as hungry as a bear. Kling mentioned that he hadn't really eaten yet either, and suggested a fabulous deli on the Stem. At eleven-thirty—fifteen minutes before the shift was officially relieved—he dashed out of the squadroom.

Sharyn was now wolfing down a pastrami on rye.

She licked mustard from her lips.

"I'm glad you called," he said. "I was going to throw myself out the window otherwise."

"Sure."

"What were you doing at St. Sab's?"

"Trying to get a cop transferred to a better hospital. Right after you called me this afternoon, an officer got shot on Denver and Wales . . ."

"The Nine-Three."

"The Nine-Three. Ambulance took him to St. Sab's, the *worst* hospital in the whole damn city. I got there at six, found out who was in charge, got the man moved before they operated. Police escort all the way down to Buenavista, sirens blaring, you'd've thought the *Mayor* was in that ambulance."

"So you were in the city, anyway . . ."

"Yes."

"So you called me . . ."

"Well, yes."

". . . just so it shouldn't be a total loss."

"Right. Also, I was very hungry. And I owed you a meal."

"No, you didn't."

"Yes, I did. How's your hamburger?"

"What? Oh. Yeah. Good. I guess," he said, and picked it up and took a big bite of it. "Good," he said.

"Why do you keep staring at me?" she asked.

"Habit of mine."

"Bad one."

"I know. You shouldn't be so beautiful."

"Oh, please."

"Why'd you walk out last night?"

"I didn't walk out."

"Well, you cut things short."

"Yes, well."

"Why?"

Sharyn shrugged.

"Was it something I said?"

"No."

"I kept trying to figure out what I'd said. All day today, I kept trying to figure it out. I almost called a dozen times. Before I finally did, I mean. What was it I said?"

"Nothing."

"Tell me, Sharyn. Please. I don't want this starting on the wrong foot, really. I want this ... well ... tell me what I said."

"You said the color I was wearing was good for me."

Kling looked at her.

"So?" he said.

"I thought you were saying that the color was good for *my* color."

"That's what I *was* saying."

"So that started me wondering if the reason you'd asked me out was that I was black."

"Yes, I know. You asked me ..."

"And I started wondering what it was you *wanted* from me. I mean, was this just de white massa hittin on de l'il house nigguh? I guess I didn't want to risk finding out that was all it might be. So I thought it'd be best if we just shook hands and said goodnight, without either of us exploring the question too completely."

She bit into the sandwich again, sipped at her beer, her eyes avoiding his. Kling nodded and took another bite. They both ate in silence for several moments, Sharyn polishing off the sandwich as if she hadn't eaten in a week, Kling working less voraciously on the hamburger.

"So what are you doing here now?" he asked.

"I don't know," she said, and shrugged. "I guess I figured you were really being nice, saying the color suited me, the color was good for me, and that this wasn't very much different from what you might have said to a blonde wearing black or a redhead wearing brown, or whatever colors it is dat de white girls wears, hmmm?"

She had done it a second time, he noticed. Falling into a sort of exaggerated black English whenever she was saying something he was sure made her uncomfortable.

"And I guess I finally realized you didn't want anything from me that you didn't want from any *other* woman . . ."

"No, that isn't true," he said.

"Which is okay, I mean, *vive la différence, n'est-ce pas?* What the hell. A man is attracted to you . . ."

"I am."

"You don't go asking is it the color of my eyes, or the color of my skin . . ."

"It is."

". . . the same way you don't go asking yourself is it because *he's* so white."

"Is it?"

"I mean, blond hair and light eyes, does he have to be *so* white? Where are the goddamn *freckles*? I mean, the first time I date a white man, couldn't he . . ."

"Is it?"

". . . be a slightly *darker* shade of Charlie, couldn't he . . ."

"The first time?"

"Yes."

"Me, too. You, I mean. You're the first black woman I've ever known. *Getting* to know, that is. That is, I *hope* I'm getting to . . ."

"Yes, you are."

"I hope so."

"I hope so, too."

"Would you like some coffee?"

"Yes, please."

He signaled to the waiter.

"Also," she said, "I thought it was kind of cute, your calling me and telling me you were willing to come all the way out to Calm's Point again, at midnight no less, for a cup of coffee. Just so we could talk awhile. I thought that was very cute. And you were *so* persistent, oh my! I thought about that phone call all the while I was driving in to St. Sab's. I began thinking This is fate, this cop getting shot, my having to drive into the city. It wasn't meant that we should leave it where we left it last night. I shouldn't have been so *rejecting* on the phone, I shouldn't have *dissed* him that way. What did the poor guy say, for God's sake? He said he liked the color of my suit. Which, by the way, *is* a terrific color for my color . . ."

"It is."

"Sure, so what was I getting so upset about? A man paying me a compliment? I kept thinking all this while I drove in, and then I put it out of my mind when I got to the hospital because the only thing I wanted to do then was find the person in charge and let him know a police department representative was here now and that the cop in there better get the best medical treatment in the world or there'd be holy hell to pay."

"Is he all right now?"

"Yes, he's all right. Shot twice in the leg. He's all right."

"I hate cops getting shot."

"Tell me about it," Sharyn said, and nodded grimly. "Anyway, I didn't think about it again, about *you* again, about your calling and being so *per*sistent on the phone, until the cop was safely on his way to Buenavista, where he won't scream in the middle of the night, thank God, and no one'll come. I was going out to my car, figuring I'd drive back out to C.P., when all at once I thought again of *you* saying you were willing to drive out there after you'd put in eight hours, just to have a cup of coffee and talk. And I thought about the cop getting shot and bringing me into the city, and I said to myself Listen, who's being the stupid one here, you or him?"

"Who was it?"

"Anyway, I was starving to death."

"Uh-huh."

"And I hate to eat alone."

"Uh-huh."

"So I called you."

"And here we are," he said.

"Alone at last," she said.

Alone with him in bed that night, she told him how frightened she'd been. How frightened she still was.

"No, no," he said, "don't worry."

Soothing her. Stroking her thighs, kissing her nipples and breasts, kissing her lips.

"Everything happened so fast," she said.

"No, no."

"Someone's bound to realize . . ."

"How could they?"

"People aren't stupid, you know."

"Yes, but how could . . . ?"

"Suppose someone saw us tonight?"

"But no one did."

"You don't know that for a fact."

"Did *you* see anyone?"

"No, but . . ."

"Neither did I. No one saw us. Don't worry."

Kissing her again. Gently. Her lips, her breasts. His hand under the gossamer gown, stroking her, touching her.

"Everything's happening so fast," she whispered.

"It's supposed to."

"They'll ask . . ."

"Sure."

"Me. You. They'll ask."

"And we'll tell them. Everything *but*."

"They're not stupid."

"We're smarter."

"They'll realize."

"No."

"Hold me, Johnny, I'm so scared."

"No, baby, no, Michelle, don't worry."

4

THE TWO BLUES SEARCHING THE ALLEY WERE COMPLAINING THAT
nobody in this city would've gave a flying fuck about a
stabbing if the victim hadn'ta been a celebrity.

"Also," one of them said, "the only perp tosses a weapon
is the pros. They use a cold piece, they throw it down a sewer
afterwards, we find it, we can shove it up our ass. A person
ain't a contract hitter, he don't throw away no weapon. Even
a *knife* costs money, what d'you think? A person's gonna
throw it away cause he just *juked* somebody with it? Don't
be ridiculous. There's switchblades cost fifty, a hundred bucks,
some of them. He's gonna throw it away cause it's got a little
blood on it? Gimme a break, willya?"

"Who's the vic, anyway," the other one asked, "we're sear-
chin this fuckin alley in the rain?"

"The fuck knows," the other one said. "I never heard of
her."

It was really raining quite hard again.

Both of the blues were wearing black ponchos, and rain covers on their hats, but their shoulders and heads were dripping wet, anyway, and the drilling rain made it difficult to see in the dark alley here at close to two o'clock in the morning, even though they were industriously fanning every inch of it with their torches. Although they hadn't expressed it quite this way, they were right about fame in that a stabbing in this city—especially so soon after there'd been so *many* stabbings in Grover Park last Saturday—was a relatively insignificant occurrence that might have gone virtually unnoticed if the victim hadn't been an actress who once upon a time had played the lead in a road show production of *Annie.* Instead, here they were in a fuckin dark alley looking for a knife that had given some unknown "star" a scratch on the shoulder.

Well, something more than a scratch maybe, but according to what each of them had seen separately on television before they'd come on tonight, Michelle Cassidy's shoulder wound had been truly superficial. How bad *could* it have been if they'd released her from the hospital within several hours of her admission to the emergency room? So if this was just a scratch here, then it couldn't possibly be the required "serious" physical injury for Attempted Murder or even Assault One. What they had here was an Assault Two, *maybe,* where there'd been just a *plain* physical injury by means of a deadly weapon or a dangerous instrument. Which is why they were looking for a knife in the rain, they guessed.

"A fuckin Class D felony," one of the blues said.

"Seven years max," the other one said.

"Get a sharp lawyer in there, he'll bargain it down to Assault Three."

"A Class A mis."

"Is what we're wastin our time on."

"This country, anything happens to you," the first blue said, "you automatically become a star and a hero. All these shmucks came back from the Gulf War, they were all of a sudden *heroes*. I can remember a time when a hero was a guy who charged a fuckin machine-gun nest with a hand grenade in each hand and a bayonet between his teeth. *That* was a hero! Now you're a hero if you just *went* to the fuckin war."

"Or if you get yourself stabbed," the other one said. "It used to be if you *defended* yourself against the perp, and grabbed the knife *away* from him, and shoved it down his fuckin throat, *then* you were a hero. Now you're a hero if you just get stabbed. The TV cameras come in on you, this is the person got stabbed on the subway tonight, folks, he's a hero, look at him, he got himself stabbed, give him a great big hand."

"A hero *and* a celebrity, don't forget," the first one said.

"Yeah, but this one here is really *supposed* to be a celebrity, though."

"You ever hear of her?"

"No."

"Neither did I. Michelle Cassidy? Who the fuck's Michelle Cassidy?"

"She's a Little Orphan Annie."

"She's *bull*shit is what she is. Anybody gets hurt in this country, he becomes a hero and a celebrity, they give him a fuckin ticker tape parade. You notice how everybody knows exactly how to be interviewed on television? There's a tenement fire and the television cameras are there, and all at once this spic in her nightgown, she just got here from Colombia the night before, she's standin in the street can hardly speak

English, she's giving an interview to the reporter, she sounds as if she's the guest star on *The Tonight Show.* 'Oh, *sí,* it wass so *terrible,* my baby wass in huh creeb in dee odder room, I dinn know *wah* to do!' An illegal from Colombia is all at once a fuckin *celebrity* givin interviews."

"She'll be doin hair commercials next week."

"Commercials for *fire* extinguishers," the first blue said, and both of them burst out laughing.

The rain kept pouring down, sobering them.

"You see any fuckin knife in this alley?" the first one asked.

"I see *rain* in this alley, is what I see."

"Let's try the sidewalk."

"The gutter."

"Maybe he threw it in the gutter."

"Maybe he took it home and tucked it under his pillow, fifty-dollar switchblade knife."

"What time you got?"

"Almost two."

"Wanna call in a pee break?"

"Too early."

"Ain't you hungry?"

"I could go for a slice a pizza."

"So let's give it a shot."

"We only been on two hours."

"More than two."

"Two and a quarter."

"In the fuckin *rain,* don't forget."

"Even so."

"Lookin for a knife don't exist."

"He coulda tossed it in the gutter."

"Knife we'll never find."

"Let's check the gutter."

Twenty minutes later, they were eating pizza in an all-night joint just off Mapes Avenue.

Seven hours after that, Carella and Kling were sitting in the squadroom going over the notes they'd taken at the theater last night. The rain had tapered a bit, but not enough to keep them from feeling that winter was still here. This was the seventh day of April. Spring had been here for two weeks and three days already, but it had been a rotten winter, and it was *still* a rotten winter as far as anyone in this city was concerned.

"The way it looks to me," Kling said, "everybody had already left the theater when she came out into that alley."

"Except the costume designer," Carella said. "According to Kendall, she stayed behind for a fitting with the costume designer."

"Woman named Gillian Peck," Kling said, and yawned. "Stage manager gave me her address and phone number, too."

"Late night?" Carella asked, and stifled the urge to yawn himself.

"I got home around three. We talked a lot."

"You and Sharon?"

"Sharyn."

"She finally agreed to let you come all the way out to C.P., huh?"

"No, she met me here in the city. Anyway, how'd you . . . ?"

"Small squadron."

"Big ears."

"*I muri hanno orrecchi,*" Carella said.

"What's that mean?"

"The walls have ears. My grandmother used to say that all the time. So who is she?"

"Your grandmother?"

"Yes, my grandmother."

"Sharyn, you mean?"

"Sharon, I mean."

"Sharyn."

"Must be an echo in this place."

"No, it's *Sharyn*. With a 'y.'"

"Ahh, *Sharyn*."

"Sharyn, yes."

"So, who is she?"

"A cop," Kling said.

He guessed it was reasonable to call a one-star chief a cop.

"Anyone I know?"

"I don't think so."

"Where'd you meet her?"

"On the job."

Which was also true, more or less.

"If all of them had already left the theater," he said, changing the subject, "any one of them could have been out in the alley stabbing her. So . . ."

"Are you changing the subject?" Carella asked.

"Yes."

"Okay."

"I just don't want to talk about it yet," Kling said.

"Okay," Carella said, but he looked hurt. "Where do we start here?"

"Steve . . ."

"I know."

"How long are we gonna beat this thing to death? She was out of the hospital a minute and a half after she checked in. She'll be back at rehearsal today, the show will go on. I've got three backed-up murders and a dozen . . ."

"I know."

"This isn't that important, Steve."

"*You* know it's not important, and *I* know it's not important, but does Commissioner *Hartman* know it's not important?"

"What are you saying?"

"Pete called me at home this morning."

"Uh-oh."

"Said he'd just got off the phone with Hartman. The Commish *and* the Mayor both wanted to know what the Eight-Seven was doing about this big star who got stabbed right outside the theater. Said they understood she'd been up here previously to report . . ."

"Three *hours* previously!"

"But who's counting? Said it didn't look good that we *knew* about threatening phone calls and still allowed . . ."

"*Allowed?*"

". . . the vic to get stabbed . . ."

"Oh yes, we allowed her to get stabbed."

"Is what the Commish told Pete. Which Pete repeated to me on the phone this morning at seven-thirty. The media's making a big deal out of this, Bert. Another feeding frenzy. Pete wants the knifer. Fast."

A uniformed black doorman asked Carella who he was here to see, please, and Carella showed him his shield and gave him Morgenstern's name. The doorman buzzed upstairs, announced Carella, and then told him he could go right up, it was Penthouse C, elevator just to the right there. A uniformed black maid opened the door for Carella and told him that Mr. Morgenstern was in the breakfast room, would he care to follow her, please? He followed her through a sumptuously

decorated apartment with windows facing the park everywhere.

Marvin Morgenstern was sitting in a bay window streaming
midmorning sunlight, wearing a blue silk robe with a blue
silk collar and a blue silk sash. Silk pajamas of a paler blue
hue showed below the hem of the robe and in the open V of
its front. He was munching on a piece of toast as the maid
led Carella into the room. "Hello," he said, "nice to see you,"
and then rose and wiped either butter or jelly from his hand,
and offered it to Carella. They shook hands, and then Morgenstern said, "Sit down, sit down. Have some coffee. Some
toast? Ellie, bring some hot toast and another cup. You want
some orange juice? Ellie, bring him a glass of juice, too. Sit
down. Please."

Carella sat.

He'd had breakfast at eight this morning, and it was now
a little past ten. Morgenstern hadn't yet shaved, but he'd
combed the sleep out of his hair, sweeping it back from his
forehead without a part. He had shaggy black brows to match
the hair, though the hair was so black it looked dyed. Maybe
the brows were dyed, too. Narrow thin-lipped mouth, bright
blue eyes, mouth and eyes seeming to join in secret amusement, though Carella could find nothing funny about assault.

"So do you know who did it yet?" Morgenstern asked.

"Do you?" Carella said.

"Who knows, the bedbugs in this city? What ideas do you
have?"

"We're still investigating," Carella said vaguely.

"Is that why you're here?"

"Yes."

"You think *I* did it?" Morgenstern said, and burst out
laughing.

"Did you?"

"I'm sixty-seven years old," he said, his laughter subsiding. "I had a triple bypass three years ago, my knee from when I had the cartilage removed twenty years ago is finally beginning to tell me when it's going to rain, and you think I stabbed my own star in an alley? Have a heart, willya? Ah, here's Ellie," he said. "Fresh coffee, too, terrific. Just set it down, Ellie. Thank you."

The maid put down a tray bearing a teaspoon, a fork, a knife, a napkin, a glass of orange juice, an empty cup and saucer, a rack of toast, and a fresh pot of coffee. Carella guessed she was no older than twenty-three, a pretty woman with sloe eyes and a *café au lait* complexion. He guessed Haitian only because so many of the new black immigrants *were* Haitian. Without uttering a word, she left the room again.

Morgenstern poured coffee, passed the cream pitcher and the sugar bowl. Carella drank his orange juice, and then reached for a piece of toast. He buttered it and put strawberry jam on it, and then bit into it. The bread was fresh and the toast was crunchy and still warm. The coffee was good and strong, too. He made himself at home.

"So tell me about the theater business," he said.

"You want to know if it was worth my while stabbing her, right?" Morgenstern said.

He still seemed secretly amused by all this.

"Something like that," Carella said.

"Like what do I stand to gain now that my star has been stabbed and everybody in town knows the name of my play," he said, and this time he smiled openly, never mind any secrets.

"*And* the date it's going to open," Carella said.

"Right, the sixteenth," Morgenstern said. "A Thursday

night. The day before Passover *and* Good Friday. That should
bring us luck, don't you think? A double whammy? So let
me tell you *just* what I'll earn if this play is a hit, okay?
Which, I'll admit, seems a good possibility. We're getting the
cover of *Time* next week, you know. It'll be on the stands
Monday."

"I didn't know that."

"Yeah. But this has become a continuing television drama,
anyway. You can't tune in a news broadcast without seeing
and hearing some mention of Michelle Cassidy, Michelle
Cassidy, Michelle Cassidy. Nothing television likes better,
right? Beautiful girl with big tits gets stabbed, they eat it up.
Wring their hands in public, but in private they're licking
their chops. I won't be surprised if they make the story a
miniseries. Not that I'm any different. In fact, if you want to
do me a big favor, you'll *arrest* somebody before we open.
Keep the story going, you know?"

"You were about to tell me . . ."

"Right, my finances. What do I stand to gain? Why did I
stab Michelle, right?"

"I didn't say you'd stabbed her."

"I know you didn't. I'm just kidding. *I* didn't say I stabbed
her, either. Because I didn't."

"I'm relieved to hear that," Carella said, and sipped at his
coffee, and then buttered and jammed another piece of toast.

"Although my piece of the show would seem to justify it,"
Morgenstern said.

"Justify what?"

"Murder."

"Uh-huh. What exactly *is* your piece of the show?"

"Which is what you asked in the first place."

"And which you still haven't answered."

"In a nutshell, I get two percent of the gross, fifty percent of the profits, and office expenses."

"What's the gross expected to be?"

"At capacity?"

"Yes."

"If we move it downtown, you mean. Which is what we'd do with a hit. So let's say we move it to a five-hundred-seat theater on the Stem. Your top ticket would go for fifty bucks on a straight play, which this is. As opposed to a musical. The top on a musical is sixty-five, seventy, it depends. So let's say a top of fifty, an average of . . . listen I've got this all broken down, what's the sense of doing it in my head?"

"Got what all broken down?"

"My business manager made an estimate for me. In case we move to the Stem."

"I guess you're anticipating that."

"Well, *now* I am, yes."

"When did he make this estimate for you?"

"Yesterday. Right after Michelle got stabbed."

"I see."

"Yeah. If you want a copy of it, I'll give it to you before you leave."

"I'd appreciate that."

"My pleasure," Morgenstern said.

"So what does your business manager estimate the profits will be if you move to the Stem?"

"In a five-hundred-seat house? At capacity? Seventy grand a week."

"In other words, Mr. Morgenstern, if this show is a hit, you'll be taking home quite a bit of money."

"Quite a bit, yes."

"How long do you figure it'll take to recoup?"

"At capacity? Thirteen weeks."

"After which you start getting your fifty-percent share of the profits."

"Yes."

"Who gets the *other* fifty percent?"

"My investors."

"How many of *those* are there?"

"Twenty. I'll give you a list of them, too, if you like."

"How much does your playwright get?"

"Freddie? Six points."

"Before or after recoupment?"

"Pre *and* post, all the way through. A straight six percent of the gross."

"Nice business," Carella said.

"Except that for every play that makes it, you've got a dozen that flop. Frankly, you're better off putting your money in mutual funds."

"I'll remember that," Carella said.

"Have another piece of toast."

"Thanks. Few more questions and I'll get out of your hair."

"Here comes the rubber hose," Morgenstern said, and smiled again.

"As I understand this," Carella said, "last night . . ."

"See? What'd I tell you?"

Carella smiled. He picked up another piece of toast, buttered it, put jam on it, bit into it. Chewing, he said, "Last night, Michelle was delayed at the theater some fifteen, twenty minutes. The *others* all broke for dinner, but she . . ."

"Yes, that's my understanding, too."

"You weren't there?"

"No. Who says I was there?"

"I thought . . ."

"Earlier maybe. But not when they . . ."

"I thought you were there during the rehearsal."

"I got there at five and left around six, six-fifteen. Right after the fight."

"Oh? What fight?" Carella asked.

"The usual bullshit."

"What usual bullshit is that?"

"The actress wanting to know *why* she's doing this or that, the director telling her to just *do* it."

"Then this fight was between Michelle and Kendall, is that it?"

"Yes. Anyway, it wasn't a *fight,* it was just the usual bullshit. You know the famous story about the phone ringing, don't you?"

"No, I don't."

"There's this scene in a play where the phone is ringing, and the actor is supposed to answer it and have a conversation with the person on the other end. So this *Method* actor wants to know what his *motivation* is, *why* does he answer the phone? The director tells him, 'Because it's *ringing*, goddamn it!' This goes on all the time, the bullshit between the actors and the director. It doesn't mean a thing."

"Who else was there? Was Freddie Corbin there?"

"No. Just the actors and the crew."

"Were they all still there when you left?"

"Yes."

"But they left the theater *before* Michelle did, is that right?"

"Yes, she had a costume fitting. The costume designer needed her for fifteen, twenty minutes."

"So the *others* all broke for dinner at six-thirty . . ."

"I think that's what Ashley was planning. Yes, I'm sure he said six-thirty."

"Which left just Michelle and the costume designer alone in the theater."

"Well, Torey would've been there, too."

"Torey?"

"Our security guard. At the stage door."

"That's his name? Torey?"

"Well, it's Salvatore Andrucci, actually. But he used to fight under the name Torey Andrews. Do you remember Torey Andrews? Good middleweight some twenty, twenty-five years ago. That's Torey."

"Know where I can reach him?"

"At the theater. You want some more coffee? I'll get the *shwartzer* to bring some."

"Thank you no," Carella said. "I've taken enough of your time."

"Then let me get that estimate for you. If you still want it."

"I still want it," Carella said.

Gillian Peck lived in a doorman building on the city's upper south side. Kling had called ahead, and when he was announced over the intercom, he could hear a British voice answering, "Yes, do send him up, please."

The woman who opened the door seemed to be in her mid-fifties, a petite, mop-topped brunette wearing a green silk-brocade tunic over matching bell-bottomed pajama pants and green slippers with a gold crest. She told him at once that she had a meeting downtown at noon—this was now ten past eleven—and she hoped this would be short. Kling promised that it would.

She led him into a living room hung with framed drawings of the costumes she'd done for what appeared to be a hundred different shows, but which she explained had been only ten. "My favorite was the *Twelfth Night* I did for Marvin," she said, beaming, and walked Kling past a series of framed sketches of figures in brightly colored costumes, the name of each character penciled in at the bottom of the drawing: Sir Toby Belch. Sir Andrew Aguecheek. Malvolio. Olivia. Viola . . .

"I love the names he gave them," she said. "Do you know what the *full* title of the play is?"

"No," Kling said.

"Shakespeare called it *Twelfth Night; Or What You Will.* I took that as a cue for the costumes. I went for an uninhibited, anything-goes look."

"I think you succeeded," Kling said.

"Yes, quite," Gillian said pensively, studying the drawings. "Well, then," she said, turning away abruptly and walking toward a seating group that consisted of a sofa done in red velvet and two side chairs done in black. She sat in one of the black chairs, perhaps because she didn't wish to appear too Christmasy in a green costume against a red background. Kling suddenly wondered if she designed her own clothes.

"Sit down, won't you?" she said, and gestured to the sofa. He sat.

She looked at her watch.

"About Miss Cassidy," he said.

"Oh dear, that poor child," Gillian said.

"You were with her last night, I understand. Just before she got stabbed."

"Yes. I fitted her for one of her costumes."

"How many are there?"

"She has three changes. This was for the one in the first act. It's white, very virginal, it's when she's supposed to be a young girl, when she first becomes infatuated with the theater. Do you know the play?"

"Not really."

"It's a dreadful stinker," Gillian said. "Quite frankly, Marvin should be grateful for all this publicity."

"I'm sure he is," Kling said.

She looked at him.

"Mm," she said. "Well, yes, I shouldn't wonder. In any case, there are three changes, the virgin white one, and then the gray one, when she sort of loses her innocence ... it's all such rot, really ... and then the red one after she's been stabbed, when God knows who or *what* she's supposed to be. Or even who's stabbed her, for that matter. It's rather a matter of life imitating art, isn't it?"

"I suppose so, yes."

"Do you have any idea who did it?"

"Not yet."

"Life imitating art exactly," she said. "In the play, nobody knows who stabbed her, either."

"Well, we're still investigating."

"It's frightening to think the person who stabbed her is still loose, isn't it? And may *remain* loose. Which wouldn't be too uncommon in this city, would it?"

"Well," Kling said.

"No offense meant."

"Where did this fitting take place, Miss Peck?"

"In Michelle's dressing room."

"At what time?"

"Six-thirty. Six thirty-five."

"How long did it last?"

"Oh, ten minutes at most."

"Till twenty to seven?"

"I'd say a quarter to."

"Then what?"

"What do you mean?"

"What did you do *after* the fitting?"

"Well, we *left*."

"The theater?"

"No, the dressing room."

"Together?"

"No. I went to the wardrobe room to hang the costume up again, and Michelle went to the loo."

"Did you see her again that night?"

"Yes, just before I left the theater."

"Where'd you see her?"

"There's a phone just inside the stage door, on the wall there. A pay phone. She was standing there as I was leaving the theater."

"Talking?"

"No. She was just dialing a number, in fact."

"What time would this have been?"

"Oh . . . ten to seven?"

"What happened then?"

"I said goodnight to Torey, and went out."

"Who's Torey?"

"The security guard."

"Where was he?"

"Sitting just inside the stage door. Where he always sits. There's a stool there."

"How far from the phone?"

"Five feet? Six feet? I really couldn't say."

"Did you see anyone in the alley when you came out?"

"No one."

"You weren't still *in* the alley when Michelle left the theater, were you?"

"No, I wasn't."

"Then you didn't see her actually leaving?"

"No, I didn't."

"And I'm sure you didn't see anyone stab her."

"That's correct."

"Where'd you go after you left the theater?"

"To meet a gentleman friend of mine."

"Where would that have been?"

"A restaurant downtown. I caught a cab just outside the theater."

"At what time would that have been?"

"At five minutes to seven."

"You know the exact time, do you?"

"Yes, I looked at my watch. I was supposed to meet my friend at seven-thirty, and I was wondering if I'd be late. The restaurant is all the way downtown."

"Which restaurant is that, Miss Peck?"

"Da Luigi. On Mersey Street."

"*Were* you late?"

"No, I got there *right* on the Dorothy."

Kling looked at her.

"The dot," she said.

Torey Andrews né Salvatore Andrucci studied the shield in the palm of Carella's hand, and then looked at his ID card again, and then said, "Is this about Michelle?"

"Yes, it is," Carella said.

"I was hoping you caught the guy by now."

"We're still investigating."

"Long as *I* ain't a suspect, huh?" Torey said, and grinned, showing a mouthful of missing teeth.

He was perhaps five feet ten inches tall, weighing in at two-forty or thereabouts these days, no longer the middle-weight he'd once been. His left eye was partially closed by scar tissue, and his nose roamed all over the center of his face, and he sounded like any of the punch-drunk pugs Carella had ever met. But there was intelligence in his lively green eyes and Carella figured he'd quit the ring before they'd managed to scramble his brains.

He was wearing what Carella had always called a "bakery-shop sweater," because this was the kind of sweater Carella's father had worn to work each morning. In Torey's case, the sweater was a collarless brown cardigan, a bit frayed at the cuffs, one of the buttons missing. He wore this with thick-waled corduroy trousers and brown loafers. He was sitting on his stool just inside the stage door. The pay phone on the brick wall painted black was some seven or eight feet away from the stool. From the stage, Carella could hear what sounded like two or three actors rehearsing a scene. The clock on the wall read twelve-thirty.

"Torey, can you tell me anything about what happened last night?" Carella asked.

"Oh, sure. It was me who called the police. I heard her screaming, I ran out there, she was laying on the ground, screaming."

"You didn't see anyone *else* in the alley, did you?"

"No. Just her. You mean the one who stabbed her? No. I wished I did."

"What'd you do?"

"I left her laying there. You ain't supposed to move any-body's hurt. I learned that when I was still in the ring. Somebody gets hit bad, you move him, it could make him worse. So I left her out there, and I come inside again and called nine-one-one. From the phone right there. They got here right away. Which is a miracle, this city."

"Can you remember seeing anyone suspicious *before* Miss Cassidy left the theater?"

"I wasn't outside."

"I meant *inside* the theater. After everyone else left."

"You mean after Miss Peck went out, too."

"Yes. You didn't see anyone suspicious in the theater, did you? Anyone who shouldn't have been here?"

"No, I didn't. Miss Peck left, and a few minutes later Michelle came up to use the phone, and . . ."

"Miss Cassidy made a phone call?"

"Yeah. From the phone right on the wall there."

"Did you hear what she *said* while she was on the phone?"

"Well, it was a very quick call."

"But did you hear it?"

"Yes, I did."

"What did she say?"

"She said . . . well, you want this exact? Because I'm not sure I can remember it *exact*."

"As close as you can remember."

"Well . . . she said like uh This is me, I'm just about to leave, something like that. And then she listened, and I guess she just said Okay, and hung up."

"Did she mention anyone's name?"

"No."

"What did she do then?"

"She came over here and we talked for a while."

"How long a while?"

"Five minutes? She kept looking at her watch . . . I figured she had to go meet somebody. But we talked for a few minutes, and then she looked at her watch again, and said, 'Well, so long, Torey,' something like that, and off she went."

"What time was this?"

"Few minutes after seven."

"How do you know?"

"Clock hanging right there on the wall," he said, and gestured with his head. "I look at it all the time. It's funny," he said. "You're in the round three minutes, it seems like forever. But here, in the theater here, I sit on my stool, I look at the clock, and I remember the old days, and it's like a movie going by too fast. Sometimes I think I won't have enough time to play all the movies inside my head. You think I'll have time to play them all?"

"I hope so," Carella said gently.

The clock on the squadroom wall read twenty minutes past one. They had sent out for lunch, and now, as they ate, they recapped what each of them had separately learned.

"Who'd she call?" Kling asked.

"Big question."

"Let me see that estimate Morgenstern gave you," he said, and Carella shoved it across the desk to him.

WEEKLY ESTIMATED BUDGET—"ROMANCE"
FOR A 500-SEAT "MIDDLE" THEATER
BASED ON A BREAK-EVEN GROSS OF $100,000

SALARIES

CAST:

MICHELLE CASSIDY	$3,000
ANDREA PACKER	$2,400
COOPER HAYNES	$2,400
MARK RIGANTI	$2,400

4 SCALE PLAYERS	@$1,000	$4,000

"Scale actors get a big one a week, huh?"

"Wanna be an actor?"

"Nope."

STAGE MANAGER		$1,400
ASSISTANT STAGE MANAGER		$1,150
A.E.A. VACATION & SICK PAY ACCRUAL		$990

"What's A.E.A.?"

"Don't know."

WARDROBE SUPERVISOR		$900
T.W.A.V./MU & HS VACATION PAY		$63

"T.W.A.V.?"

"Some kind of union, I'll bet."

"MU? HS?"

"Don't know."

GENERAL MANAGER		$1,500
COMPANY MANAGER		$977
PRESS AGENT		$1,085
PRODUCTION ASSISTANT		$500
ATTORNEY		$350
ACCOUNTANT		$250
BOOKKEEPER		$200
CASTING DIRECTOR		$250
DESIGNERS	2@$175	$350
		$24,165

THEATER

RENTAL GUARANTEE	$6,500
BASIC PERSONNEL & EXPENSES	$22,500
ADDITIONAL STAGE CREW	$1,195
	$30,195

PROMOTION, PUBLICITY AND ADVERTISING

PRINT ADVERTISING	**$9,000**
RADIO ADVERTISING	**$3,000**
TELEVISION ADVERTISING	**0**

"Guess they don't believe in the power of the tube, huh?"

"Guess not."

THREE-SHEET-MAINTENANCE	**$200**
BUSES, CABS, PHONE BOOTHS, ETC.	**$3,000**
PRINTING, MAILING 7 PHOTO REPRO	**$150**

"What's a three-sheet?"

"Beats me."

PRESS AGENT OFFICE & EXPENSES	**$250**
SPECIAL PROMOTION	**$400**
	$16,000

ADMINISTRATIVE AND GENERAL

PROGRAM INSERTS, ETC.	**$80**
LEAGUE DUES AND FEES	**$500**

"As the monkey said while peeing into the till . . ."

"This is running into a lot of money," Carella said, and both men began giggling like schoolboys.

PRODUCER OFFICE EXPENSE	**$750**
GENERAL MANAGER OFFICE EXPENSE	**$400**

"You can skip over the rest of the administrative and general expenses," Carella said. "Look down to the next section."

Kling looked:

ROYALTIES AT GROSS OF:	**$100,000**	
AUTHOR	6.00%	6,000
STAR	.00%	0

"Michelle isn't getting a piece of the action, I see."

"None of the actors are."

"Big winner is the author."

"*Bigger* winner is Morgenstern."

"Not according to this."

DIRECTOR	2.00%	$2,000
PRODUCER	2.00%	$2,000
TOTAL ROYALTIES	10.00%	$10,000

"He *also* gets fifty percent of the profits."

"Nice. Does he own the *theater,* too?"

"I don't think so."

THEATER PARTICIPATION

Projected % Rate	5.00%	$5,000

"So what've we got here?"

"Add it up."

TOTAL ESTIMATED WEEKLY OPERATING

RECAP

IN A 500-SEAT HOUSE

WITH: $50.00 TOP TIX

NET: $45.75 AVG TIX

ESTIMATED CAPACITY GROSS:	$183,000
ESTIMATED EXPENSE AT CAPACITY:	$112,925
ESTIMATED WEEKLY PROFIT AT CAPACITY:	$70,075

"Morgenstern gets half of that," Carella said. "Plus his two percent and his office expenses."

"You think he did it?"

"No."

"Then who did?"

"Whoever Michelle phoned before she left the theater."

5

THE SECRETARY IN THE SMALL WAITING ROOM OF JOHNNY Milton's office on Stemmler Avenue and Locust Street was on the telephone when the detectives arrived at three o'clock that Tuesday afternoon. She glanced up briefly, signaled to the bench on the wall opposite her desk, listened for another moment, and then said, "I can understand how you feel, Mike, but he really *is* on a conference call, and I don't know how long he'll be."

She listened again, rolled her eyes, and said, "Well, that isn't true, Mike, he talks to you *all* the time. *When?* What do you mean *when?*" she said, and rolled her eyes again. "Whenever there's anything to report, he calls you. Well, that's not true, either. He's always got things to report to you. Mike, you just got back from a dinner club date in Boston, who do you suppose got *that* for you, if not Johnny. What? No, I'm sure that wasn't two months ago. February? Really? Was it in *February*? Then I guess it *was* two months ago. Gee. Even so, he's working for you all the time, Mike, I promise you. Ooops, there goes the other phone," she said, although nothing else in the office was ringing. "I'll tell him you called, he'll get right back to you. Nice talking to you," she said, and hung up, and expelled her breath in exasperation.

"Actors," she said, and then, realizing that the two men standing near the bench across the room were cute enough to be actors themselves, and might just possibly *be* actors, she said in explanation, "Hitchcock was right," and recognized she might only be compounding the felony although neither of the two seemed to understand the reference, which was to Hitchcock constantly saying all actors were cattle, which she'd read in a magazine in a doctor's office, never having met the man.

"Can I help you?" she asked, smiling pleasantly and sitting up straighter in her chair, the better to impress in her somewhat tight red sweater. The blond one stepped away from the wall with the framed eight-by-tens of Johnny's clients on it, and crossed over to the desk, a sort of leather fob falling open in his right hand to reveal a gold shield that had the name of the city on it, and the city's seal in gold on blue enamel and the word DETECTIVE under it, and under that 87TH SQUAD.

"Detective Kling," he said. "My partner, Detective Carella," nodding toward him as he, too, approached the desk. "We'd like to talk to Mr. Milton, please."

"Oh," she said. "Sure," and immediately picked up the phone and hit a button on its base, giving the lie to the conference-call story she'd just told the actor named Mike. "Mr. Milton," she said, "there are some detectives here to see you." She listened, nodded, and said, "Yes, sir, right away," and replaced the phone on its base. "Just go right in," she said, and indicated a wood-paneled door to the right of her desk.

Johnny Milton was dressed for spring sunshine this afternoon, although it was still raining outside his window. Wearing a pastel blue V-necked sweater over a yellow shirt open at the throat, beige slacks, and tasseled loafers, he looked like a producer on a Hollywood lot, rather than an agent in an office the size of the lieutenant's back at the old Eight-Seven. Instead of mug shots, however, the walls here were covered with framed posters of shows in which Milton's clients had presumably performed. Some of the shows were familiar to Carella, if only by their titles. Most of them rang no bell at all. Milton's right hand was extended as he came around the desk.

"Gentlemen," he said, "nice to see you again," and shook hands first with Carella and then with Kling. "Sit down, please. Just move that stuff, here let me get it," he said, and went to a sofa laden with what Carella guessed were scripts in variously colored binders. Milton carried them to his desk, dropped them on it unceremoniously, motioned for them to sit, and then went behind the desk and sat himself. The sofa was one of those narrow little love seats upholstered in a very dark green velvet fabric. The detectives sat side by side on it, their shoulders touching.

"Michelle's fine," Milton said at once. "If you're wondering." He looked at his watch. "Rehearsing right this minute, in fact."

"Good," Carella said. "Mr. Milton, had she mentioned any of these threatening phone calls to you?"

"Not until yesterday. I was the one who advised her to go to the police."

"Ahh," Carella said.

"Yes."

"Did she tell you the man sounded like Jack Nicholson?"

"Yes. But, of course . . ."

"Of course."

". . . he *isn't* Jack Nicholson. You understand that, don't you?"

"Yes, we do."

"Jack Nicholson is in Europe right now, in fact, on location."

"So he couldn't have been the man who stabbed Michelle in that alleyway," Carella said, deadpan.

"Exactly what I'm saying," Milton said.

"Any idea who that man might have been?" Carella asked.

"No."

"Do any of your clients do Jack Nicholson imitations?"

"No. Not to my knowledge, anyway," Milton said, and smiled.

"Mr. Milton," Kling said, "do you remember where you were last night when you heard Michelle had been stabbed?"

"Yes, I do. Certainly. Why?"

"Where would that have been, sir?"

"At a steakhouse on the Stem. Stemmler Avenue," he added, explaining the abbreviation as if the detectives had just got off a boat from Peru.

"Do you remember the name of it?" Carella said.

"O'Leary's Steakhouse."

"On the Stem and North Twelfth?"

"Yes."

"All the way uptown, huh?"

"Michelle was supposed to meet me there. It's close to the theater."

"Three, four blocks away, in fact."

"Yes."

"What time were you supposed to meet?"

"I made a reservation for seven."

"But she never showed."

"No. Well, you know what happened."

"Yes. She got stabbed as she was leaving the theater. Apparently on her way to meet you."

"Apparently."

"What'd you do when she didn't show?"

"I called the theater."

"What time was that?"

"Seven-fifteen, seven-twenty. That was when I learned what had happened."

"Oh?" Kling said.

Both detectives looked at each other.

"I thought you heard the news on the radio," Carella said.

"No, Torey told me what had happened. The play's security guard. *Romance*. The play she's in. He told me she'd been stabbed and they'd taken her to Morehouse General. So I caught a cab and rushed right over."

"I got the impression you'd heard the news on the radio," Carella said.

"Really? What gave you that impression?"

"Just the way you said it."

"What I said was I'd just heard the news."

"Yes, and rushed right over."

"Right."

"Made it sound as if you'd heard a news broadcast."

"No, I didn't. It was Torey who told me about it."

"I understand that now."

The detectives looked at each other again.

"According to Miss Cassidy, you and she are living together, is that right?" Kling asked.

"That's right."

"Where do you live, sir?"

"Her apartment. What *used* to be her apartment, till we decided to take the plunge. Live together, I mean."

"And where's that?" Carella asked.

"The apartment? On Carter and Stein."

The Eighty-eighth, Carella thought.

Carter and Stein was just on the edge of Diamondback, in what used to be the area's Gold Coast back in the late twenties and early thirties. In those days, Diamondback was exclusively black, and the high-rise buildings on Carter Avenue between Stein and Ridge were populated with entertainers, musicians, artists, businessmen, politicians, all the elite of Isola's black society. The buildings still afforded a splendid view of Grover Park, an inducement that had caused an enterprising black developer to renovate them into doorman buildings which downtown honkies had snapped up in a minute. These adventurous whites wouldn't have been quite so bold if the buildings had been offered for sale a scant twelve blocks farther uptown. *Living* in the heart of Diamondback was a bit different, Charlie, from going uptown to Mama Grace's for a down-home supper of chitlins, black-eyed peas, and grits. But Carter Avenue was still relatively safe for this city, and you couldn't beat the price or the view of the park.

Diamondback was *still* predominantly black. In fact, one of its more clever nicknames was Diamond*black*. But Hispanics from Colombia and the Dominican Republic—as opposed to the Puerto Ricans who were now third-generation citizens—and other immigrants, many of them illegal, from Pakistan, Vietnam, Korea, Bangladesh, Afghanistan and the planet Venus had begun infiltrating the area in ever-expanding pockets, foreign to most of the longtime residents and cause for cultural clashes of a minor scale—so far. The mix was a volatile and dangerous one. Except along Carter Avenue, where Johnny Milton lived with Michelle Cassidy in an apartment that used to be hers alone.

"She's also your client, is that right?" Carella asked.

"Yes."

"Which came first?"

"She was my client before we started a personal relationship, if that's what you mean."

"When was that?"

"Seven years ago."

"The personal relationship?"

"Yes."

"How about the business relationship?"

"That goes back a long while."

"How long a while?"

"Since she was ten. She was a child actress, you know . . ."

"Yes."

"I got her the touring company of *Annie*. She played Annie. The starring role."

"So you've known each other how long?"

"Thirteen years."

"Neither of you is seeing anyone else, are you?"

"No, no. It's the same as if we're married."

"Would you say your relationship is a good one?"

"Very good. The same as being married."

"Then it has its ups and downs, huh?" Carella said. "Same as being married."

"Yes. Exactly the same."

"How'd you react when she told you about the threatening calls?"

"I told you. I advised her to go straight to the police."

"Any idea why she waited so long to tell you?" Kling asked.

"No."

"Because apparently the calls . . ."

"Yes, I know . . ."

". . . started on the twenty-ninth of March . . ."

"Yes, I know . . ."

"But she didn't tell you about them till yesterday."

"I think she was hoping they would stop."

"*You* never talked to this man, did you?" Carella asked.

"No."

"What I mean, you didn't answer the phone and have someone in a Jack Nicholson voice asking for Miss Cassidy, did you?"

"No, never."

"Any hang-ups?"

"Oh, sure. This is the city."

"Wrong numbers, like that?"

"Yeah, like that."

"Anyone ever say 'Sorry, wrong number' in a Jack Nicholson voice?"

"No. The wrong numbers are foreign voices mostly. Hispanic, Asian, Solly, long numbah. They don't know how to dial a goddamn phone, you know."

Carella made no comment.

"What time did you get to O'Leary's?" Kling asked.

"I told you. Seven."

"On the dot?"

"Few minutes before, maybe. My reservation was for seven."

"When did you start getting nervous?"

"About her not showing up?"

"Yes."

"About ten after. I knew they were supposed to break for dinner at seven. This is a play in rehearsal, you understand, everything's racing against the clock, everything's sliding downhill toward opening night. If the dinner break is at seven, that *means* seven, and it means you're back at eight, to pick up where you left off. The theater's, what, five minutes from O'Leary's? I gave her till a quarter after, and then I went looking for a phone."

"Who answered the phone at the theater?"

"Torey, I told you. There's a phone backstage. The minute I asked to speak to Michelle, he said, 'Hold on tight, Johnny. Michelle just got stabbed in the alley outside.' "

"His exact words?"

"Exact. I asked him where they'd taken her, and he told me Morehouse. So I left the restaurant and went right over."

"By taxi?"

"Yes."

"Left the restaurant at what time?"

"Soon as I got off the phone. Twenty after seven? Twenty-five after?"

"Went straight to the hospital."

"Well, yeah. You were there when I walked in, what time was it? Quarter to eight, something like that?"

"Around then," Carella said. "Mr. Milton, thanks for your time, we appreciate . . ."

"Are you gonna *catch* this guy?" Milton asked.

"We hope so," Kling said. "Thanks again, sir, we appreciate your time."

The secretary in the small waiting room was on the phone again when they walked out, explaining to Mike the Actor that Mr. Milton had had an unexpected visit, but that he was

free to talk to him now. She smiled at Kling as they walked
out, and then buzzed the inner office. In the hallway outside,
as they waited for the elevator, Carella said, "Let's drive
uptown."

"Sure," Kling said. "The theater first? Or O'Leary's?"

"The theater," Carella said.

No knife.

Such was what the sodden blues had reported upon their
return to the station house late this morning, and neither
Carella nor Kling had reason to doubt the diligence of their
search. Nonetheless, he and Kling made another pass at the
alley and the stretch of sidewalk and gutter in front of the
theater, and confirmed in the riddling rain that indeed there
was no knife.

None that they could find, at any rate.

Besides, they weren't here primarily to search for a knife.

They were here to clock the time it took to walk from the
theater to O'Leary's Steakhouse on the Stem.

They'd eliminated at once the possibility that whoever had
stabbed Michelle Cassidy had *run* off after committing the
dastardly deed; in this city, a running man attracts attention.
So Kling hit the stopwatch button on his complicated digital
watch, and together they began walking at a good clip, out
of the alley, turning left under the theater marquee with the
red-lettered title ROMANCE on a black background, moving
quickly past the posters announcing the April sixteenth opening of the play, Kling's watch ticking away, both men striding
out briskly like the youngsters they no longer were, but who
was counting, up toward the corner of Detavoner Avenue
where a red light stopped them, ticking, ticking, WALK, the
traffic sign flashed, and they crossed the avenue that was still

under construction after God knew how many years, but who was counting, nobody in this city counted, up toward Sexton Avenue, the watch ticking, ticking, and finally they reached Stemmler Avenue itself, the *Stem* of legend and lore, and made a hasty turn at the corner and headed uptown toward North Twelfth. Kling hit the button again the moment they pushed through O'Leary's entrance door. The time was twenty-seven minutes past twelve. It had taken them exactly five minutes and forty-two seconds to get here, and they'd been counting.

The place was already packed with its lunchtime crowd, and everybody was too busy to talk to a pair of cops who'd been walking fast in the spring rain. But Carella mentioned the magic name "Michelle Cassidy," and in this celebrity-mad city, in this celebrity-worshipping nation, all at once everybody had all the time in the world to discuss the darling little thing who'd been stabbed in a theater alley, as reported on three television newscasts at eleven last night, and as plastered all over the front pages of the city's two tabloid dailies early this morning.

"Michelle Cassidy, yes," the headwaiter said. "She comes here frequently. They're rehearsing just up the street, you know."

Well, four blocks away, Kling thought. And five minutes and forty-two seconds.

"She was in *Annie,* you know. On the road."

"Yes," Carella said, "so we've been told."

Steak joints in this city tended to get noisy as hell. O'Leary's was no exception. The place was filled with raucous business-men in suits and vests who sat ham-hocked at tables with pristine white tablecloths and sparkling glassware, blowing smoke in the air, blasting laughter to the rafters, causing the

place to reverberate with thunderous sound. Carella wondered
why steak joints seemed to bring out the worst in men. None
of them would have behaved this way in a tearoom.

"We understand she was supposed to be here last *night*,"
he shouted over the noise.

"Is that right?" the headwaiter said.

He was as big as the noise in the place, a man with side
whiskers and a belly that started under his chin, wearing a
dark suit and a plum-colored tie fastened to his shirt with
a modest diamond stickpin. Carella thought he looked like
a British barrister in a Dickens novel. He sounded like one,
too, come to think of it.

"With Johnny Milton," Kling said.

"Oh, yes, the agent. Yes, he was here. I didn't know she
was supposed to join him."

"What time did he get here?" Carella asked.

"Let me check the book."

He moved toward his little podium like a galleon under
full plum-colored sail, flicked pages like a conductor leading
an orchestra, mumbling to himself as he scanned the reservation entries, "Johnny Milton, Johnny Milton, Johnny Milton,"
and finally stabbing at the page with a plump little forefinger,
and looking up triumphantly, and saying, "Here it is, seven
o'clock."

"Was he *here* at seven?" Carella asked.

"Well, I don't know," the headwaiter said.

"Could you try to remember, sir?"

"He may have been a few minutes late, I don't know."

"How late?" Kling asked.

Michelle had stepped into that alley at a few minutes past
seven. Say two, three minutes past seven. Add to that the five
minutes and forty-two seconds it took to walk here fast . . . .

"Did he get here at *five* past seven?" he asked.

"I don't know."

"Seven past?"

"Eight past?"

"*Ten* past?"

Both of them zeroing in. *Trying* to zero in.

"I have no way of knowing, really."

"Would anyone *else* know?"

"One of your waiters?"

"Do you remember where you seated him?"

"Well, yes, I do. But I doubt anyone . . ."

"Which table would it have been, sir?"

"Number six. There near the bar."

"Would that waiter be here now?"

"The one who had that table last night?"

"Gentlemen, really . . ."

"At seven?"

"Or seven-fifteen?"

"Around that time?"

"Yes, he's here. But, really, you can see how crowded we are. I can't possibly pull him off the . . ."

"We'll wait till lunch is over," Carella said.

The waiter's name was Gregory Stiles, and he was a thirty-two-year-old aspiring actor, which did not make him exactly unique in this city. He remembered serving Johnny Milton, because he knew Milton was an agent, and he himself had been looking for a new agent ever since his last one moved to Los Angeles. Stiles had straight black hair, dark brown eyes, and an olive complexion, which made it difficult for him to get many acting jobs because everyone assumed he was Latino, and there weren't too many roles for Latino actors in this city—or in this country, for that matter—unless you were a Latino actor who also sang and danced, in which case you could get a part in a summer stock production of *West Side Story,* maybe.

In the movie *Walk Proud,* which was about Chicano gangs in L.A., the starring Chicano role had been played by Robby Benson, a very good actor who happened to be an Anglo. The Chicano community raised six kinds of hell about this, even though the film created more jobs for Chicano actors than had previously been available since the Mexican Army stormed the Alamo and killed John Wayne. Unfortunately, Stiles hadn't been living on the Coast when the movie was made, and so he'd missed out on a career opportunity. He was still annoyed that he looked so fuckin Hispanic when in fact his forebears were British.

He told all this to the detectives after the lunchtime hubbub had subsided, at ten minutes to three that afternoon, over coffee at a small table near the doors leading to the kitchen, where the dishwashers were busily at work. The dishwashers at work were almost as noisy as the businessmen had been at lunch, though not quite.

"He told me he was waiting for someone, but that he'd have a drink meanwhile," Stiles projected over the clatter of dishes and pots and pans and someone singing in what sounded like Arabic. "He ordered a Tanqueray martini on the rocks, with a twist."

"What time was this?" Kling asked.

"Exactly fifteen minutes past seven," Stiles said.

Both detectives looked at him.

"How do you happen to know the exact time?" Kling asked

"Because I'd just got off the phone with my girlfriend."

Which did not answer the question.

"Do you always call her at a quarter past seven?" Carella asked.

Which seemed a logical thing to ask.

"No," Stiles said. "As a matter of fact, *she* called me."

"I see," Carella said.

Which he still didn't.

"What time did she call you?" Kling asked reasonably.

"About five after seven. She'd just been asked back for a second reading, and she wanted me to know about it. She's an actress, too. She also waits tables."

"So she called you at five after seven . . ."

"Yes, and I took the call in the booth there . . ."

Nodding toward a phone booth at the end of the bar.

". . . where I could see the room and also the clock over the bar. I saw Mr. Milton when he came in, and I saw him when Gerard led him to the table. The headwaiter. Gerard."

"What time did Mr. Milton come in?"

"I didn't look at the clock when he came in. But I *did* look at it when Gerard led him to the table a few minutes later."

"Why'd you look at the clock then?"

"Because I knew I'd be on in the next ten seconds. So I told Mollie I had to go, and I hung up, and the time on the clock was a quarter past seven."

"You're sure about that?"

"Positive."

"So he sat down at a quarter after seven, and told you he was expecting someone, and ordered a Tanqueray martini . . ."

"On the rocks, with a twist."

"Then what?"

"About ten minutes later, he went to the phone. Same phone over there. The booth at the end of the bar."

"That would've been around seven twenty-five."

"Around then. I didn't look at the clock again. I'm just estimating."

"Then what?"

"He came back to the table, threw down a twenty-dollar bill, and ran out."

"Didn't ask for a check?"

"Nope. Just assumed the twenty would cover it, I guess. Which it did, of course. *More* than."

"Seemed in a hurry, did he?"

"Was Roadrunner in a hurry?"

"What time did he leave the restaurant, did you happen to notice?"

"I would say around seven-thirty. But again, that's just an estimate."

"But you're absolutely certain . . ."

"Was Nostradamus certain?"

". . . that he sat down at the table at a quarter past seven?"

"Positive."

"And came into the restaurant a few minutes before then?"

"Yes. Well, I took Mollie's call at five after, and he hadn't yet come in, I didn't see him standing at the door with Gerard till a few minutes later. If I had to make a guess, I'd say he got here about ten after."

"Ten after seven."

"Yes. And Gerard went through the greeting routine, and the shaking of hands, and all the maître d' bullshit, and then brought him to the table and sat him down at a quarter past seven on the dot. Which is when I looked at the clock, and said goodbye to Mollie, and hung up."

"Thank you, Mr. Stiles."

"*De nada*," he said, and grinned.

* * *

He had been on the phone with Mike the Whiner for almost forty minutes, and then had got involved in what seemed like a hundred *subsequent* phone calls, and then had gone out for a meeting with a producer who was doing a revival of a play called *The Conjuror,* which he'd seen at the University of Michigan some twenty-five, twenty-six years ago, but which had never made it to Broadway . . . or anywhere *else,* for that matter. Why the producer wanted to revive it was something beyond Johnny's ken, but he listened patiently as the play was outlined and then took notes on the actors and actresses required for the cast. He got back to the office at a little past five, called the theater and was told by the stage door guy that everyone had already quit for the day. So he'd called Michelle at the apartment and got no answer there, and kept trying every ten minutes or so until finally he reached her at close to six o'clock. She told him she'd just walked in the door.

"I was starting to get worried," he said.

"Why?"

"The cops were here to see me," he said.

The door to his office was closed, but Lizzie was still outside at her desk, and she had ears like a rabbit, so he automatically lowered his voice to a whisper.

"When?" Michelle asked.

"This afternoon."

"Why didn't you call me?"

"I did. As soon as I could. You'd already left the theater."

"I didn't leave the theater till five o'clock!"

"I had a meeting."

"What'd they want?"

"Fishing expedition," he said, and shrugged. "They think I'm the one who stabbed you."

He heard her catch her breath. There was a long silence on the line. Then she said, "They accused you?"

"No, no, they're not stupid. But they were asking how long we've known each other, how we got along . . ."

"Uh-oh."

"Yeah, what time I ate dinner, what time I found out you'd been stabbed . . ."

"This is very bad, Johnny."

"No, I think I covered it nicely."

"Don't you see what they were trying to find out?"

"Oh, sure. They were running a timetable in their heads. Trying to figure did I have time to stab you and then run over to O'Leary's."

"Which is just what you did."

"Yeah."

"So what'd you tell them?"

"I told them I had a seven o'clock reservation. Which, by the way, I did."

"What'd they say?"

"They wanted to know what time I *got* there, never mind what time the reservation was for."

"Johnny, we're in trouble."

"No, no. I told them I got there a little before seven."

"They'll check. We're in trouble, Johnny."

"Who's gonna remember exactly what time I got there? Come on, Meesh."

"Someone'll remember. You shouldn't have lied, Johnny. It would've been better to tell the truth."

"The restaurant is my *alibi*!"

"Some alibi, if you weren't there."

"What'd you want me to say? That I didn't know *where* I was? You're getting stabbed in a fuckin alley, and I can't account for where I was?"

"You could've said you were home. Getting *ready* to go to the restaurant. Or you could've said you were trying to catch a *cab* to the restaurant. There's no way they can check on a man standing on a street corner waving at taxis. Anything would've been better than telling them you were already *in* the restaurant, which they can check in a minute. They'll be back, Johnny, you can bet on it. They're probably on their way back right this minute."

"Come on, Meesh, stop tryin a get me nervous."

"You'd better start thinking up another story. For when they come back and ask you how come the people at the restaurant don't remember seeing you there at seven."

"I'll tell them my watch was running fast."

"Then you better set it fast right this minute."

"Meesh, you're really getting all upset about nothing. They bought my story. There's no *reason* for them to . . ."

"How do you know they bought it?"

"They both thanked me for my time."

"And that means they bought your story, huh?"

"What I'm saying is they didn't seem suspicious."

"Then why were they asking you all those questions?"

"Routine."

"What else did they ask you?"

"Who remembers?"

"*Try* to remember."

"They wanted to know where we live, and how long you'd . . ."

"Did you tell them?"

"Yes."

"You gave them the *address* here?"

"I told them Carter and Stein."

"Oh, Jesus, they'll find me! They'll come here!"

"No, no."

"What else did you tell them?"

"I told them you'd been my client since you were ten years old, and that we've known each other for thirteen years. They wanted to know if either of us was seeing anyone else . . ."

"That's good."

"It is?"

"Sure. It means they were thinking it could've been somebody else. Not you, a third party. What'd you tell them?"

"That it was the same as being married, and that we had a very good relationship."

"Good."

"Yeah, I thought so. And then they wanted to know did I have any clients who did Jack Nicholson, and why you'd waited so long to go to them about the calls, you know . . ."

"Yeah."

". . . and how it was my idea that you go see them. They wanted to know . . ."

"That was stupid."

"What was?"

"Telling them it was *you* who sent me to the police. Makes it sound like you masterminded the whole fucking thing. Johnny, we're in trouble, I know it."

"No, they were just trying to find out who the guy *was*, the guy making the calls. Wanted to know if *I'd* ever talked to him . . ."

"Sure, because they were already thinking the calls were bullshit . . ."

"No. No, I don't think so."

"Was all this *before* or *after* they asked about the restaurant?"

"Before."

"Sure, they were closing in."

"No."

"They'll be back, Johnny."

"I'm telling you no."

"I'm telling you yes."

"Why would they? When I asked them were they gonna catch this guy, the blond one—you remember the blond one?"

"What about him?"

"He said he hoped so. That they'd catch him."

"Yeah, *you*. He was talking about *you*."

"No, he was talking about the guy who stabbed you in the alley."

"Yeah, who was *you*."

"Yeah, but they don't know that."

"I'll tell you, Johnny, if they come here asking questions, I'm gonna say I don't know a fucking thing about it."

"Good, that's exactly what you should say."

"No, you're not hearing me."

"What am I not hearing?"

"I'm going to say I didn't know anything about it."

"Right."

"I'll tell them you must've dreamt it all up on your own."

"On my . . . ?"

"Without my knowledge."

There was a silence on the line.

"I'm not going down with you, Johnny . . ."

"You helped . . ."

"I'm gonna be a star, Johnny."

"You helped me *plan* it!" he shouted.

"Prove it," she said, and hung up.

She had double-locked the door, and put the chain on, and angled the Fox-lock bar firmly in place, but she was still scared he might come in through the window or whatever, one of the heating vents even, he could be a crazy bastard when he wanted to. The moment she'd hung up she'd realized how stupid it had been to tell him in advance what she would do if push ever came to shove. Now she sat here wondering whether she ought to get out of the apartment altogether, go crash with any one of a hundred unemployed actresses she knew in this city, even take a hotel room someplace till the cops arrested him, which she guessed should be any minute now, the way they were closing in on him.

How could he have been such a jackass, telling them he was someplace he couldn't *possibly* have been at the time of the stabbing? Didn't he *realize* they'd time the distance from the theater to O'Leary's? Didn't he *know* they'd check his alibi? Even if they didn't for a minute suspect there was some kind of conspiracy here, even if they never once imagined this was all planned to call attention to her as the star of a show about to go down the drain, even if they were every bit as stupid as all the other cops in this city, didn't he *know* they'd suspect him if only because he was the significant *other*? Didn't he read the newspapers?

What'd he think? That everything he saw on television and in the movies was the way it was in real life? All those complicated murder plots? All those shrewd schemes that would net millions and millions of dollars for the person clever enough to hatch them and execute them? Baloney. If you read the papers, you knew that most murders had nothing to do with brilliant planning. Most murders these days were either murders committed during the commission of some *other* crime, or else they were murders between people who knew each other. A little while ago, it used to be random killings, strangers knocking off strangers for no apparent reason. But now, the pendulum had swung back to the family circle again, and people who loved each other were busy slitting each other's throats. Husbands and wives, sweethearts and lovers, brothers and sisters, mothers and sons and fathers and uncles, *these* were the people who were killing each other these days. She knew because she'd done a lot of research for this dumb play she was in.

One of the things that *had* to've occurred to the police was that the guy making threatening calls in a Jack Nicholson voice might have been none other than the guy who was currently sleeping with the victim, who by the way had been the same guy sleeping with her for the past seven years, give or take, and not counting the times his hands were up under her skirt when she was twelve or thirteen. If Michelle Cassidy gets stabbed in a dark alley coming out of a theater, who are the cops going to think did it, some crazed Puerto Rican drug dealer named Ricardo Mendez or whoever? No, they are going to think *Boyfriend,* they are going to think Johnny Milton, they are going to think there's something wrong with that relationship there, because that's the way they're *trained* to think. They're trained to think mother father son daughter boyfriend girlfriend goldfish. Even if they never once think it's a scheme to put my name up in lights, they'll look to Johnny.

He should've realized that, and he should've been ready for whatever they'd thrown at him, instead of giving them an alibi that wouldn't wash. The weak son of a bitch would probably begin sniveling the minute they went back and began turning the screws on him. They'd come here pounding on her door next, wanting to know what part she'd had in the scheme. Me, Officers? *Moi?* Why, I don't know what you're talking about, sirs. She knew all about interrogations because of this dumb play she was in.

She looked at her wristwatch.

Seven-thirty, dark outside already. Maybe he didn't plan on coming home at all, maybe she'd scared him into running for China or Colorado, wherever. Maybe she could relax. No Johnny Milton, no cops, just her name up above the title of the play in big blazing lights,

M*I*C*H*E*L*L*E C*A*S*S*I*D*Y!

Speaking of which.

She turned back to the blue-bindered script in her lap.

While perspiring over whether that lunatic would come break down the door or something, she'd been trying to go over her lines in the scene where the Detective takes her aside—takes the *Actress* aside—and talks to her confidentially about what he thinks is going on, a very difficult scene to play in that no one *in* the play knew what was going on because their genius playwright, Frederick Peter Corbin III, hadn't bothered to mention anywhere in the entire script who it was that stabbed the girl, excuse me, the goddamn *Actress*. So the scene was like two people talking underwater. Or sinking in quicksand. The *Detective* doesn't know what's going on, and the *Actress* doesn't know what's going on, either, and neither would the audience. Which is why it had become necessary in the first place to stab her in the alley, not the Actress in the play, but the actress in real life, Michelle Cassidy, if she was ever going to *get* anywhere in this fucking business.

> THE DETECTIVE
> What I'm trying to get at, miss, is
> whether or not <u>you</u> saw the man, woman,
> person who stabbed you as you were
> coming out of the restaurant?

> THE ACTRESS
> No, I didn't.
>   (pause)
> Did <u>you</u>?

She hated it when a playwright—*any* playwright and not just their genius playwright, Frederick Peter Corbin III—underlined words in a script to show his actors exactly which word or words he wanted stressed. Whenever she read a line like "But I *love* you, Anthony," with the word *love* underlined for indicated emphasis, she automatically and perversely read it every which way but what the playwright had heard in his head, how *dare* he intrude upon her creativity that way? Sitting around a table at a first reading, she would say, "But *I* love you, Anthony," or "But I love *you,* Anthony," or "*But* I love you, Anthony," or even "But I love you, *Anthony!*"

> THE ACTRESS
> No, I didn't.
>   (pause)
> Did <u>you</u>?

> THE DETECTIVE
> Well, no, of course not, I was nowhere
> <u>near</u> the restaurant when you were
> stabbed.
>
> THE ACTRESS
> I <u>realize</u> that. I just thought . . .

All those fucking underlined words.

> . . . you might have been suggesting
> that I <u>saw</u> who stabbed me when
> actually, you know, I <u>didn't</u>.
>
> THE DETECTIVE
> Neither did I.
>   (pause)
> Because, you see, I was wondering . . .
> if <u>I</u> didn't see you get stabbed, and if
> you <u>yourself</u> didn't see the person who
> stabbed you, if <u>no</u> one, in fact,
> actually <u>saw</u> you getting stabbed . . .
>   (pause)
> Then <u>did</u> you, in fact, actually <u>get</u>
> stabbed?

What a dumb fucking play, she thought, and was about to
put the script down when the doorbell sounded, startling her.
She hesitated a moment, not saying anything, sitting quite
still in the easy chair with its flower-patterned slipcovers, the
open blue-bindered script in her lap, the lamp behind her
casting light over her shoulder and onto the script and spilling
over onto the floor.

The doorbell sounded again.

Still, she said nothing.

From outside the door, a voice called, "Michelle?"

"Who is it?" she asked.

Her heart was pounding.

"Me," the voice said. "Open the door."

"Who's me?" she said, and rose from the easy chair and placed the script down on its seat, and then walked to the door and looked through the peephole flap, and said in relief, "Oh, hi, just a sec," and took off the chain, and released the Fox lock, and then unlocked the dead bolt and the Medeco lock and opened the door wide and saw the knife coming at her.

6

REEKING OF GARLIC AND UNIDENTIFIABLE EFFLUVIUM, DETECtive Fat Ollie Weeks oozed into the squadroom, spotted Meyer Meyer sitting alone at his desk, and announced, "Well, well, well, well, well, well, well, *well*," in his world-famous imitation of W. C. Fields, which was more and more beginning to resemble Al Pacino doing the blind marine in *Scent of a Woman*. Meyer looked up wearily.

In all truth, Ollie resembled W. C. Fields more than he did Al Pacino, not for nothing was he called *Fat* Ollie Weeks. This Wednesday morning, the eighth day of April, a gray and dismal but not yet wet reminder of the day before, Ollie was wearing a white button-down-collar shirt open at the throat, a brownish sports jacket with mustard stains on it, rumpled darker brown slacks, and a pair of scuffed brown loafers which, Meyer noted with surprise, had a penny inserted in the leather band across each vamp, would wonders never.

"How'd you like *Schindler's List*?" Ollie asked pointedly.

"I didn't see it," Meyer said.

"You didn't go see a picture about your own *people*?"

Meaning Jews, Meyer figured.

He did not feel he had to explain to a bigot like Ollie that the reason he hadn't gone to see the movie was that he thought it might be too painful an experience. Unlike Steven Spielberg, who in countless articles preceding the release of the film had confessed that making the movie had put him in touch with his own Jewishness, or words to that effect, Meyer had been in touch with his own Jewishness for a very long time now, thank you. And unlike Spielberg, Meyer did not believe that the Holocaust had been in any danger of becoming "a footnote to history" before this particular movie came along. No more than dinosaurs were a footnote to history before *Jurassic Park* roared into theaters all over the world. There were Jews like Meyer who would *never* forget the Holocaust even if there hadn't been a single Hollywood movie ever made about it.

Meyer's nephew Irwin, who had been known affectionately as Irwin the Vermin when he was but a prepubescent child, had since grown into a somewhat rabbinical type given to rolling his eyes and davening even when asking someone to please pass the salt. He had seen *Schindler's List* and had pontificated that this wasn't a movie about the Holocaust here, this was a movie here about a man finding in himself depths of feeling and empathy he had not before known he'd possessed. "What this movie is about is a flower growing up through a concrete sidewalk, cracking *through* that sidewalk and spreading its petals to the sunshine, is what this movie is all about," Irwin had proclaimed at Aunt Rose's house last night.

Meyer had said nothing.

He was thinking that here was a Jew who'd gone to see a movie which, according to its director, had been designed to make people *remember* there'd been such a thing as the Holocaust, and instead it had caused Irwin to *forget* there'd been a Holocaust and to remember instead that flowers could grow through sidewalks.

Now here was Fat Ollie Weeks, in all his fetid obesity, standing before Meyer's desk like a fat Nazi bastard, demanding to know why Meyer had chosen not to go see a movie that might cause him to weep.

"You think all that really happened?" Ollie asked.

Meyer looked at him.

"All that stuff?" Ollie said.

"What brings you here?" Meyer asked, attempting to change the subject.

"The stuff they say the Nazis did to the Jews?" Ollie persisted.

"No, they made it all up," Meyer said. "What brings you here?"

Ollie looked at him for a moment, as if trying to decide whether this wise Jew here was putting him on or what, telling him the whole fuckin Hologram had been invented, whereas Ollie knew there wasn't a Jew in the world who believed that, who was he trying to kid here? Or maybe he'd finally seen the light himself, and realized governments could stage things like fake moon landings and six million Jews getting exterminated. He let the whole thing go because, to tell the truth, he didn't give a shit one way or the other, six million Jews getting killed on the moon, or six fake astronauts flying over Poland.

"I think we're gonna be working together again," he said, and leaned across Meyer's desk and nudged him in a ham-fisted gesture of camaraderie. Meyer instinctively backed away from the unctuous reek. How had he got so lucky? he wondered. There he'd been, sitting behind his desk, minding his own business, a good-looking man if he said so himself, thirtysomething but still hale and hearty although entirely bald, tall and burly with bright inquisitive blue eyes—if, again, he said so himself—wearing suspenders that matched the cornflower blue, a gift from his wife Sarah at Christmas, or Chanukah, or both, because each was celebrated in turn at the Meyer household, when all at once comes a two-ton tank smelling of diesel oil and farts, announcing that they'd be *working* together again, *oi vay'z mir.*

"On what?" Meyer asked.

"On this girl got stabbed and slashed twenty-two times—and incidentally murdered, by the way—in apartment 6C at 1214 Carter Avenue in the Eighty-eighth Precinct, which happens to be where I work, ah yes," he said, falling into his W. C. Fields mode again. "Whereas I understand, m'boy, that the vic was *previously* stabbed right here in the old Eight-Seven, although a mere superficial wound, ah yes."

"What are you saying?"

"Michelle Cassidy."

"Was *murdered*?"

"Twenty-two times over."

"When?"

"Sometime last night. When she didn't show for rehearsal this morning, somebody at the theater called nine-one-one, and they dispatched a car from the Eight-Eight."

"Michelle *Cassidy*? The actress Kling and Carella . . . ?"

"Is that who was working it?"

"Yeah," Meyer said. "In fact, they got a search warrant this morning to . . ."

"*What* search warrant?"

"To toss the agent's office."

"*What* agent?"

"The one living with her."

"They shouldn'ta done that," Ollie said, and scowled darkly. "This is *my* case."

Ollie was annoyed that they'd gone around him—a difficult task under any circumstances—to obtain their warrant while *his* people were still conducting a search of the crime scene. Carella explained that when they'd applied for the warrant, they hadn't known the apartment on Carter Avenue had *become* a crime scene. They were merely looking for a weapon possibly used in an assault, and they reasoned that Milton wouldn't have left that weapon in the apartment he shared with the assault *victim*. It was Carella's guess that the warrant would have been denied if Michelle Cassidy hadn't been mentioned in it some half dozen times; even judges of the superior court watched television and read newspapers.

"Point is . . ." Ollie said.

"Point is, we've got the knife," Nellie Brand said.

They had called her in because the court-ordered search of Johnny Milton's office on Stemmler Avenue had yielded surprisingly good results. Nellie was an assistant district attorney, dressed for work this morning in a smart suit the color of her sand-colored hair, a blouse a shade lighter, darker brown panty hose, and brown leather shoes with French heels. Carella liked her style. She always looked breezy and fresh to him.

"Moreover," she said, "there appears to be blood caked in and around the hinge. If Milton wasn't cleaning chickens, I want to know where that blood came from. And if the lab can match it with Michelle Cassidy's . . ."

"Goodbye, Johnny," Kling said.

"Let's go talk to him," Carella said.

The Q and A took place in Lieutenant Byrnes's corner office at eleven twenty-seven that Wednesday morning. Present in addition to the three detectives and Nellie was a female video technician from the D.A.'s Office, and Lieutenant Byrnes himself, who sat in the swivel chair behind his desk trying not to appear too excited about his detectives maybe cracking this celebrity case so soon. He could see naked greed gleaming in Ollie Weeks's eyes. Ollie had caught the squeal this morning. This was a hot collar, and Ollie wanted it. Byrnes was ready to defend it to his death.

Milton had been read his rights the moment they found the knife and slipped the cuffs on him. The video technician turned on the camera, and Nellie read Miranda yet another time, advising Milton again that he was entitled to a lawyer if he wished one. Milton said, again, that he'd done nothing, had committed no crime, had nothing to hide, and therefore was in no need of legal representation. Every other person in the room figured these were famous last words.

"Do you recognize this?" Nellie asked, firing from the hip and aiming straight between the eyes, even though the weapon she held in her hand was a knife in a clear plastic bag. No knife, no case, she was thinking. Get to it. Nail him fast.

"I recognize it, yes," Milton said.

"Is this the knife Detectives Carella and Kling found in your office at 1507 Stemmler Avenue?"

"It appears to be that knife, yes," Milton said.

"Well, is it or isn't it?" Nellie said.

"I believe it is."

"Yes or no?"

"Yes, it is."

"Does this knife belong to you, sir?"

"No, it does not," Milton said.

"This knife . . ."

"Is not mine, that's correct."

"This knife the detectives found in your office . . ."

"Is not mine. I never saw that knife before the detectives found it."

"Came as a surprise to you, did it?"

"Oh, yes."

"Detectives pulling books from your bookcase . . ."

"Um-huh."

". . . and they spot a switchblade knife you never saw before, huh?"

"Never."

"You know, do you not, that from the moment the detectives removed several books from the shelf and spotted the knife . . ."

"I don't know how it got there. Someone must have put it there."

"Well, *who* if not you?" Nellie said. "You realize, don't you, that from the moment the knife was discovered, no one has touched it with a naked hand? Not the arresting detectives, not me, not anyone in the police department or connected with the District Attorney's Office. The detectives were wearing white cotton gloves when they conducted their search . . ."

"Yes, I saw that."

"And when they found the knife, they dropped it into a plastic evidence bag, and that's where it's been since. No one has touched this knife with a naked hand. Except the person who hid it behind those books."

"I don't know how it got there."

"But you *do* know, do you not, that what appears to be blood is caked in and around the hinge of that knife?"

"No, I didn't know that until just this minute."

"You know, do you not, that this knife will be sent to the police laboratory where it will be determined whether or not the suspect substance is, in fact, blood?"

"I would assume so. But it's not my knife. I don't care where you send it."

"Mr. Milton, do you know that we can take your fingerprints whenever we want to?"

Milton looked surprised.

"Is that something else you didn't know until just this minute?" Nellie asked.

"You don't have the right to take my fingerprints. I didn't commit any crime."

"Yes, we do have the right, believe me, Mr. Milton."

"I would have to ask a lawyer if you have that right."

"Would you like to call your lawyer now?"

"I only have an entertainment lawyer."

"Would you like to call a *criminal* lawyer?"

"I'm not a criminal. And I don't *know* any criminal lawyers."

"If you like, I can give you the names of ten high fliers who'll come up here in a minute."

"Anyway, why would I *need* a criminal lawyer? I didn't commit any crime."

"Be that as it may, you've been arrested for a crime, and *any* lawyer will tell you that we can take your fingerprints without permission. Under the Miranda ruling, fingerprinting you without permission would *not* be taking incriminating testi . . ."

"I won't *give* you my permission."

"We don't *need* your permission. We can fingerprint or photograph you without permission, Mr. Milton, that is the long and short of it. The same way we can ask you to submit to a blood test or a Breathalyzer test . . ."

"No, you can't."

"Yes, we can. These are all *non*-testimonial responses and are permitted under the ruling."

"I don't know what that means."

"It means we're going to take your prints and compare them with whatever's on that knife. And it means we're going to compare the blood on that knife with Michelle Cassidy's blood, and if the fingerprints match and the blood matches, then we've got you stabbing her and killing her, Mr. Milton. That's what it . . ."

"*Killing* her? What?"

"Killing her, Mr. Milton."

"What the hell are you talking about?"

"You want to tell me if this is your knife?"

"I already *told* you it's not my knife. And I didn't . . ."

"You want us to go through the whole dog and pony act, is that it?"

"I don't know which dog and pony act you mean."

"The fingerprinting, the comparison tests . . ."

"You're not *allowed* to fingerprint me."

"Fine, we're not allowed to," Nellie said, exasperated. "So I guess we'll just have to break the law right this minute by doing what we're not allowed to do. Fellas, you want to take him out and print him?" she said, turning to where Carella and Kling sat watching and listening.

"I want a lawyer," Milton said.

"Lieutenant, can you get a lawyer for this man, please?"

"I want my *own* lawyer."

"Your entertainment lawyer?"

"Better than some kid fresh out of law school."

"Fine, get him up here, maybe he'll entertain us. Meanwhile, we'll print you. Give us something to discuss when he gets here."

"You can't print me before I talk to my lawyer."

"Print him," Byrnes said flatly.

Harry O'Brien—no relation to Bob O'Brien, the squad's own hoodoo cop—came into the squadroom at a little past one that Wednesday afternoon, announced that he'd been contacted by Milton's personal attorney and then produced a card identifying himself as a partner with the law firm of Hutchins, Baxter, Bailey and O'Brien. He shook hands with Milton and then Nellie, nodded to the assembled cops, and said, "So what is this?"

He was a man in his fifties, Nellie guessed, well-toned and tanned, with gray hair and a neatly trimmed gray mustache, wearing a double-breasted gray nailhead suit with a smart, solid blue silk tie. He half sat on, half leaned against the lieutenant's desk, his arms folded across his chest, giving an impression of casual ease in a cops-and-robbers environment.

"This is about Murder Two," Nellie said.

"Oh?"

Face expressing mild surprise, as if Milton's *entertainment* lawyer hadn't already told him this on the phone.

"Who is supposed to have murdered whom, may I ask?"

Faint derisive smile on his face now. His pose, his manner, the smile, even the expensive hand-tailored suit all said Johnny Milton would be out of here in ten minutes flat. Over my dead body, Nellie thought.

"Mr. Milton is being charged with murder in the second

degree," she said dryly. "Did you want to talk to your client about it before we proceed further?"

"Thank you, I would appreciate that," Milton said.

They all left Byrnes's office. Outside in the squadroom, none of them said very much. The lab had already come back with a double match on fingerprints and blood. They had Milton cold. Nellie wasn't even willing to do any deals here. This was Murder Two, plain and simple, and Milton was looking at twenty-five to life.

Some ten minutes later, O'Brien opened the door to Byrnes's office, poked his head out into the corridor, smiled under his gray mustache and said, "Mrs. Brand? Ready when you are."

They filed back into the lieutenant's office again.

"Would you like to tell me what you think you have?" O'Brien said.

"Happy to," Nellie said, and laid it all out for both of them. She told them that Milton's fingerprints matched the latent impressions lifted from the knife found in his office, that the residue substance clogged in the hinge of the knife was indeed blood and that moreover it matched the AB blood group of Michelle Cassidy, who had been stabbed and slashed to death the night before. She pointed out that Miss Cassidy shared her apartment on Carter Avenue with Mr. Milton and that the investigating detectives from the Eighty-eighth Squad had found no evidence of forcible entry to the apartment. It was her assumption that Mr. Milton had his own keys to the apartment. If she was wrong in this assumption, she wished Mr. Milton would correct her when the questioning was resumed. *If* it was resumed.

"That's it," she said.

"My client is willing to admit to the assault on Michelle

Cassidy on the night of April sixth," O'Brien said. "But he had nothing to do with her murder."

"No, huh?" Nellie said.

"No," O'Brien said.

"You're trying to deal an A-1 felony down to a Class D, is that it?" Nellie said, and shook her head in amazement.

"Better than that," O'Brien said. "I'm looking for Assault Three, a Class A *mis*."

"Why should I buy that?"

"Because you've got nothing that puts my client in that apartment last night."

"Where *was* he last night?"

"Why don't you ask him?"

"Does that mean I can question him now?"

"Sure. I've only just met the man, but I'm convinced he's got nothing to hide."

Nellie nodded. The technician turned on the video camera again. Milton was read his rights again, this time in the presence of his attorney, and he ascertained that he was willing to answer questions. The dog and pony act began.

"Mr. Milton, did you stab Michelle Cassidy on the night of April sixth at approximately seven P.M.?"

"I did."

Good. That nailed down the assault.

"You previously told Detectives Carella and Kling that you were in a restaurant named O'Leary's at that time, didn't you?"

"Yes."

"So you weren't quite telling them the truth, is that right?"

"I wasn't."

"In fact, you were lying."

"Yes."

"You were instead in the alley outside the Susan Granger Theater, stabbing Miss Cassidy."

"Yes."

"With this knife?" Nellie asked, and showed him the knife in the plastic evidence bag.

"With that knife, yes."

"Then, contrary to what you told me earlier, this knife *is* yours."

"Yes, it's my knife."

"And are you the person who hid it behind the books in your office?"

"Yes."

"So when you said earlier . . . tell me if I'm quoting you incorrectly . . . when you said, 'I don't know how it got there. Someone must have put it there,' referring to this knife, you were not telling the truth then, either, were you?"

"I was not."

"You were lying again."

"I was lying."

"This *is* your knife, and you *did* hide it behind those books in your bookcase."

"Yes."

"And you now say you used this knife to stab Michelle Cassidy on the night of April sixth."

"Yes."

"How about last night? Did you use this knife to stab her *last* night?"

"No, I did not."

"Did you use some *other* knife to stab her last night?"

"I didn't stab her last night."

"You stabbed her *Monday* night, but not last night."

"That's correct."

"Would you care to explain that, Mr. Milton?"

Milton turned, looked at his attorney. O'Brien nodded.

"Well . . ." Milton said.

And now he told Nellie and the assembled detectives how the idea had been Michelle's from the very start . . . well, *premised* on something he'd said while they were in bed together this past Sunday night. She'd been complaining about how *stupid* the play was, *Romance,* the play they were rehearsing, and Johnny had mentioned that the play had pretensions of being something it couldn't ever possibly be, there was simply no *way* you could turn a murder mystery into a silk purse. He'd gone on to explain that the minute anybody stuck a knife in somebody else, all attention focused on the victim, and all anybody wanted to know was whodunit.

Which wasn't such a bad idea, he'd thought.

Focusing attention on the victim.

Which he'd said aloud.

To Michelle.

"It wouldn't be such a bad idea to get some attention focused on *you,*" he'd said, "never mind the dumb *play.*"

Well, if there's anything an actress loves, it's getting attention focused on her. The minute he mentioned this thought— what was actually just a passing thought, an idle thought, a whim, you know—Michelle wanted to know what he meant, what *kind* of attention? He had mentioned somebody sticking a knife in a person, which happens in the play, of course, and now she picked up on that, saying it was too bad some nut out there didn't get it in his head to stab *her,* the way the girl in the play gets stabbed, which would certainly focus a lot of attention on her, and wouldn't hurt the play besides, since a stabbing is what happens in it. The whole damn audience would be sitting there waiting for the stabbing scene, knowing that Michelle had been stabbed in real life, though not as seriously as the girl in the play, who almost gets killed from what she could determine, although it was such a goofy play that the next minute she's up off the floor and answering the Detective's questions, *sheeesh*.

"Too bad there *isn't* some nut out there," she'd said, and they'd lain there in each other's arms, quiet for a while, and then she said, "Why does it have to be some nut?"

"What do you mean?" he'd said.

"Why don't we *get* someone to do it? Stab me. Not too seriously. Just seriously enough to focus attention on me. As the victim."

Well, they'd discussed this for a while, back and forth, and she finally agreed with his opinion that if you ever hired somebody to do something like that, it always came out in the wash. Whoever did the job always came clean for one reason or another, and it would all lead right back to them and have the opposite effect from the one intended.

"Why can't it be someone we know real well?" Michelle said. "Who does the stabbing, I mean."

So they batted *this* around for a while, back and forth, trying to think of anyone they knew who could be trusted first to stab her not too seriously and then to keep his mouth shut afterward . . .

"Or even hers," Michelle offered.

. . . but they couldn't come up with anyone, male or female, who they felt they could absolutely, positively trust to pull this off and not implicate them later on.

"How about *you*?" Michelle suggested.

The idea of him stabbing her did not immediately appeal to him. He wasn't sure, first of all, that he could succeed in stabbing her "not too seriously," as she kept putting it, because he was not a surgeon, after all, and he had no idea what arteries or veins might be inside her chest or her shoulder that could rupture and cause her to bleed to death if he hit one of them by accident. So she lowered the strap of the sheer purple baby-doll nightgown she'd been wearing that night, and showed him her shoulder, and together they started poking and probing, trying to figure out how to stab her without doing *too* much harm. They finally figured that he could just *cut* her rather than actually *stab* her, and they decided to do it the following night, when the cast broke for dinner.

"But it was her idea," Milton said.

"To focus attention on her."

"Yes. First to go to the cops and tell them she'd been threatened . . ."

"Which she did."

"Yes. It was also her idea to say the person calling her sounded like Jack Nicholson."

"I see," Nellie said.

"Yes. Because Nicholson sounds very menacing even when he isn't trying to be. The whole idea was to get media attention."

"Which is exactly what happened," Nellie said.

"Yes. We got a lot of attention."

"So why'd you kill her?"

"Now, now, Counselor," O'Brien said.

"Why'd you kill her, Mr. Milton?"

"I didn't."

"When's the last time you saw her, Mr. Milton?"

"When I left the house yesterday morning."

"Do you have your own keys to the apartment, by the way?"

"I do, yes."

"What time did you leave yesterday morning?"

"Around nine."

"Lock up after you?"

"No. Michelle was still in the apartment."

"Where'd you go?"

"To my office. These detectives came to see me there around eleven o'clock."

"What time did you leave the office?"

"I went out for lunch around twelve-thirty, I guess it was."

"Who with?"

"Producer named Elliot Michaelman."

"Did you go back to the office after lunch?"

"I did."

"What time would that have been?"

"A little after three."

"When did you see Michelle again?"

"I didn't."

"You didn't see her from when you left the apartment at nine that morn . . . ?"

"That's right."

"Well, didn't you go *back* to the apartment, Mr. Milton? Isn't that where you *live*?"

"Yes, but I didn't go there last night."

"Why not?"

"Because we had a fight on the phone."

"Oh?" Nellie said, and saw the warning glance O'Brien shot Milton. "When was this?" she asked at once.

"I guess around six o'clock. I tried the theater as soon as I got back from a meeting, but they'd already stopped rehearsing for the day, so I kept calling the apartment every ten minutes till I reached her."

"And you say this was around six o'clock."

"Yes. She'd just come in."

"What'd you fight about, Mr. Milton?"

"I told her the detectives here had come to my office, and she was worried they might be getting suspicious."

"That doesn't sound like a fight to me."

"Well, she finally said that if they came to the apartment asking questions, she would say she didn't know anything about it, that I must've dreamt up the whole thing on my own, without telling her about it. She told me she wasn't going down with me, she was going to be a star."

"Then what?"

"I told her she was the one who'd *planned* the damn thing, for Christ's sake! So she said 'Prove it' and hung up."

"How'd you feel about that?"

"Rotten."

"In addition to feeling rotten, did you also feel *angry*?"

"No, I just felt rotten. I thought we were supposed to love each other. I wouldn't have gone along with her scheme if I hadn't loved her. I did it for her. So she really *could* become a star. I've known her since she was *ten*, I've been grooming her all that time."

"And now she tells you you're on your own, right?"

"In essence, yes."

"If they catch you . . ."

"Yeah."

". . . she knew nothing about it."

"Yeah."

"*She* gets her shot at stardom . . ."

"Well, yeah."

". . . while *you* go to jail for assault."

"I wasn't thinking about jail. I was thinking we were supposed to love each other."

"So you decided to kill her."

"No, I didn't kill her."

"You had nothing to lose anymore . . ."

"No . . ."

"So you went back to the apartment . . ."

"No, I didn't. I never left the office. I sent out for a sandwich and a bottle of beer . . ."

"When? What time?"

"Around six."

"It was delivered at six?"

"Six-fifteen, six-twenty."

"Who delivered it?"

"Some black kid. I ordered it from a deli on the Stem."

"Name of the deli?"

"I have it in the office. On one of those menus they slide under the door."

"But you don't know the name of the deli offhand."

"I don't."

"How about the kid who delivered your order? Know him?"

"By sight."

"You don't know his name?"

"No."

"And you say he delivered your sandwich and beer . . ."

"And some fries."

". . . and some fries at six-fifteen, six-twenty."

"Yes, around then."

"Then what?"

"I ate."

"Then what?"

"I went to sleep."

"You went home to sleep?"

"No. I slept in the office."

"Anyone *see* you sleeping there?"

"No. But I was there when Lizzie came in this morning. My secretary. Elizabeth Campieri."

"Found you *sleeping*, did she?"

"No, I was awake by then."

"Is there anyone who can say with certainty that you were in that office all last night?"

"No, but . . ."

"Is there anyone who can say with certainty that you didn't *leave* the office after your sandwich was delivered at six-twenty, and *go* to Michelle Cassidy's apartment, and *open* the several locks with your keys, and *stab* . . ."

"I didn't . . ."

". . . her to death? Is there anyone who *saw* you where you say you were? Or is this another alibi like the one you had for the night you stabbed her in that theater alleyway? Are you lying yet another time, Mr. Milton?"

"I am telling you the God's honest truth. I did not kill Michelle."

"He done it," Ollie said. "Go for the jug, Nellie."

She knew Ollie Weeks only casually, having seen him in the corridors of justice on one or another occasion, but he was already calling her Nellie. Also, he seemed not to have bathed in a while. But she agreed with him.

"He's admitted to the assault," she said. "That's open and shut. And I think we've got enough cause to arrest him on the homicide, too."

"I don't think so," Carella said.

They all turned to him.

They had asked O'Brien and Milton to wait in the squad-room outside while they deliberated. Lieutenant Byrnes was still seated in the swivel chair behind his desk. Ollie was overflowing a straight-backed chair near the windows. Nellie had moved across the room now, as far away from him as possible. Carella stood alongside Kling, near the bookcases opposite Byrnes's desk.

"What bothers you?" Byrnes asked.

"Motive," Carella said.

"She threatened to burn him," Ollie said. "That's motive enough."

"I think he's right," Byrnes said.

"What does he gain by killing her?" Carella said.

"If he doesn't kill her, he goes down for the assault."

"We've got him on that, anyway."

"He done her *before* he knew that," Ollie said. "He was still figuring if he done her, he'd walk."

"If I bring both charges on the same indictment," Nellie said, thinking out loud, "O'Brien can take his misdemeanor plea and shove it."

"Why not charge Milton with just the assault?" Carella said.

"Oh, I see," Ollie said. "You get the assault collar and I get *bupkes,* is that it?"

"You can have *both* collars," Carella said.

"By rights, both collars are *ours,*" Byrnes said.

"Let's not debate credit here," Nellie said. "If there's no real evidence to support the homicide, then frankly the assault isn't *worth* more than a mis. But I think Milton *did* kill her, so how about that?"

"Hooray for you, lady," Ollie said.

"If we lock him up for Assault Two," Carella said, "we can explain to the court that we're still *investigating* the homicide . . ."

"That'll make a strong case, all right," Nellie said.

"It will if we find the evidence we need to back up a . . ."

"Come on, Steve, we've got circumstantial coming out of our ears."

"I don't think so. The blood on that knife was caked into the hinge. Really dry blood. The girl was killed . . ."

"So how long does it take for blood to dry?" Ollie said. "He done her last night, you think the blood's still gonna be *wet*?"

"No, but . . ."

"The blood's gonna be *dry*," Ollie said. "Same as blood from two days ago, three days ago, dry is dry, there are no gradations of dry. What are we talking here, martinis?"

"Okay, why'd he keep the knife?"

"They do that all the time," Ollie said, and waved the question away. "Nobody says these guys are rocket scientists."

"A man's looking at Murder Two, and he hangs on to the weapon?"

"I'd have thrown it down the nearest sewer," Kling said.

"Then why didn't he toss it after the *assault*?" Byrnes asked.

"Right," Ollie said. "If he didn't toss it after he stabbed her the *first* time, why would he toss it the *next* time around?"

"Because it would cost more to *keep* it," Carella said.

"Only your pros think that way," Ollie said.

"He was looking at fifteen on the assault, anyway," Nellie said. "If he didn't toss the knife *then* . . ."

"Fifteen years isn't life."

"It ain't chopped liver, either. Besides, the man's an *agent*," Ollie said scornfully. "What does he know about how much time you can get for what? This isn't a pro here, this is an amateur."

"Steve," Nellie said, "I wish I could agree with you on this one . . ."

"Just give us a chance to run it down, that's all I'm asking. If we tell the arraigning judge we're investigating a linked homicide, he'll set a juicy bail on the assault. That means Milton stays inside while we develop a good case. If there *is* one."

"I've already got a good case," Nellie said.

"I don't think so," he said.

"I'm sorry," she said.

"Nellie, if Milton *didn't* kill her, the *real* murderer . . ."

"What makes you . . . ?"

". . . walks."

". . . think he didn't kill her?"

"Gut instinct."

The room went silent.

"What do you want?" Nellie asked.

"I told you. Lock him up on the assault, let us pursue the murder investigation. If we come up empty, you can always tack on the second charge."

"Today's what?" she asked no one.

Byrnes looked at his desk calendar.

"The eighth," he said.

"Okay, our 180.80 Day is six days from arrest. That means on the fourteenth, I *have* to indict Milton on one or more felony charges or else release him on his own recognizance. Here's what I'm willing to do. I'll arraign him for both the assault *and* the murder . . ."

"Good," Ollie said.

". . . but I'll ask my bureau chief to talk to the Chief of Trial Division . . ."

"What for?" Ollie askd.

"So *he* can go to the Chief of Detectives and explain the situation to him."

"*What* situation?"

"That one of his best detectives has doubts and is still investigating the homicide."

"I don't *have* any goddamn doubts!" Ollie said.

"Steve, you've got till the morning of the fourteenth. Bring me something better by then, or I'll indict Milton for the homicide."

"Thanks," Carella said.

"You meant *him*?" Ollie said.

7

Bert Kling danced like a white man.

Oh dear Lord, he was the *worst* dancer she had ever danced with in her life, even though it had been *his* idea to go dancing this Wednesday night. She'd said, Sure why not? A man asks you to go dancing, you figure he's got to be a good dancer, no? A lousy dancer doesn't ask you to go dancing, he asks you to go bowling. But, oh my, was he *terrible*!

She'd dressed up all slinky and smooth in the same smoky blue color he'd admired, a different dress but the same shade of blue that matched her eye shadow—if it ain't broke, don't fix it. The dress was very short and very tight, the only such outrageous dress she owned, what she used to call a fuck me dress when she was still in medical school and trying to attract the attention of any single eligible black man in D.C.; five to one the ratio was said to be in that town, women to men, that is; five to one, honey, count 'em. Outrageous or not, the man had said the color was good for her, so why not accommodate him again? Besides, the only other smoky blue outfit she owned was the suit she'd worn on their first date, so this was it, take it or—Ooops, sorry. No, my fault.

She looked good in certain shades of green, too, come to think of it, maybe she should have dressed all verdant and vernal tonight. But it wasn't easy being green, you could so easily slip into looking like an uptown ho. Anyway, how did this get to be all about *color*? But that's what this *was* all about, wasn't it? About whether there was anything more to this besides his being white and her being black and maybe being attracted to each other only *because* he was white and she was black. It certainly wasn't about him being Fred Astaire.

The band was pretty good, considering half the musicians in it were white, including the bass player, who she always figured was the very heart and soul of any band. Six pieces up there on the bandstand in this small place down in the Quarter, a bit too smoky for a surgeon's comfort, but he seemed as much disturbed by the air quality as she was. Maybe the smoke was affecting his dancing. *Something* had to be affecting his dancing, because in all truth she had never known a man or boy who was quite as stiff and awkward as he was. Was he counting inside his head? Was that it? She was afraid to speak for fear she would throw off the count, welcome to Transylvania. She was wearing high-heeled blue shoes fashioned almost entirely of straps. A single wafer-thin sole and then straps, straps, straps. Showed off her legs to good advantage, she felt, come step into my parlor, let me bite you on zee neck.

She thought it was very cute that he was such an awful dancer, but she wished he wouldn't step quite so often on her feet in their strappy shoes. "Ooops, sorry," he would say each time, and she would say, "No, my fault," and then she began wondering if he really *thought* it was her fault, if somehow he believed that *she* was the lousy dancer. Well, no, surely, he *had* to know how clumsy he was. But then why had he asked her to go dancing?

At the table again—smoke drifting their way, the band playing a soft slippery tune that slithered on the air, low and rife with funky tenor sax riffs—she put it in a kinder, gentler way. Didn't say How come you chose to take me *dancing* of all things, you endearing oaf? Said instead, "How'd you happen to pick this place?"

"I thought it might be fun," he said, and gestured around vaguely to include the entire room, which—she now noticed—was populated with an uncommonly high mix of salt-and-pepper couples. Had he known this when he chose the spot?

"Where'd you learn to dance?" she asked.

"Oh, a bunch of guys used to . . . this was when I was a kid, you know?"

"Uh-huh."

"I grew up in Riverhead. When the neighborhood was still good."

Meaning what? she wondered. That it was now *black*? And therefore *no* good?

"This guy Frank had a big basement in his house, a finished basement, and we used to go down there and dance."

"Boys and girls, you mean?"

"I *wish*. No, it was just the guys. Frank was a very good dancer, he was teaching the rest of us to dance. We took turns leading and following. It was good training."

Yes, I can see the results, she thought.

"Where in Riverhead?" she asked.

"Cannon Road. Used to be black, Irish and Italian when I was growing up. Never any trouble there. Even when there was rioting in Diamondback, we all got along fine in Riverhead. No more. That's all changed."

She nodded.

"I can remember my father telling me . . . this was at the time of the big riots, I was just a little boy . . . I remember him saying, 'If you spread any of this filth, you won't be able to sit for a week, Bert. I'll fix you so you'll be lucky if you can even *walk*.'"

Is that why you're with a black woman tonight? she wondered.

"What happened Saturday was nothing compared to the trouble back then," he said. "I'll never forget it."

"Do you still live in Riverhead?" she asked.

"No, no. I have a small apartment right here in Isola. Near the Calm's Point Bridge."

"When did you leave?"

"Riverhead? Right after the war. When I got back from the war."

She did not ask him which war. In America, there'd been a war for any man coming of age at any given time. Most of these men were trying to forget whichever war had occupied their time and consumed their youth. She had never once met a man who wanted to talk about his wartime experiences. Which said a lot for recruiting posters.

"You're a good dancer," he said.

Us folks sho has rhythm, she thought.

"I'll bet you could teach me more than Frank did."

"Maybe I could," she said.

"Next time we go out there," he said, nodding toward the small dance floor.

"Okay."

The waiter brought a fresh round of drinks. There was a two-drink minimum in the place. Plus a cover charge. She realized this was costing him more than he could easily afford on his detective's salary. Everywhere around them, mixed couples drank, and talked, and danced, and held hands, and occasionally kissed. She wondered again how he'd happened to choose it.

"How'd you know about this place?"

"I asked Artie."

"Who's Artie?"

"Artie Brown. One of the guys on the squad. He's black."

"Brown is black, huh?"

"He thinks that's how his great-great-grandmother got the name, in fact."

"How do you mean?"

"She was a slave. He thinks her master gave her the name Brown because of her color. It's just a theory, he doesn't know for sure."

"When did you ask him?"

"I never did. He just happened to mention it one time."

"I meant about this place."

"Oh. Yesterday. I told him I was dating a black girl, and I asked him if he knew anyplace where we'd feel comfortable. While we were getting to know each other."

"What'd he say?"

"He recommended this place."

"And *do* you feel comfortable here?"

"Yeah, I guess so. Do you?"

"I don't know. It seems to be trying too hard, maybe."

"Maybe so."

"How'd he feel about your dating me?"

"Artie? How *should* he feel?"

"The black-white thing, I mean."

"It didn't come up."

"How do *you* feel about it?"

"The black-white thing?"

"Yes."

"I'm hoping it works for us."

She looked at him.

"I'm hoping we can one day go wherever we want to go, and just be us, without having to worry about looking like everyone around us."

"Is Brown your partner?"

"Sometimes. We work it a little different at the Eight-Seven than in some other precincts. We team up with different people all the time. Makes it more interesting. Also, it gives us an opportunity to exchange information about the bad guys and what they're doing."

"You didn't answer my question."

"I'll tell you the truth, Shaar," he said, shortening her name, rhyming it with the first syllable in Paris, "I thought you might feel uncomfortable in a place where there were only white people."

"How about a place where there are only *black* people?"

"Like in Diamondback, you mean?"

"Yes."

"I think *I* might feel uncomfortable in a place like that," he said.

"So you asked Brown to recommend a place where we would *both* feel comfortable."

"Yes. But I didn't know everything would be divided right down the middle. Three white guys in the band, three black guys. One white bartender, one black. A black girl for every white guy, a black guy for every white girl."

"Like painting by the numbers," she said.

"Yeah. Would you like to get out of here?"

"Where would you suggest?" she asked.

"Top of the Hill," he said.

The Hill Building was in midtown Isola on Jefferson Avenue. They had taken a taxi uptown, and now—at ten o'clock on a wide-awake, big-city, middle-of-the-week night—they walked into the lobby and stood behind a red velvet rope, where a man in a green uniform and a green hat kept parceling eight or ten people at a time into an express elevator that ran to the fifty-eighth floor of the building. They had no reservations. Kling was worried. Big-shot detective, How about Top of the Hill? How about when we *get* there a haughty headwaiter takes one look and sends us on our way, Sorry, buster, no room at the inn.

Well, how could that possibly happen? Handsome blond detective in a dark blue suit, beautiful black woman in a complementary blue dress, anyone should be *delighted* to have us in their midst, add a touch of elegance to the joint. *Come in, come in, sir, come in, miss, would you care for a table by the window where you can look out over the entire city? Lovely night, isn't it, sir?* Otherwise, just flash the tin and slip him a few bucks ... did people *do* that in fancy places like Top of the Hill?

He kept planning strategy all the way up to the fifty-eighth floor, where they transferred to another elevator going up to the sixty-fifth floor and the roof of the building. The elevator doors opened onto a plush reception area at one end of which were the glass entrance doors to the restaurant and lounge,

beyond which a twinkling nest of lights beckoned romanti-
cally. He knew at once that he'd made the right spontaneous
choice. But . . .

Oh, God, there he was, a stout penguin, all white and black,
standing at a podium just inside the entrance doors. Kling
would rather have faced a bank robber with a nine in each
fist. Boldly, he led Sharyn to the doors, opened one for her,
and allowed her to precede him into a view of the city that
was utterly dazzling, lights stretching from here to the farthest
tip of the island and beyond, bridges that seemed to span
continents, stars racing to the planets and beyond, to solar
systems yet unimagined. He almost caught his breath. There
was the sound of music coming from somewhere deep in the
room, soft and danceable. There were lighted votive candles
in crystal holders in the center of round tables with polished
black tops. There were waitresses in white blouses and long
black skirts slit up the leg to the thigh, everyone and everything
in black and white, when you were in love, the whole universe
was black and . . .

"Sir?"

The penguin. He, too, in black and white, *that* hadn't
changed. Chest puffed out, staring down the length of his
nose.

"Sir?"

A bit more imperiously this time. A *king* penguin, Kling
figured.

"Detective Bert Kling," he said, "Eighty-seventh Squad."

There was a moment, but only a moment.

And then, beaming, the penguin said, "Yes, sir, how do
you do, sir, a pleasure to have you with us. My name is
Rudolph, will there be just the two of you, Mr. Kling?"

"Just the two of us, yes, thank you," Kling said, bewildered.

"Will that be for supper, sir, or just cocktails?"

"Sharyn?"

"Just cocktails, please."

"Just cocktails, please," Kling said.

"Just cocktails, yes, Detective Kling, this way, please, I have a lovely table by the window."

It was not until Rudolph was seating them that Kling realized what this was all about.

"That was speedy work you and your mates did on that actress who got stabbed," Rudolph said.

"Oh," Kling said. "Thank you."

"Speedy work indeed. Enjoy the view. Enjoy the music, I'll send your waitress at once. Let me know if there's anything I can do for you."

"Thank you, Rudolph."

"My pleasure, Detective Kling. Miss," he said, and bowed to Sharyn, and then moved swiftly from the table.

"Well!" she said.

"Imagine what'll happen if Fat *Ollie* stops by," Kling said, shaking his head.

"Fat who?"

"Ollie. Who shared the collar. You'll have to meet him sometime. No, on second thought . . ."

"I forgot to congratulate you," she said.

"Our friend Rudolph must've seen us on television," Kling said. "There were cameras waiting when we took Milton out to the van."

"I saw it," she said.

"Was I okay?"

"You looked very cute," she said.

"But did I *sound* okay? Steve wouldn't say a word . . ."

"Steve?"

"Carella. We worked the assault together. He doesn't think Milton did the homicide."

"Was Fat Ollie . . . ?"

"The one standing on my right. The one hogging the camera."

"Ah, yes."

"Then you saw him."

"How could I *miss* him?"

"The power of television, huh?" he said, still amazed, shaking his head. "Boy."

A waitress materialized.

"Sir?" she said, smiling.

Her manner told him she watched television, too.

"Sharyn?" he asked.

"Beefeater martini, pair of olives," she said, "straight up and very cold."

"Johnnie Black, on the rocks," Kling said, "a splash."

"Water?"

"Soda."

"Would you care to see menus?"

"Sharyn? Anything?"

"Maybe something to nibble on," she said.

"I'll bring the menu," the waitress said, and clicked off on her black high heels, long legs showing in the slit skirt.

Sharyn turned immediately to the window, where the lights of the city lay spread below like a nest of sparkling red and white and green and yellow jewels. "This is *glorious*," she said.

"Listen," he said.

She looked toward the bandstand, where a quartet sounding very much like George Shearing's had just begun a new tune. She listened for only a moment, recognizing the song at once.

" 'Kiss,' " she said.

"Let's dance," he said.

"Love to," she said.

They moved onto the polished dance floor. She slid into his arms. He held her close.

Kiss . . .

It all begins with a kiss . . .

"I'm a lousy dancer," he said.

"You're very good," she lied.

"You'll have to teach me."

But kisses wither

And die

Unless

"This is much better, isn't it?"

"Much."

The first caress

Is true.

Kiss . . .

"See? We're doing it already."

"What are we doing already?" she asked.

She was thinking What we're doing is dancing too close already. We're going to get arrested already. Good thing you're a celebrity hero cop—at Top of the Hill, anyway.

"We're going wherever we want to go," he said, "and we're just being us, without having to worry about looking like everyone around us."

"We could *never* look like everyone around us," she said.

"That's because you're so beautiful," he said.

"No, it's because you're so handsome," she said.

"And such a good dancer," he said.

"Thank you," she said.

"I meant *me*," he said.

"Of course, exactly what *I* meant," she said.

So hold me tight and whisper
Words of
Love
Against my eyes.
And kiss me sweet and promise
Me your
Kisses won't be lies.

"We are, you know," she said.

"Are what?"

"Going to get arrested."

"That's okay, I'm a cop."

"So am I."

"I find it hard to think of you as a cop."

"I find it hard, too," she said, and moved in very tight against him.

He caught his breath.

She caught hers, too.

Kiss . . .
And show me, tell me of
Bliss . . .

"I love this song," she said.

"I love it, too."

Because I know I
Will die
Unless

"Sharyn?" he said.

"Yes?"

"Nothing."

This first
Caress
Is true.

* * *

The rehearsal had ended at ten-thirty and now the play's producer, director and playwright sat in the darkened theater, whispering low, considering their chances. There was no doubt in any of their minds that the murder of Michelle Cassidy would immeasurably help the show's prospects. They were all beginning to think they had a hit on their hands.

"*Plus,*" Kendall said, "Josie's a hundred times better than Michelle *ever* was."

"Or ever *would* have been," Morgenstern said.

They were giving Corbin the needle, of course. He had been the only holdout in casting Josie Beales over Michelle. As playwright, he'd had the final say. Now Michelle's understudy had inherited the role by default, and the play was better for it. Even Corbin had to admit it.

"I admit it," he said. "She's better. She makes the play come alive. I admit it. Now drop it."

"The point is," Kendall said, "how do we capitalize on what's happened?"

"I got a call from Wally this afternoon," Morgenstern said. He liked to think he was either Flo Ziegfeld or David Merrick. He had worn a black homburg and a black topcoat to the theater this evening. The topcoat was draped over the seat beside him, but he was still wearing the hat. Wally Stein was the play's press agent, as opposed to its advertising representative. "He told me *Time*'s still doing the cover story."

"Great," Corbin said.

"Be better if we could get Josie in the story someplace," Kendall said.

"She's already in it," Morgenstern said.

"When did this happen?"

"They interviewed her this morning. Murdered star's replacement, how does she feel about it, all that shit."

"When are they running it?"

"*Next* week's issue, they've delayed it. Big picture of Michelle on the cover."

"Do we have any pictures of her getting stabbed?" Corbin asked.

"In the play, do you mean?" Morgenstern said.

Kendall looked at him.

No, in her *fuckin* apartment, he thought, but did not say because this was the play's producer here.

"Yes," he said, "Wally has publicity photos, and we've also got display photos for outside the theater."

"Of her getting stabbed?" Corbin insisted.

"Yes, I'm sure we do."

"We ought to get them over to *Time*."

"I'm sure Wally's already thought of that," Morgenstern said. "But we've got to be careful about this, you know. We don't want to look like vultures. In fact . . ."

"You're right, we've got to express the proper grief," Kendall said.

"Which is why I was thinking . . ."

"Wally should start feeding the media some material on the play's *content,*" Corbin said. "I don't want people coming to see it just because Michelle happened to get killed."

"Well," Morgenstern said, "why*ever* they come see it is fine with me, so long as they come see it. The thing is not to make it *appear* that's what we're looking for. Which is why I thought I might announce that we're closing the play."

"Closing it!"

"Out of respect for the dead, all that shit."

"*Closing* it!"

"We're sitting on a multimillion-dollar hit here!"

"Besides, this is a good play here," Corbin said.

"Especially now with Josie in it."

"I've already *admitted* I made a mistake . . ."

"All right, all right."

". . . so stop about Josie already."

"Anyway, the mistake's been corrected," Morgenstern said. "And I would never *dream* of actually closing it."

The men fell silent.

Their separate breathing was the only sound in the darkened theater.

"You know . . ." Morgenstern said.

"Mmm?"

"They'll be coming to us again, you know."

"The media?"

"No. The police."

"Mmm."

"The one with the Chinese eyes, especially."

"The one with the Italian name."

"Furillo."

"Furella."

"Carella."

"Whatever."

"He'll want to know."

"Know what?"

"How much we're getting out of this thing."

"What do you mean?"

"He's already asked me. He'll ask again, now that Michelle's dead."

"That's what they look for."

"Motive, do you mean?"

"Love or money. Those are the two motives."

"But they've already arrested her agent."

"I'll bet you any amount of money he didn't do it."

"He's crazy enough to have done it."

"But he didn't."

"Anyway, *all* agents are crazy."

"But he didn't kill Michelle, I'll bet my share of the gross on it."

"That's what he'll keep harping on. Gross. Net. Profits. Royalties. Carella."

"I don't think so. He's already made his arrest."

"Did you *see* that fat one?"

"On television, do you mean?"

"Yeah. The fat one."

"*He* sure as hell thinks Johnny did it."

"But not Carella. You didn't see *Carella* on camera, did you? *I* didn't see Carella on camera."

"Because he doesn't believe it."

"Which is why he'll be back, believe me."

"Why?"

"To ask about our financial arrangements again."

"Well, my lousy six percent isn't worth killing for."

"Neither is my two."

They both looked at Morgenstern.

"Hey, come on, fellas," he said.

Looking at him over the rim of her glass, she asked him why he'd trimmed Sharyn to Shaar earlier tonight. He was still trembling inside from having held her so close. He found it difficult to remember having called her Shaar.

"When did I call you Shaar?" he asked.

Not putting his hands on the table because he was sure they were shaking.

"When you were saying you thought I might feel uncomfortable in a place where there were only white people."

"Do you feel uncomfortable now?"

"No."

"Well, do you feel *comfortable*?"

"Yes."

"Even though everyone around us is white?"

"I'm not seeing anyone around us."

"Do you think if we went to a place in Diamondback, *I* wouldn't see anyone around us, either?"

"I think if we went to Diamondback, you'd be made for a cop in ten seconds flat. They'd probably shoot you the minute you walked through the door."

"That's racist."

"But realistic."

"How about you? Would they shoot you?"

"I doubt it."

"How come? You're a cop."

"Do I look like a cop?"

"You look like a sexy, beautiful woman."

"I *feel* like a sexy, beautiful woman."

"So I called you Shaar, huh?"

"Yes. You said, 'I'll tell you the truth, Shaar.'"

"I guess maybe I did."

"Why?"

"I guess I was feeling very close to you."

"My mother's the only one in the world who ever called me Shaar."

"Is that good or bad?"

"It's just peculiar. That you should pick my mother's pet name for me."

"I'm sorry, I didn't realize it was a special . . ."

"No, I kind of like your using it."

"Then I'll . . ."

"But not all the time."

"Okay, only . . ."

"Only when you're feeling very close to me."

"I'm beginning to feel close to you *all* the time."

"Then we'd better be careful," she said.

"Why?" he said, and suddenly put his big trembling hands on the table and covered her hands with them.

"Oh dear," she said.

The waitress was back.

"Another round?" she asked, smiling at Kling.

"Sharyn?"

"Yes, okay," she said.

"I'm glad you caught that guy," the waitress said, and swiveled off.

"*She* thinks you're cute, too," Sharyn said.

"Who?"

"The waitress."

"What waitress?" he said.

Alone with her in bed that night, he tried to tell her what was troubling him about the Cassidy murder. She listened intently, lying back against the pillows, head turned toward him, eyes wide, trying to visualize these people he was talking about.

"You see, Johnny Milton just had no reason to *kill* her," he said. "Stabbing her accomplished everything he wanted to happen. His client is suddenly a star, she's in a play where she gets *stabbed*, he's got all the media dogs barking at her heels, so why *kill* her? No reason for it at all. Stabbing her already served the purpose. Stabbing her put both her *and* the play on the map. So why kill the golden goose? No way. I can't see it. Where's the motive?

"Love or money, that's it, it's either one or the other. He stabs her, he can expect to *lose* money, so scratch that. Love? *Is* there another guy or girl in the picture, who knows? Maybe there *is* a man out there who was somehow involved with her, or a woman, for that matter. One thing you learn about homicides is never to take anything for granted, nothing is *ever* what it seems to be. So maybe it's love, okay, that's a possibility. I don't think we've got a crazy loose out there, this doesn't look like a crazy to me. So it's either love or money, the same old standbys, you can count on them every time, love or . . . excuse me, honey, but are you falling asleep?"

She nodded vaguely.

Smiling, he leaned over and kissed her on the cheek and then found her mouth and kissed her lips and then looked into her eyes and said, "Goodnight, Teddy, I love you."

And she signed with her right hand *I love you, too,* and turned out the light, and then snuggled up close to him in the dark.

8

CARELLA AND KLING WERE ON THEIR WAY OUT OF THE SQUAD-
room when this big black guy who looked like a contract
hitter for either the Crips or the Bloods came up the iron-
runged steps leading to the second floor. From above, Carella
saw the top of a red and blue knit hat, brawny shoulders in
a black leather jacket, and the clenched ham-hock fists of a
man in one hell of a hurry. He figured he'd better get out of
the way fast before he got stampeded. Kling, younger and
more foolhardy, said to the top of the man's head, "Help you,
sir?" They were both surprised when he looked up sharply
and—lo and behold—it was Detective/Second Grade Arthur
Brown, dressed for what was undoubtedly a waterfront plant
since Carella now noticed the baling hook hanging from his
belt.

"How'd it go last night?" Brown asked.

"Barney's, you mean?" Kling said.

"Yeah. Well, *all* of it."

"We left kind of early."

"Too Oreo, huh?"

"Yeah. Kind of unnatural."

"I was worried about that. But I figured . . ."

"No, listen, it worked out fine. We both felt the same way about it."

Carella figured this was the woman Kling didn't want to talk about just yet. But here he was, babbling about her to Brown.

"Who *is* this woman, anyhow?" Brown asked.

Good question, Carella thought.

"You don't know her," Kling said.

"What's her name?"

"Sharyn."

"Irish girl, huh?" Brown said, and burst out laughing for no reason Carella could fathom.

"With a 'y,' " he offered helpfully. "The Sharyn."

"Now *that* makes more sense," Brown said, still laughing. "Black folks don't know how to spell their own kids' names. Where'd you . . ."

What? Carella thought.

". . . end up?"

What?

"When you left Barney's, I mean."

"Top of the Hill."

"Hoo-boy!" Brown said. "I figured her being black and all, Barney's might ease the way. But it turned out to be overkill, huh?"

"Yeah, it really was, Artie."

Carella stood by silently.

"How black *is* she, anyway? Is she black as me?"

"Nobody's as black as you," Kling said, and Brown burst out laughing again.

Carella suddenly felt like an outsider.

"Well, is she the color of this banister here?" Brown asked.

"A little darker."

"That makes her blacker than me."

"No, I don't think so."

"You think you'll be seeing her again?"

"Oh, sure. Well, I hope so. I mean, *she's* got a say in it, too."

"Cause if you'd like to some night, maybe Caroline and me could join you, go out for Chinks or something, if you think you'd like that. Both of you."

"Let me ask her."

"Might be nice, you know?" Brown said. "You ask her, okay?"

"I will."

"Is the Loot in yet?" Brown asked, and started charging up the stairs again.

"Artie?" Kling called after him.

"Yeah?"

"Thanks."

"Hey, man," Brown said, and disappeared from sight.

Together, Kling and Carella went down the iron-runged steps in silence, their footfalls clanging as if they were in armor. He was wondering why Kling hadn't told him Sharyn was black. Surely, he didn't think . . .

"We'd better hurry," Kling said. "I told her ten o'clock."

End of discussion, Carella guessed.

Sitting and smoking in her dressing room at the theater, wearing rehearsal clothes that consisted of a shirred purple tube top, white boating sneakers without socks, and low-slung jeans that exposed her belly button, Andrea Packer snubbed out her cigarette the moment they entered the room, like a kid who'd been caught sneaking a drag in an elementary school toilet.

Nineteen years old if she was a day, lean and coltish, her long blond hair pulled back in a ponytail held with an elasticized band the same color as her precarious purple top, she stood at once, extended her hand, told Kling she was sorry if she'd sounded distracted on the phone, but she'd been studying her new lines, Freddie had put in a whole new scene, would he like a cup of coffee or something, there was a big coffeemaker on the table near the stage door where Torey stayed. All of this in a breathless rush that made her sound even younger than she was.

"I thought you'd be coming alone, Mr. Kling," she said, making the focus of her interest immediately apparent, and flashing him a brown-eyed glance and a radiant smile that in tandem could have melted granite. She then turned her chair so that her back was almost to Carella, who understood body language about as well as any other detective in this city. He felt suddenly useless. In fact, he felt invisible.

Kling explained that they were here because they'd been told that she and Michelle had shared a dressing room here in this small rehearsal theater . . .

"Yes, that's true. Well, now Josie and I do."

. . . and they were wondering if Michelle might have mentioned anything to her that could possibly throw some light on her murder.

"Confidential girl talk, huh?" she said, and smiled again at Kling.

"Anything she might have said about anything that was troubling her, or annoying her, or . . ."

"*Everything* annoyed her," Andrea said.

"How do you mean?" Carella asked.

"Well . . ."

They waited.

Carella moved around in front of her so that he could see her face and her eyes. Outmaneuvered, she sat in the chair before the dressing-table mirror, her hands spread on her thighs, and looked up into their faces. In a tiny little girlish voice, she said, "I don't wish to speak ill of the dead," and lowered her eyes.

"We know how difficult it must be for you," Carella said, bullshitting her.

"I'm sure you do, sir," she said, bullshitting him right back, and then raising her eyes to meet Kling's, excluding Carella as effectively as if she'd again turned her back to him. "The thing is," she said, "and I'm not the only one who felt this way, Michelle was a total pain in the ass with an ego out of all proportion to her talent. Well, look what she put him up to doing. Johnny, I mean."

"What was that, Miss Packer?" Kling asked.

"Stabbing her in the alley," Andrea said.

From the stage, Kling could hear the other actors running a scene over and over again. In high school, he had played Christian in *Cyrano*. He had fallen madly in love with the girl playing Roxanne, but she'd had eyes only for the guy playing the lead, a kid named Cliff Mercer who almost didn't need the fake nose they stuck on his face every night. Kling had once thought seriously of becoming an actor. That was before the war. That was before he saw friends getting killed. After that, acting seemed a frivolous occupation.

"Was there any prior indication that she and Mr. Milton were planning to stage a stabbing incident?" Carella asked.

Without looking at him, she said, "If you mean did she tell me Hey, guess what, Johnny's gonna stab me tomorrow night so I'll get a lot of publicity and become a big movie star, no. Would you advertise it in advance?" she asked Kling.

"Did she tell you she wanted to be a movie star?"

"*Everybody* wants to be a movie star."

Not me, Carella thought.

"As you probably know," Kling said, "Mr. Milton has *admitted* stabbing her . . ."

"Yes, it's all over the papers, all over everything, I'm sick of it already. This is a good play. We don't need cheap publicity to guarantee its success."

But it couldn't hurt, Carella thought.

"I guess you also know," Kling said, "that Mr. Milton denies having killed her."

Andrea shrugged. The tube top slipped a bit lower on her breasts. Automatically, she grabbed it in both hands and yanked it up.

"What does that mean, Miss Packer?" Carella asked.

"What does what mean?"

"The shrug."

"It means I don't *know* who killed her. It could've been Johnny, it could've been anybody. What I was trying to say before is that *nobody* liked her. That's a plain and simple fact. Ask anybody in the show, ask anybody *working* the show, nobody liked her. She was an arrogant, ambitious, untalented little bitch, excuse me, with delusions of grandeur."

But tell us how you *really* feel, Carella thought.

"When you said earlier that *everything* annoyed her . . ."

"Everything, everything," she said, and rolled her eyes at

Kling. "The play, the scenes in the play, the lines in the play, her costumes, her motivation, the sun coming up in the morning, *everything*. She kept wanting to know who *stabbed* her! As if that mattered. Freddie's play surmounts cheap suspense. It supersedes the genre, it subverts it, in fact. If Michelle had understood her part in the slightest, she'd have realized that. This isn't a mystery we're doing here, this is a *drama* about a woman's triumph of will, an epiphany brought about through a chance stabbing, an almost *casual* stabbing, accidental, random, totally meaningless in the larger scheme of things. So Michelle kept wanting to know *who* stabbed her. Is it the waiter, is it the butler, is it the upstairs maid? I swear to God, if I'd heard her ask one more time who stabbed her, *I'd* have stabbed her, right in front of everybody."

"You seem to have a good understanding of the character she was playing," Carella said.

"You have to understand the conceit of the play," Andrea said to Kling, smiling, "its internal machinations. Michelle was playing a character listed in the program only as the Actress. That's the part Josie is doing now. It's the starring role. *I'm* playing someone called the Understudy. Well, an understudy is supposed to know all the lines and moves of the person she may have to replace one night, because of illness, or accident or . . ."

Or death, both detectives were thinking.

"So whereas I wasn't Michelle's *real* understudy, I *was* her understudy in the *play*, and knowing all of her lines and moves was part of my preparation for the role."

"Of Understudy."

"In the play."

"In the play, yes."

"*Josie* was her understudy in real life. Which is why she took over the part when Michelle got killed."

"Did you ever think *you* might get the part?" Carella asked.

She turned to him. Looked him dead in the eye.

"Me?" she asked.

"Since you knew all her lines and moves?"

"Surely not as well as Josie does."

"But did it ever occur to you, once Michelle was dead, that you might get the starring role? Since you knew all the lines and moves?"

"It occurred to me, yes. But not because I knew all her lines and moves."

"Then why did it?"

"Because I'm a better actress than Josie is."

"Do you feel any resentment about Josie getting the part? An understudy? Taking over the starring role? While you— an actress in an important *supporting* role . . ."

"Of course," Andrea said.

"You resent it," Carella said, and nodded.

"Sure, wouldn't you?" she asked Kling.

"I guess," he said. "Miss Packer," he said, "there are questions we have to ask, I hope you understand this doesn't mean we suspect you in any way of having killed Michelle Cassidy. But there *are* certain routine questions . . ."

"You sound like Mark."

"Who's Mark?"

"Riganti. He plays the Detective. In the play. That's the sort of thing he would say."

"Well, it's the sort of thing we *do* say."

"I understand," she said softly, and lowered her eyes again.

"So maybe you'd like to tell us where you were on Tuesday night between seven and eight o'clock," Carella said.

"I was wondering when you'd get to that," she said, the brown eyes snapping up to his face. "All that business about knowing the part, and resenting Josie . . ."

"As my partner explained . . ."

"I know, I'm not a suspect. Especially when I tell you where I was."

"Where were you?"

"Aerobics class."

"Where?" Kling asked.

"Which one of you is Mutt?" she asked. "In the play, Freddie writes all about Good Cop, Bad Cop. Mutt and Jeff, isn't that what you call them?"

"Where's your aerobics class?" Kling asked.

"You must be Jeff."

"I'm Bert. Can you tell us . . . ?"

"Hello, Bert. It's on Swift. I'll give you a card. Would you like a card?"

"Yes, please."

"I was there on Tuesday night from six-thirty to seven forty-five. Then I went home. Check it out."

She turned toward the dressing-table mirror, reached for her handbag where it sat among a dozen or more makeup jars and powder puffs and brushes and liner pencils, snapped open the bag, rummaged in it for a moment, and handed Kling a card.

"The instructor on Tuesday was a woman named Carol Gorman. You'd better call first, she's not there all the time."

"We will. Thanks for your . . ."

"Andy?"

They all turned to where a strapping young man in watch cap and overalls was standing in the doorway.

"Sorry," he said, "I didn't realize . . ."

"Come in, Chuck," she said. "Have you met Mutt and Jeff?"

Madden looked puzzled.

"Good Cop/Bad Cop," she said. "Detectives Carella and Kling."

"Saw you the other day," Madden said. "How are you?" Turning to Andrea again, he said, "Ash wants to run the Understudy/Detective scene ten minutes from now."

"We just ran it," Andrea said dryly.

Once upon a time, a detective named Roger Havilland worked out of the Eight-Seven. He abruptly stopped working there when someone tossed him through a plate-glass window. But before his untimely demise, he'd once remarked, "I love this city when the coats come off."

He'd been referring to women, of course. *Women* taking off their coats, hell with the men. He and Carella had been strolling along Hall Avenue in the sunshine, and Havilland had been admiring the girls prancing by. *Girls* back then, not *women*. Nobody was quite as ready to take offense back then. Except Havilland, perhaps, who'd been a hater of monumental proportions. No one missed him. Enough police department bigots had risen to take his place. Oddly, though, on a beautiful spring day like today, Carella remembered the one memorable thing Havilland had ever said.

I love this city when the coats come off.

Today, the *women* had taken off their coats. Even the women who were only sixteen years old were prancing by in celebration of spring. The skirts were even shorter now than when Havilland had made his immortal remark, and the girls, the *women,* the *persons* of contrasting sex were now wearing thigh-high black stockings, some of them exposing garter belts, below the hems of their teeny-weeny skirts. It was a nice time of the year to take the air, especially down here in the Quarter.

Carella had always felt this part of the city was the most vital, a self-contained enclave of the eccentric and the eclectic, a city within the city proper, honoring its own established morals and mores, its own rules of acceptable behavior, most of it outrageous. A girl walked by wearing . . .

Well, she really *was* a girl, if twelve counted, anymore.

. . . what appeared to be a caftan, white with black trim at the hem and the long flowing sleeves. Over this, she wore an assortment of dangling, clanging chains, and a black fez beneath which her blond hair cascaded. She was barefooted, her feet caked with the grime of the city. She smiled at him as she went past. He wondered if his own daughter would one day dress like a camel driver and smile blissfully at every passing stranger.

The sun felt good on his shoulders and head.

He did not want to go indoors, he did not want to work on a day like today.

But Frederick Peter Corbin III was waiting.

Bodies by Rhoda was on the second floor of a red brick building on Swift Avenue, not far from the old Federal Bank Building. Kling had got there a half hour earlier and had been told by a woman with frizzy black hair and leotard and tights to match that Carol's Step-and-Stretch class was still in progress and wouldn't break till eleven. It was now ten minutes to the hour, and he sat patiently on a bench in the reception area, looking through a plate-glass window at a wide variety of women jumping and bouncing in the air. He could not hear any music behind the glass, but he suspected some was being played, otherwise the sight would have been entirely bizarre.

The women began pouring out of the room at about five past the hour, all of them sweating, all of them looking flushed and invigorated. He asked a somewhat beefy blonde who Carol might be, and she pointed out a trim brunette wearing a shocking-pink leotard and black tights, rewinding a tape at the player across the room. The room smelled vaguely of female perspiration. He caught his own reflection in what seemed a dozen mirrors as he crossed to the far corner.

"Miss Gorman?" he asked tentatively.

She turned. Faint surprised look on her freckled face. Green eyes wide. Lips slightly parted. No makeup on her cheeks, eyes or mouth. Fresh-faced kid of twenty-one, twenty-two, he guessed.

"Yes?" she said.

"Detective Kling," he said, "Eighty-seventh Squad," and showed her the shield. She seemed impressed. Nodded. Waited.

"I wonder if you can give me some information about this past Tuesday night . . ."

"Yes?"

". . . that would've been the seventh of April."

"Yes?"

"Were you here that night?"

"I think so. Tuesday? Yes, I'm sure I was. Why? What happened?"

"Were you teaching a class from six-thirty to seven forty-five that night?"

"Yes. Well, from six-thirty to seven-*thirty,* actually. Gee, you sound stern. Something terrible must have happened."

"I'm sorry," he said, "I didn't mean to . . ."

"I mean, you don't *look* stern, but you sure do *sound* stern. Very."

"I'm sorry," he said again.

"What is it that happened?"

"Nothing," he said. "This is a routine inquiry."

"Into what?"

"Do you know a woman named Andrea Packer?"

"Yes?"

"Was she in that class on Tuesday night?"

"Oh, this is about the actress who got killed, right? Michelle whatever. Someone told me Andy was in the same play with her."

"Yes," he said. "*Was* Miss Packer in that class?"

"Yes, she was. Is that what she told you?"

"That's what she told me."

"Well, she was telling the truth."

"I figured she might be," Kling said, and sighed.

In fact, even before he'd shlepped away the hell over here, he'd been dead certain she'd been telling the truth. Not once in his entire time on the force, as uniformed officer *or* detective, had anyone given him an alibi that later turned out to be false. Not once. Well, maybe once, but if so he couldn't remember when. Well, actually, yes, he could remember some guy telling him he was at a movie when actually he was out chopping up his mother-in-law. But never had anyone told him *This* is where I was at such and such a time on such and such a night and—

Well, wait a minute. How about that jackass Johnny Milton, who'd told them he was at O'Leary's at seven when he didn't get there until seven-fifteen, the jackass. A person had to be crazy to tell you he was someplace he wasn't when there were people who could absolutely state otherwise. Yet each and every goddamn alibi had to be checked out against the likelihood that the person was lying, which he'd have to be an idiot to do, when it was so easy to verify.

"Why didn't you simply *call*?" Carol asked.

Another good question.

He hadn't simply *called* because then he wouldn't have been able to ascertain that the person to whom he was speaking on the telephone was not being coerced into saying Yes, Andrea Packer was here bouncing around on Tuesday night. Over the phone, you couldn't tell if someone was holding a gun to a person's head. So what you did, you marched all the way over to Swift Avenue and waited on a bench while a lot of women you didn't know jumped in the air to the accompaniment of unheard music, and then finally you talked to the alibi and got the answer you knew you'd get all along. Sometimes, he thought he might enjoy being a fire fighter.

"Have you had lunch yet?" Carol asked.

"No," he said.

"Would you like to join me?" she asked. "There's a very good deli just around the corner."

He thought of Sharyn.

"Thanks," he said, "but I've got to get back to the office."

"Where's that?" she asked.

"The Eight-Seven? Uptown. Just off the park."

"I might stop in sometime."

"Uh-huh," he said.

"See what a police station looks like."

"Uh-huh. Well, thanks for your help, Miss Gorman, I appreciate it."

"Thanks for coming by," she said, and raised one eyebrow.

* * *

Freddie Corbin was telling Carella that non-fiction writing wasn't really writing, *anyone* could write a non-fiction piece. In fact, all non-fiction writing was just "What I Did Last Summer" over and over again. Carella didn't think he could write a non-fiction piece; he even had trouble writing detective reports.

They were sitting in a small sun-washed room Corbin called his study, "Not because I'm affected," he said, "but because a portrait painter had this apartment before I took it, and he used to paint in this room he called his study. As painters are wont to do," he added, and smiled.

Two side-by-side windows were open to a mild April breeze that wafted up from a small garden two stories below. A fire escape crowded with red geraniums in clay pots was just outside the windows. Corbin was sitting in a black leather swivel chair behind his desk. Carella was in a chair across the room. The playwright had been interrupted while rewriting several scenes in his play, but he seemed in no hurry to get back to the work at hand. Carella wanted to know what Corbin knew about Michelle Cassidy. Instead, Corbin wanted to tell him what he knew about writing.

"So let's dismiss non-fiction as something any child of eleven can do," he said, "and let's dismiss most forms of *fiction* as writing that requires *no* discipline whatever. The novel, in particular, is by definition a form that *defies* definition. Moreover, most novelists at work today are writing as poorly as the people writing *non*-fiction. What it's come down to, if a person can successfully string together nine or ten plain words to fashion a simple sentence, then he or she may be dubbed 'author' and be permitted to go on *author's* tours and speak at Book and *Author* luncheons and generally behave like a *writer*."

Carella couldn't see the distinction.

"An *author*," Corbin went on, seemingly reading his mind, "is anyone who's written a book. The book can be a diet book, or a cookbook, or a book about the sex life of the tsetse fly in Rwanda, or it can be a trashy woman-in-jeopardy mystery, or a high-tech novel about a missing Russian diplomat, or any one of a thousand poorly written screeds or palimpsests. An *author* doesn't need to study literature, he doesn't need to take any courses in the craft of writing, all he needs to do is impulsively and ambitiously sit himself down in front of a computer and write as badly as he knows how to write. In this great big land of the literary jackpot, if he writes badly enough, he may hit it really big, therefore qualifying as a bona fide *author* entitled to go on book tours and television talk shows. A *playwright*, on the other hand, ahhh-*hah*!"

Carella waited.

"A playwright is a *writer*," Corbin said.

"I see," Carella said.

"The living stage is the last bastion of the English language," Corbin said. "The last arena permitting exploration of character in depth and with perception. It is the final stuttering hope for beauty and meaning, the last stand, the *only* stand of the word itself. That's why I write, Mr. Carella. That's why I wrote *Romance*."

Though Carella couldn't remember having asked him.

"Now you may ask . . ."

I wish I could ask about Michelle, Carella thought.

". . . why I've chosen to express myself in terms of a mystery. But *is* my play a mystery? Oh, yes, there is a stabbing in it, an attempted murder, if you will, but the *focus* of the play is not upon the perp, as you call it, but instead on the vic, as you call it. Unlike the mysteries you deal with every working day of your life . . ."

Carella was thinking that in police work there *were* no mysteries. There were only crimes and the people who committed those crimes. He was here today because someone had committed a most grievous crime against Michelle Cassidy.

". . . in a straight play occurs at the *end* of the story," Corbin was saying. "And this change, this epiphany, can take many different shapes and forms. It can occur as insight, or simple recognition, or even the realization by a character that he or she will *never* change, which in itself is a change of sorts. In a *mystery,* on the other hand, the change takes place at the very beginning of the story. A murder is committed, there is an aberration in the normal orderly flow of events . . . a *change,* if you will. And a hero or heroine comes into the story to investigate, ultimately finding the killer and *restoring* order, *correcting* the change that took place in the beginning. So you see, there's a vast difference between a straight play and a mystery play. *Romance* is not a mystery. I will not think kindly on any critic who treats it as such."

"There's a danger of that happening now, don't you think?" Carella said.

Trying to get Corbin back to the matter at hand. Which was not writing the great American drama, but was instead this investigation into an aberration in the normal orderly flow of events as personified by the body of Michelle Cassidy with its twenty-two stab and slash wounds.

"Do you mean because of the publicity attendant on Michelle's murder?"

"Yes. Linked with the fact that there's a stabbing scene in the play itself. Some critics . . ."

"Fuck the critics," Corbin said.

Carella blinked.

"I don't write for critics. I write for myself and for my public. My public will understand that I don't write cheap mysteries, never have, never will. My public . . ."

"I understood . . ."

"*Those* were *not* mysteries. Excuse me, were you about to mention *Blue Badge* and . . . ?"

"Actually, I didn't know the . . ."

"*Blue Badge* and . . ."

". . . titles of . . ."

"*Street Nocturne,* yes. The two novels I wrote about New York City cops. But those weren't *mysteries,* they were novels about cops."

"Right, procedur . . ."

"No!" Corbin shrieked. "*Not* procedurals. *Never* procedurals. And not *mysteries,* either. They were simply *novels* about *cops.* The men and women in blue and in mufti, their wives, girlfriends, boyfriends, lovers, children, their head colds, stomachaches, menstrual cycles. *Novels.* Which, of course, I now recognize as a form inferior to that of the spoken word on the stage."

"How did you feel when Michelle first got stabbed?"

"The first time? In the alley?"

"Yes."

"To be honest?"

"Please."

"I felt good. Because of the publicity the play was attracting. Mind you, *Romance* is a wonderful play, but it doesn't hurt to have all this attention focused on it, does it?"

"According to Johnny Milton . . ."

"*That* piece of shit."

". . . the idea was originally Michelle's."

"I wouldn't be surprised. Very ambitious girl, very opportunistic."

"How do you feel about her *murder*?"

"Terribly saddened."

Carella waited.

"A regrettable occurrence," Corbin said. "But I must be honest with you. I still feel good about the publicity we're getting. *Unless* it turns against us. Unless it makes my play look like a cheap mystery."

"How well did you know Michelle?"

"I was the one who held out for hiring her—against Ashley's wishes *and* Marvin's, too—but he has no taste at all. Well, I take that back. He did, after all, decide to produce *Romance*. But Michelle was hired for the role because *I* insisted on it."

It occurred to Carella that his question hadn't been answered. He tried again.

"How well did you know her, Mr. Corbin?"

"Not at all well, I'm sorry to say. One misses life's little opportunities, doesn't one? And then it's all too often too late."

"Which of life's little opportunities do you mean?" Carella asked.

"Why, the opportunity to have known her better."

"How do you feel about the actress replacing her?"

"Josie? I think she's wonderful. In fact, I have to admit that I may have made a mistake not hiring her in the first place."

"Feel better with her in the part, do you?"

"Yes, actually. I think our chances are better. Even *without* the fuss over Michelle's death, I think we stand a much better chance with Josie in the role."

"And, of course, if the play turns out to be a tremendous hit . . ."

"I would be gratified, of course. But the value of the play is intrinsic to the play itself. Ten years from now, a hundred years from now, *whatever* the critics say, the play will stand on its own."

"Still, you would enjoy a hit, wouldn't you?"

"Oh, yes, certainly."

"A hit would mean a lot to you moneywise, wouldn't it?"

"Money's not the important thing."

"Six percent of the weekly gross . . ."

"Yes, but . . ."

"Capacity gross is estimated at a hundred and eighty-three thousand dollars."

"*If* we move downtown."

"Well, you'll certainly move downtown if the play is a hit."

"Yes."

"So six percent of the gross comes to almost eleven thousand dollars a week."

"Yes, I know."

"You've calculated it?"

"Many times."

"Close to six hundred thousand a year."

"Yes."

"A play like *Romance* could run for how long?"

"Who knows? If the reviews are raves, and if we move downtown? Five years, six years, who knows?"

"So there's quite a bit of money involved here. If it's a hit."

"Yes."

"And with Josie Beales in the starring role, and with all the publicity Michelle's murder has generated, the likelihood of a hit becomes . . ."

"I feel I should tell you," Corbin said, "before you ask . . . I have no alibi whatsoever for the night Michelle got killed."

Carella looked at him.

"None," he said. "I was here alone in the apartment, coincidentally working on the scene where the Actress gets stabbed. The scene in the play. So you see . . ."

Corbin smiled.

"I'm completely at your mercy."

They regrouped at three that afternoon.

Carella wasn't surprised to learn that Andrea's alibi had checked out. Kling was very surprised to learn that Corbin had no alibi at all.

"Maybe immortal writers don't need alibis," Carella said.

Hoping to catch Josie Beales at the theater, they called ahead, but Chuck Madden told them she was already gone for the day.

"You may want to try her at home," he said. "Though actresses are never home."

"How do you mean?" Carella asked.

"Auditions, readings, classes, benefits, they're never home."

"Did she say she was going to one of those? An audition or . . ."

"I'm just the stage manager," he said airily, "nobody ever tells me anything." Carella knew that exactly the opposite was the case. It was part of a stage manager's job to know where everyone involved with a show could be reached at any given time of the day. "Let me check my book," he said, "give you her home number, it's at least worth a shot." Carella could hear him leafing through pages. "Yeah," he said at last, "here it is," and read it off. "Otherwise, you can try the Galloway School later tonight. I see she has a class there on Thursdays."

"Do you have a number for it?"

"Yeah, right here, it's on North Loring," Madden said, and read off the number.

"When's your next rehearsal?" Carella asked. "In case we miss her."

"Tomorrow morning at nine."

They tried Josie at home, and left a message on her answering machine. They called the Galloway School and were told that classes tonight began at eight o'clock and that indeed Josie Beales was enrolled in a class called Advanced Performing Skills.

They'd both been working since eight o'clock this morning.

But they sent out for sandwiches and Cokes, and started typing up their reports, waiting for it to be eight o'clock tonight.

9

THE GALLOWAY SCHOOL—OR MORE ACCURATELY THE GAL-
loway School of Theater Arts, as the sign downstairs
announced it—was on the third floor of a building that had
once been a hat factory. Kling wanted to know how Carella
had known this. Carella said there were just some things a
good detective knew, kid. A scene was in progress as they
slipped into the vast room. Some thirty or so students sat on
folding chairs watching Josie Beales and an older man going
through an aria intended to break the heart, Carella figured.
In it, the old man was telling his daughter he had cancer and
had been given thirty days to live. Josie didn't seem to have
much to do in the scene except listen. She did that very well,
brown eyes glistening with tears as the old guy told her about
all of life's little missed opportunities. Carella wondered if
Freddie Corbin had written the scene. They stood at the back
of the room, listening and watching. On the folding chairs,
there was a lot of respectful fidgeting.

When the scene ended, a bearded man in the front row personally critiqued it, and then called for reactions and responses from the assembled students on the hard wooden folding chairs. A half hour later, he called a break and Josie and the old guy went out into the corridor together. She was standing by a radiator in front of a very tall window, smoking, when they joined her. The old guy was nowhere in sight. Josie's strawberry-blond hair was piled on top of her head. She was wearing blue jeans and a white T-shirt, and she looked very young and fresh and innocent. But she was twenty-one years old and an experienced actress. And she had inherited the starring role in *Romance* from another actress who'd been brutally stabbed to death.

"How's it coming along?" Kling asked.

"Oh fine. Well, you know, I *knew* all the lines and stage directions already, I was her understudy, you know, this wasn't like coming into something cold, taking over cold for somebody. Chuck rehearses all the understudies—Chuck Madden, our stage manager—three, four times a week, so really we're pretty much up on it."

She had stubbed out her cigarette and was leaning against the radiator now, arms folded across her chest, a defensive posture, Carella noticed, but nothing else about her seemed guarded. Rail thin in the tight-fitting blue jeans and T-shirt, she appeared almost waif-like. Brown Bambi eyes wide in a pale white face crowned with masses of reddish-blond curly hair, her mouth lipstick-free, a single ruby-red earring in . . .

She saw where his eyes had wandered.

"This isn't an affectation," she said.

Carella looked puzzled.

Her hand went immediately to her right ear, tugged the

earlobe there. "I *lost* the other one," she said, "I can't imagine where. I *know* I had both of them on at rehearsal today."

"I'm sure things have been pretty frantic," Carella said.

"Well, yes, but understudies are used to going on at a moment's notice, you know, if anybody gets sick or anything. So I really do know the part."

"Must be a strain, though," Carella suggested.

"A strain? How?"

"I mean replacing a murder victim," he said softly, and watched her eyes.

"Yes," she said, "it's a terrible thing, what happened to Michelle. But this is show business, am I right? The show must go on, isn't that so?" Eyes clear and bright, eyes unflinching. "And what you said, replacing her, this isn't really *replacing* her, it isn't as if she was *fired* so I could take the role, it isn't that at all. I was her understudy and something happened to her, and so I'm going on in her place, but that isn't *replacing* her, is it? You don't *really* think it's *replacing* her, do you?"

"Only in a manner of speaking," Carella said, and kept watching her eyes.

"Well," she said, and shrugged. "I feel awful about what happened to Michelle, but I'd be lying if I didn't say I feel happy for *myself,* for getting the opportunity to play the leading role in a play that now ... well, this'll sound terrible, too. But, you know, we really *do* have a shot now. With all the publicity the play's getting, I mean. I know that's awful, we wouldn't be *getting* the publicity if someone hadn't killed Michelle, but that's the simple truth of the matter. She got killed and now there's a lot of focus on the play. And a lot of focus on *me,* too—there, I said it before you did," she said, and smiled.

"I wasn't about to say it," Carella said.

"Neither was I," Kling said.

"No, but you were thinking it, weren't you? You've *got* to be thinking it. If it wasn't Johnny who killed her, then it had to've been somebody else, am I right? The papers said he admitted stabbing her but not *killing* her. So, okay, what you're thinking—the police, I mean, not you two individually, though I'm sure *you're* both thinking it, too—what *all* of you are thinking is that it must've been somebody who had a lot to *gain* from her murder, am I right? So who gains more than her understudy? Who gains more than *me*? If I go out there and do a good job in this play that everybody's already talking about *weeks* before it opens, I'll get to be a star. Me. Little Josie Beales. So, *sure,* I can understand why you're wondering where I was the night she got killed."

"In fact . . ." Carella said.

"Sure," she said, and nodded.

". . . *where* were you, Ms. Beales?"

"I had a feeling you'd ask that right on cue," she said, and smiled again.

"You understand . . ."

"Sure," she said. "I'm the one who got the part. I'm the one who gets a shot at stardom. So, sure. But did I *kill* Michelle to get it?"

"No one's suggesting . . ."

"Oh, please, guys, why are you here otherwise?"

"A routine visit," Kling said.

"Routine, my ass," she said, and smiled yet again.

Carella wondered if the smile was an actress's trick. Or even an actress's tic. He realized all at once that with an actress, you could never tell when she was *acting.* You could look into her eyes from now till doomsday, and the eyes would relay only what she was performing, the eyes could look limpid and soulful and honest, but the eyes could be acting, the eyes could be lying.

"From what I understand," she said, and paused dramatically, very serious now, almost solemn now.

"According to the newspapers and television," she said, and paused again.

He was thinking she was a very good actress.

"Poor Michelle was . . ." she said.

The word caught in her throat.

"*Killed* . . ." she said.

One *hell* of an actress, he thought.

". . . around seven-thirty, eight o'clock on Tuesday night."

"That's right."

"In her apartment on Carter and Stein."

"Yes."

"In Diamondback."

"Yes."

"A black neighborhood all the way uptown," Josie said.

Kling wondered why she'd felt it necessary to comment on the racial breakdown of the neighborhood. He wondered, too, how Sharyn might react to such an observation. Or was Josie merely establishing that the neighborhood, black or otherwise, was all the way uptown?

"Yes," he said. "A black neighborhood."

"Which doesn't mean a black person killed her," Josie said.

"That's true," he said.

"But who did?" she asked, and opened the brown eyes wide. "If not Johnny, and not some black junkie burglar . . ."

Black again, he noticed.

". . . breaking into her apartment and killing her . . ."

Which wouldn't have been a bad supposition, except that

there'd been no signs of forcible entry, something they hadn't reported to the media, and something she could not possibly have known unless Michelle had unlocked the door for her and opened it on a knife.

"Then who?" she asked.

Kling said nothing. Carella said nothing. They both knew when somebody more talented was taking the spotlight.

"Me?" she asked.

They still said nothing.

"Was *I* in Diamondback on Tuesday night at seven-thirty, eight o'clock? Was *I* on Carter and Stein?" she asked. "All the way uptown?"

They waited. Sometimes, if you waited long enough, they outsmarted themselves.

"Was *I* up there doing Michelle in her own bed?"

Michelle had been killed in the doorway to her apartment. Nowhere—not in the papers, not on television—had it even been *suggested* that she'd been killed in bed.

"Were you?" Kling asked.

"I was taking a singing lesson," she said, and smiled. "All the way *down*town."

"All the way downtown where?" he asked.

"In the Quarter. On Sampson Street," she said. "My teacher's name is Aida Renaldi, I've been taking from her for four years, I go every Tuesday night at seven—unless there's a performance or a rehearsal. On Tuesday, we quit rehearsing at five. I was downtown at ten to seven. My lesson started at seven and ended at eight. I went directly home afterward. I'll give you Aida's card if you like."

"Thank you," Kling said.

She searched in her purse, decided she didn't have a card after all, and wrote down an address all the way downtown.

Carella had just come from all the way downtown. He did not feel like going all the way downtown again.

"Call her first," Josie said. "She's very busy."

"I will," he said.

"I didn't kill Michelle," Josie said. "In fact, I feel very sorry for her."

She looked suddenly mournful.

"But at the same time," she said, "I feel happy for myself."

Aida Renaldi was delighted that one of the detectives visiting her was Italian. She didn't know that Carella thought of himself as American, perhaps because he'd been born in the United States and had never been informed otherwise. Aida, on the other hand, had been born in Milan, Italy, and rightfully considered herself Italian since she was still an Italian citizen here in the country on a work visa. In fact, she planned to go *back* to Italy as soon as she'd saved enough money to finance an operatic career interrupted by marriage, childbirth and divorce, not necessarily in that order.

Aida was forty-six years old and she weighed a hundred and eighty-seven pounds, which qualified her as a diva in at least one respect. Her hair was dyed a midnight black and she was dressed like a Gypsy when Carella and Kling arrived at her studio later that night. Both detectives figured she had just done a performance of *Carmen*. Instead, she had just given a lesson to a girl who did not know Verdi from Puccini, but who—like Aida—was hefty enough to entertain operatic aspirations. The girl smiled at Kling on the way out. Carella noticed that a lot of girls smiled at Kling. He wondered again who Sharyn might be.

During the interview with Aida, the teacher sat at the piano and sang an impromptu aria from *Butterfly,* discoursed might-

ily on the benefits of knowing both French *and* Italian if one
desired to sing opera . . .

"German no matter too much, eh?" she said.

. . . told them she far preferred Domingo to Pavarotti, and
incidentally confirmed that Josie Beales . . .

"Nize-a girl . . ."

. . . had been there for a singing lesson on Tuesday night
between seven and eight o'clock.

"Nize-a voice," she said.

"So what's this all about?" Carella asked out of the blue.

This was now a little past ten that night, and they were
eating what cops always ate whenever they had a chance,
hamburgers and fries, in a coffee shop on Avery and West, a
block from Aida Renaldi's studio apartment.

"What's *what* all about?" Kling asked, and bit into a hamburger dripping with ketchup and mustard.

"I always thought we could talk about . . ."

"We can . . ."

". . . anything together. I always felt . . ."

"So do I . . ."

"Like a goddamn older *brother* to you . . ."

"Yes, me, too, but . . ."

"So what's this about you're dating a *black* girl and you
can't tell me about her? I mean, god*damn* it, Bert, what the
hell is *that* about, you can't tell me about a *black* girl you're
dating, you have to tell *Artie* about her, you can't tell *me*
about her? What the hell do you think I am, some kind of
racist *jackass*? What the hell *is* this, Bert?"

"Wow!" Kling said.

"Yeah, wow, *shit*!" Carella said.

"I just didn't know how you'd feel," Kling said.

"Oh, terrific!" Carella said. "Compound the felony, tell me you don't know how I'd feel about a black-white relationship, tell me . . ."

"I'm sorry."

"Sure, kid, terrific!"

"I just don't know how I feel *myself*!" Kling said, and both men looked at each other in startled surprise, and just then the bigot of the universe walked in.

"I've been tracking you all over this fuckin city," Fat Ollie Weeks said, and shoved his way into the booth. "Hey, miss!" he yelled, and ordered three hamburgers and a side of fries. "My lieutenant says if it turns out Johnny Milton done the girl, the Eight-Eight definitely wants the homicide collar."

"So take it," Carella said. "*If* it turns out that way."

"Sure. Meanwhile, when Nellie indicts next Tuesday . . ."

"*If* she indicts."

"She'll indict. And by then we'll have a strong case to back her up."

"What do you mean?"

"My loot wants me to keep digging."

"For*get* it!" Carella snapped.

"What's wrong with you?" Ollie asked, looking offended. "If Milton done this, you should be *glad* we're lendin a hand here."

"No, we've got two different agendas here," Carella said. "*We* want to catch whoever killed Michelle Cassidy. All *you* want to do is nail Milton."

"That's one and the same person, pal."

"We don't think so."

"*Who* don't think so? Your lieutenant? Nellie? I was there, remember? *You're* the only one don't think so. They'd both be *grateful* if I came up with something makes the case stronger. If I can get people who'll testify . . ."

"What people? What are you talking about?"

"People who knew both Milton and the girl. People who can say . . ."

"Ollie, stay away from this! The people who knew them are the people we're already talking to. If you screw this up . . ."

"Hey, come on, screw it up! What's the *matter* with you?"

"You hear me, Ollie? Keep out of it. Come on, Bert."

"Where you going? What's the matter with you?"

"Enjoy your hamburgers," Kling said.

Whenever Mark Riganti played a detective, which was often, he prepped for the role by wearing a fake pistol in a shoulder holster day and night. The gun was weighted to give it heft and it had come from the factory in the same bluish-black color as a real .38 Smith & Wesson. Riganti had purchased it before toy manufacturers realized that somebody shoving a fake gun into a shop owner's face could cause him to wet his pants and open his cash register as easily as a real gun could. This gun *looked* real and it *felt* real and it made Riganti feel like a real cop. Truth was, even without the gun, he'd played so many detectives in his lifetime that sometimes he felt more like a cop than he did an actor.

Riganti had played a detective in the movie *Fuzz* which had been about policemen in Boston, and he had played a detective in the movie *Without Apparent Motive* which had been about policemen on the French Riviera, and he had played a detective in the movie *Blood Relatives* which had been about policemen in Toronto, and he had played a detective, albeit in Asian disguise, in the movie *High and Low,*

which was about policemen in Yokohama. In the play
Romance, which was about policemen in New York, he played
a detective investigating the stabbing of an actress performing
in a *play* called *Romance,* go figure it. A *fake* play called
Romance in a *real* play called *Romance,* where nobody gets
to kiss the girl.

At eleven o'clock that night, he was sitting barefooted at his
kitchen table, wearing his fake gun in a real leather shoulder
holster, and real faded blue jeans, and a white long-sleeved
shirt with the sleeves rolled up, the way detectives everywhere
rolled them up, he supposed. Open on the table before him
was his script for *Romance,* which now included several new
scenes typed on blue paper by their illustrious playwright and
handed to the cast at rehearsal this afternoon. If anything, the
new stuff made the play even worse than it had been. Riganti
figured they were all lucky Michelle had been killed.

This was a shame in one respect, though, since before her
death Riganti had considered her a likely prospect for a bed-
mate if the play enjoyed a long run. One of the reasons Riganti
had become an actor was that you got to meet a lot of good-
looking women and in some plays you got to kiss them and
in some instances you got to lay them. Offstage. In *many*
instances, in fact. In fact, Riganti was willing to give two-to-
one odds that actors in plays got laid more often than detectives
in police stations. Which was neither here nor there. What
was here at the moment was this terrible play with its rotten
new scenes Riganti had to memorize before tomorrow's
rehearsal at nine A.M. Usually, Riganti got this or that aspiring
young actress to run lines with him, the better to entice her
into the bedroom. But there was no time for fooling around
tonight. Tonight, there was only the drudgery of having to
learn all this uninspired crap from Freddie.

THE DETECTIVE
Did you ever once think <u>you</u> might get
the part?

THE UNDERSTUDY
No, I didn't.

THE DETECTIVE
It never occurred to you that if the
actress in the <u>leading</u> role . . .

Riganti hated speeches with underlined words in them.

THE UNDERSTUDY
Never.

THE DETECTIVE
. . . got <u>killed</u> . . .

He also hated *interrupted* speeches. The hardest thing to
do onstage was to interrupt another actor and make the inter-
ruption seem convincing.

THE UNDERSTUDY
Never, never, <u>never</u>!

THE DETECTIVE
. . . then <u>you</u>, as her understudy . . .

THE UNDERSTUDY
How many times do I . . .

THE DETECTIVE
. . . might inherit the role?

THE UNDERSTUDY
. . . have to tell you?

THE DETECTIVE
You as understudy might most
naturally <u>replace</u> her?

THE UNDERSTUDY
I never entertained such an ambit . . .

A knock sounded on the door.

Startled, Riganti looked first at the locked door and next at the clock on the kitchen wall.

Ten minutes past eleven.

He had been burglarized twice since moving into this apartment eight months ago. Now some son of a bitch was at the door at ten minutes past eleven.

"Who is it?" he yelled.

"Mr. Riganti?" a voice yelled back.

"Who is it?"

"Police," the voice said.

Yeah, bullshit, Riganti thought.

He got up from the table, went to the door, and placed his ear to the wood, the way he had done many times before while playing a cop. Simultaneously, he slipped the fake pistol from its shoulder holster, holding it alongside his free ear, the barrel pointed up at the ceiling, the way cops did in plays and in movies. He could hear nothing but heavy breathing in the hallway outside. Another knock sounded on the door, close to where his ear was pressed to it, causing him to jump back a step. His heart was pounding.

"You hear me in there?" the voice said.

"I hear you. How do I know you're a cop?"

"Open the door, I'll show you my shield."

Shield. That was a good sign. Riganti had been in many plays and movies where you could tell a fake cop because he called his shield a badge. Only civilians called a police shield a badge. Riganti turned the thumb bolt, made sure the night chain was in place, and opened the door a crack. He was looking out at a very fat man holding up a gold-and-blue-enameled detective's shield.

"Detective Oliver Weeks," the man said, "Eighty-eighth Detective Squad. I'm investigating the murder of Michelle Cassidy, would you please open the door?"

"Let me see your ID card," Riganti said.

The fat man made an exasperated sound, and then took out his wallet and fished through it for a laminated card which he held up to the crack in the door. The seal of the city's police department was on the card, and so was a color photograph that looked very much like the person holding up the card, and there was also the name he'd just given Riganti, typed across the face of the card, DETECTIVE/FIRST GRADE OLIVER WEEKS, with a matching signature below it.

Riganti figured the guy was really a detective.

He took off the night chain, and opened the door wide, forgetting that the fake pistol was in his right hand and not back in its holster. Ollie saw the gun and immediately reached for his own very real pistol in a clamshell holster on his right hip. Riganti realized at once what was happening. He yelled, "It's fake, I'm an actor, for Christ's sake I'm an *actor*!" Ollie remembered that the man he was here to see was, in fact, an actor. But he'd been a cop for too long a time now, so he immediately barked, "Drop the gun!" which Riganti was only too tickled to do. Ollie kicked it across the kitchen floor.

"I almost shot you," he said.

"Yeah, tell me about it," Riganti said.

He was having a little difficulty breathing.

"You got a permit for that piece?" Ollie asked.

"I told you. It's fake."

"It looks real."

"That's the idea."

"Why you packing a fake gun?"

"I told you. I'm an actor."

"Yeah?" Ollie said.

"I play a detective in this play we're doing."

"Oh, yeah, right."

"You scared the shit out of me," Riganti said.

"Me, too," Ollie said. "You got anything to drink here?"

"What do you mean?"

"Something medicinal?"

"Like booze, do you mean?"

"Yeah, like booze, beer, wine, whatever."

"Are you allowed to drink on duty?"

"No," Ollie said, and sat at the kitchen table.

"I think I have some beer in the fridge," Riganti said.

"Yeah, beer'll be fine."

"That's very interesting," Riganti said, going to the refrigerator and opening it. "You're not allowed to drink on duty, but you're accepting a beer from me."

"Yeah, that's very interesting, all right," Ollie said. "What kind of beer is it?"

"Heineken."

Ollie watched as he popped the caps off two green bottles. Riganti handed him a glass and one of the bottles.

"I almost blew your fuckin head off," Ollie said. "Cheers."

He drank straight from the bottle. Riganti poured his beer into a glass, and then sat opposite Ollie at the table.

"So what do you know about this creep who killed her?" Ollie said.

"Who do you mean?"

"Her agent. Johnny Milton."

"I don't know him too well."

"How about the girl?"

"Michelle?"

"Yeah. How well did you know her?"

"Well, we were in rehearsal together for three weeks when she . . ."

"What does that mean? Were you boffin her?"

"No. Certainly not."

"Why certainly not? Are you gay?"

"Of *course* not."

"Why of course not? Lots of actors are gay."

"But not me."

"Did you know he was living with her? The agent?"

"That's what we began to realize."

"Who's we?"

"All of us. The cast, the crew. It got to be pretty evident."

"That they were living together."

"Yes."

"Why do you think he killed her?"

"I'm not sure he did."

"You think there might've been some other guy she was involved with?"

"Do you always conduct an interrogation this way?"

"This ain't an interrogation."

"Then what is it?"

"Two guys sittin around talkin, havin a few beers."

"No, really, I'm interested in the process. I play a lot of detectives, you see."

"Uh-huh."

"Casting directors think I look like a cop."

"They do, huh?"

"You think I look like a cop?"

"I think you look a little faggoty to be a cop."

"I already told you . . ."

"I'm not sayin you *are* a fag. I'm only sayin you *look* like one. For a cop, anyway."

"Well, casting directors find me authentic-looking."

"Do *I* look like a cop?" Ollie asked.

"No."

"What do I look like?"

A fat tub of shit, Riganti was tempted to say, but didn't.

"You look like an actor *playing* a cop," he said.

"No kidding?" Ollie said. "Is there any more of this beer?"

"Sure, let me get you another one."

"An actor, huh?" Ollie said. "I wished I was."

"It's not as easy as you think," Riganti said, and carried another bottle of beer to the table. He uncapped it, slid it across the table to Ollie, and then sat down at the table and picked up his own unfinished glass again.

"Thank you," Ollie said, and tilted the bottle to his mouth, and took a long swallow. Wiping his lips with the back of his hand, he said, "You think she was cheatin on him?"

"Not from what I could gather."

"Then why'd he kill her?"

"Well, that's *your* assumption. I'm not sure he did."

"One cop to another," Ollie said, and winked, "why do you think he killed her?"

"One actor to another," Riganti said, "why do *you* think he killed her?"

"Cause he's a fuckin liar," Ollie said.

"How do you know that?"

"I was there when they were questioning him."

"I do a lot of questioning, too," Riganti said.

"Me, too," Ollie said.

"What's your technique? During a questioning?"

"I ask questions, the perp answers them. What do you mean, technique?"

"Well, do you *prepare* for a questioning in any way?"

"Prepare?"

"Yes. The way I use a fake gun to . . ."

"I almost blew your fuckin brains out."

". . . put me in a detective's frame of mind. I carry that gun with me everywhere I go. On the subway, in a restaurant, wherever. Because a gun is a vital part of being a detective, isn't it?"

"Oh sure."

"Take away a detective's gun, you take away his penis."

"Well . . . sure."

"Carrying the gun helps me *live* the part, do you see?"

"Sure."

"It's my way of preparing for the role."

"Sure."

"So how do *you* prepare?"

"Prepare?"

"Yes. For questioning someone."

"I don't."

"You don't?"

"I just go in, I say Where the fuck *were* you last Tuesday night, you little shit? He don't answer me, I keep at him. I keep tellin him this can go easy, it can go hard, it can go however he wants. You help me, I'll help you. You want a local jail, you want a state pen, you want niggers fucking you in the ass? Tell me where you were, you dumb shit!"

"Uh-huh."

"Like that," Ollie said, and picked up his bottle, drank, set it down again, belched, and said, "Sorry."

"For example," Riganti said, "suppose you were questioning this girl who . . . well, here, take a look," he said, and picked up the *Romance* script in its binder, pulled his chair closer, and said, "This scene here. How would you approach it? The scene I have with the girl."

"What girl?" Ollie asked.

"Her understudy."

"Whose understudy?"

"The girl who got killed."

"The Cassidy girl?"

"Well, no, this is in the play."

"I hear it's a dumb fuckin play."

"It is."

Ollie picked up the script. Squinting at it, he asked, "Why are these pages blue?"

"They're new pages. They're blue to differentiate them from the original pages. We can have blue, yellow, pink, green, sometimes even *purple* pages before all the revisions are done."

"These are hard to read, blue fuckin pages."

"They are."

Ollie kept squinting at the script. At last, reluctantly, he reached into his jacket pocket and took out an eyeglass case. The glasses he pulled from it were little Ben Franklin glasses. He suddenly looked like a fat scholar.

"For reading," he explained apologetically.

"I wear contacts myself," Riganti said consolingly.

Adjusting the glasses on his nose, Ollie cleared his throat as if he were about to read aloud, but then didn't. Silently, he read the page. Turned it. Read another one.

"You're right," he said, shaking his head, "this *is* a dumb fuckin play."

"I told you. But . . . just for the hell of it . . . how would *you* conduct this questioning?"

"This questioning right here?"

"Yeah. Where he wants to know whether she's ever thought of . . ."

"Yeah, I see it," Ollie said. "What I'd do, I'd say 'Look, miss, let's be realistic here, okay?' This is a *girl* I'm talkin' to, right?"

"Yes."

"Cause you have to clean up the act a little with a girl. I mean, you can't talk to a girl the way you can talk to a fuckin *thief,* you understand me? You got to be more gentle. So what I'd say . . . *what's* her name?"

"She doesn't have a name."

"What do you mean she doesn't have a name?"

"She doesn't. She's just called the Understudy."

"So what do you *call* her, if she doesn't have a name?"

"I don't call her anything."

"That makes it harder."

"How so?"

"Because say her name is Jean, you can start by tellin her 'Look, Jeannie, let's be realistic here, okay?' You use the diminative, you understand, You say Jeannie, instead of Jean. You put yourself on personal terms with her right away. Unless she don't even *have* a fuckin name, which makes it difficult."

"That's a good point."

"Nobody in the *world* doesn't have a name."

"Except in this play."

"Yeah," Ollie said, shaking his head, and looking at the script again, and then saying, "But even *without* a name, what

I'd say is 'Look, miss, let's be realistic here, okay? Do you expect me to believe you're understudyin the starring role in this play, and the girl gets killed and you never even once think Gee, maybe *I'll* get to go on in her place? Don't you ever go to the fuckin *movies,* miss? Didn't you ever see a movie where the star breaks her leg and the understudy has to go on for her? And all these fuckin workmen are sittin up on these little catwalks, high above the stage where the lights are hangin, and they all catch their fuckin breaths when she starts singin? And this old guy who pulls the curtain is standin there with his fuckin mouth open in surprise and a little old lady with costumes in her hands and pins stickin in her dress is standin there like *she* got struck blind, too, and all over the fuckin theater they're *amazed* by what this understudy is doin, you mean to tell me you never *saw* that movie, miss? Let's be *realistic,* miss.' Is what I would say to her."

"Wonderful," Riganti whispered. "Thank you."

"You ever get to kiss a girl in any of these plays you're in?" Ollie asked.

"Oh sure."

"What does a gay guy do when he has to kiss a girl in one of these plays?"

"I wouldn't know."

"I'm not sayin *you're* gay, you understand. I'm just wonderin how they'd *feel* about something like that. You think they go home afterwards and wash out their mouths with soap?"

"I'm sure they don't."

"I was just wonderin. You ever *throw* yourself into any of these scenes? Where you have to kiss a girl in one of these plays?"

"Oh sure."

"But somebody's gotta do it, I guess, huh?" Ollie said, and grinned like a shark.

"Still, it's not as easy as you think."

"Hey. It must be *very* difficult, soul-kissin some strange girl in front of ten thousand people."

"It is."

"I'll bet. You ever have to play a nude scene with one of these girls?"

"Oh sure."

"What do they tell these girls when they want them to take off their clothes?"

"Who do you mean?"

"Whoever it is that tells them to take off their clothes."

"The director, you mean?"

"Yeah, what does he tell them?"

"Well, if the scene calls for it . . ."

"Yeah, let's say the scene calls for it."

"He'll just say, 'People, we'll be doing the scene now.' Something like that."

"And she just takes off her clothes, right?"

"If the scene calls for it."

"Are there any scenes in *this* play where they have to take off their clothes?"

"No."

"Michelle Cassidy didn't have to take off her clothes any-place in this play, did she?"

"No."

"So her boyfriend couldn'ta been annoyed by anything like that, huh?"

"No."

"So what got him mad enough to stab her twenty-two times?"

"*If* he did it," Riganti said.

"Oh, he did it, all right," Ollie said.

"Maybe Andy did it."

"Who's he?"

"She. Andrea Packer. She plays the Understudy. Remember the scene you just read . . . ?"

"Yeah, right."

Ollie was thoughtful for a moment.

Then he said, "No, it couldn'ta been her. Nor the *other* actress, either."

"Why not?"

"Cause they're actresses," he said.

"What does that . . . ?"

"They both had to've seen the movie," he said.

10

THE MOMENT CARELLA GOT OUT OF BED, HE CALLED RIGANTI, hoping to set up an interview for later that Friday. Riganti told him a detective had already interviewed him last night.

"What detective?" Carella asked.

"Ollie Weeks," Riganti said. "He was very valuable."

Carella wondered what *that* meant.

"If you have a few minutes later on," he said, "maybe we can . . ."

"Oh, sure, but I'll be rehearsing from nine to . . ."

"Few other people I want to talk to at the theater, anyway."

"Well, sure, come on down," Riganti said. "Happy to talk to you."

Valuable *how*? Carella wondered, and hurried into the shower.

A traffic jam on the Farley Expressway delayed him for a good forty minutes. He did not get to the theater till ten past nine. He scanned it quickly, relieved to see that Ollie hadn't beat him to the punch again.

Riganti, in jeans, Italian loafers without socks, and a loose-fitting cotton sweater, was already onstage with Andrea Packer. This morning, she was wearing a moss-green wrap-around mini, orange-colored sneakers and an orange-colored T-shirt with no bra. Her long blond hair was stacked on top of her head like a small sheaf of wheat.

Riganti was trying to explain something to their director and their playwright, who both sat in what Carella now realized were their customary seats out front. Carella stood at the back of the theater, his eyes adjusting to the dark, trying to see if anyone else was sitting out there.

". . . a more realistic approach," Riganti was saying. "To the scene."

"Let me understand this," Kendall said. "Are you saying that you and Andy got here early this morning . . ."

"Eight o'clock," Andrea said.

Carella had called Riganti at seven-thirty.

". . . to read this scene we're about to rehearse?" Kendall asked.

"To go over it," Riganti said.

"To do an *improv* on it, actually," Andrea said.

"An improv?" Corbin asked.

"Well, yeah. Actually," Riganti said.

"On the new *scene*?" Corbin asked.

"Just to see if we could get a handle on it," Riganti said.

"Find a way into it," Andrea said.

"Find a realistic approach to it," Riganti said.

"My new *scene*?" Corbin asked.

"Well . . . yes. Your . . . uh . . . new scene."

"Which is terrific, by the way," Andrea said.

"Really terrific," Riganti said. "We were just trying to get a handle on it, is all."

"By doing an *improv*?" Corbin asked.

"By trying . . ."

"An *improvisation*? On my new *scene*?"

"Just to try for a little added reality," Riganti said, and turned to Andrea for assistance.

"To go for that additional touch of realism," she said, and smiled helpfully.

"I think it's quite real *enough*, thank you," Corbin said. "And by the way, improvs are for acting classes, and this happens to be a play in rehearsal. So let's just run the new scene, if you don't mind. The way I wrote it, please. *My* words, please."

"I'm curious to see what they've come up with," Kendall said casually. "How long will this take?" he called to the stage.

"Ten minutes," Riganti said.

"Why don't we see it, Freddie?" Kendall said. "What possible harm can it do?"

"What possible *good* can it do?" Corbin asked. "We've got eight new pages to . . ."

"It's just an exercise," Kendall said. "Loosens them up."

"Ashley . . ."

"If it's good for them, it might be good for the scene. Let's see it, Mark!" he called to the stage.

"Ashley . . ."

"What we tried to do . . ." Riganti started.

"Don't tell it, show it," Kendall said.

"Thank you," Riganti said, and nodded to Andrea, who immediately sat in a straight-backed wooden chair, and folded her hands in her lap, and lowered her head. The stage and

the theater went silent. There were just the two actors on
stage with a work light and a chair, getting ready to do an
improvisation for a director, a playwright and a detective in
a hushed darkened theater. Riganti started circling the chair.
Carella watched intently. Riganti didn't say a word, just kept
circling the chair.

"Look, miss," he said at last, "let's be realistic here, okay?
Do you expect me to believe . . . ?"

"Those aren't my words," Corbin said in a whisper that
carried clear to where Carella was standing at the back of the
theater.

"It's an improv," Kendall said in an equally loud whisper.

"I won't have them changing . . ."

"For Christ's sake, let's just *hear* the thing!"

The theater went silent again.

On the stage, the two actors looked out into the darkness,
puzzled, waiting for instructions.

"Again, please," Kendall said softly.

Riganti hesitated a moment. Then he nodded to Andrea,
who struck the same pose she had earlier, hands folded in
her lap, head bent. Riganti began circling the chair again.
Carella thought he did that very well, circling the chair.
"Miss," he said at last in a voice that sounded gruffly familiar,
"let's be realistic here, okay? Do you expect me to believe
you're understudyin the starring role in this play, and the girl
gets killed and you never even once think Gee, maybe *I'll*
get to go on in her place?"

"I never once thought that, no," Andrea said.

"Don't you ever go to the fuckin *movies,* miss?"

"Of *course* I go to the . . ."

"Didn't you ever see a movie where the star breaks her leg
and the understudy has to go on for her?"

"These are *not* my words!" Corbin whispered.

"Shhh!" Kendall whispered.

". . . and all these fuckin workmen are sittin up on these little catwalks," Riganti said, "high above the stage where the lights are hangin, and they all catch their fuckin breaths when she starts singin? And this old guy who pulls the curtain is standin there with his fuckin mouth open in surprise," Riganti said, circling the chair like a shark closing in for the kill, "and a little old lady with costumes in her hands and pins stickin in her dress is standin there like *she* got struck blind, too, and all over the fuckin theater they're *amazed* by what this understudy is doin," Riganti said, and stopped dead in front of Andrea and pointed his finger into her face and shouted, "You mean to tell me you never *saw* that scene, miss?"

"Yes, I saw that . . ."

". . . you never saw that *movie,* miss?"

"I saw that movie, but . . ."

"Then let's be *realistic* here!" Riganti shouted, and suddenly turned off the character he was playing, suddenly stopped being this raging detective in the scene he was improvising, becoming in the wink of an eye simply the self-effacing actor Mark Riganti again, standing there in jeans and a floppy sweater and Italian loafers without socks, smiling weakly and turning for approval to where Kendall and Corbin were sitting in the sixth row center in the dark.

"Bravo," Kendall whispered.

"Bravo, my *ass!*" Corbin shouted, and stormed out of the theater.

"If there is one thing I absolutely despise," Kendall said, "it's writers. I would truly be the happiest person on earth if

I could direct the telephone book. Give me a handful of trained actors and I could make a hit out of the telephone book, I promise you."

They were sitting in the delicatessen alongside the theater alley where Michelle Cassidy was first stabbed. Kendall had called a half-hour break after calming down his actors and promising them their playwright would be back after he'd got over his little fit of pique.

"Which I'm not sure he really will, by the way—unless he's a better actor than anyone in the cast."

"How do you mean?" Carella asked.

Both men were drinking coffee. Carella didn't really give a damn about writers *or* telephone books, although he guessed *somebody* wrote even telephone books. But he let Kendall talk. When a person talked, you learned a little something about him. And sometimes, incidentally, about the person who'd been killed.

"Well, this was a monumental explosion, this was rage of heretofore unseen proportions!" Kendall said, and rolled his eyes. "How dare they *this,* how dare they *that,* I'm going directly to the DGA, I'll have their heads . . ."

"The what?"

"What?" Kendall said. "Oh. The DGA. The Dramatists Guild. Of America, that is. Where else, Poland? Freddie threatened to go there and have all the actors fired, have *me* fired for encouraging them to subvert his play . . . his exact word, by the way, subvert . . . went out of the theater in high dudgeon. Now either this was the performance of the century, designed to let everyone know exactly who's in charge here and don't fuck with *me,* mister, or else he really was enjoying a totally childish temper tantrum unproductive to the collaborative theatrical effort."

"Which do you think it was?"

"A tantrum," Kendall said. "The trouble with writers—*especially* writers in the theater, where they do, in fact, have *outrageous* control—is that they mistakenly believe *their* contribution to the creative process is the most important one. Which, of course, is absolute drivel."

"Mr. Kendall," Carella said, "as I'm sure you know, we're still investigating the murder of . . ."

"Yes, I assumed that's why you were here," Kendall said dryly.

"Yes. That's why I *am* here, in fact. In fact, we can save a lot of time . . ."

"On the night Michelle was killed," Kendall said, "I was with Cooper Haynes."

"Who's Cooper Haynes?"

"He's the gentleman who plays the Director in *Romance.* I use the term advisedly. Gentleman, that is. Most actors aren't. But Coop is a dignified, courteous *gentleman,* thank God for small favors. He thought it might be valuable if he had an in-depth conversation with a *real* director. This, mind you, all this time *after* we went into rehearsal. Suddenly decided he ought to know what a *real* director was all about if he was to portray effectively a director *onstage.* They're such children, really, even the best of them. So I spent several hours with him, holding his hand, trying to convey the essence of . . . when I say holding his hand, by the way, I don't mean that literally. Coop is a happily married man with three children, straight as an arrow."

"And you?"

"Is that a question? And if so, what does it have to do with Michelle's death?"

"You raised the subject," Carella said.

"So I did. I *am* homosexual, Mr. Carella, yes. I am currently living with a set designer named José Delacruz, who is similarly gay and fifteen years my junior. I will be forty-seven in October. If my arithmetic is correct, the last time I looked he was thirty-two. And, by the way, he was there *with* us on the night Michelle was killed."

"There with you and Cooper Haynes, do you mean?"

"Yes. Well, not in the same *room,* we were working in the living room, and Joey was in his studio down the hall. He did the revival of *Moon for the Misbegotten,* did you happen to see it?"

"No."

"Pity."

"Anyway, that's where I was, and that's who was with me. As Casey Stengel used to say, 'You could check it.'"

"When you say that's where you were . . ."

"My apartment. 827 Grover Park North."

"Which you share with Mr. Delacruz."

"As of the moment, yes. I do not believe in long-term relationships. Life is short and time is swift."

"Speaking of which . . ."

"He got there at seven."

"Cooper Haynes?"

"Precisely seven."

"And left when?"

"Around ten. He would have stayed longer if Joey hadn't begun making ugly sounds about how late it was getting. They're such children, really."

"Actors, do you mean?"

"Actors, writers, set designers, costume designers, anyone involved in the theater."

Except directors, Carella noticed.

"Well, maybe not the technical people," Kendall said. "Your stage managers, your lighting people, your musicians if it's a musical. But anyone on the so-called *creative* end, dear God, *spare* me," he said.

"Did Mr. Haynes leave the apartment at any time between seven and ten?"

"No, we were together all that time."

"Didn't go down for a sandwich or anything?"

"We have ample food and beverage in the house, thank you."

"Step outside for a smoke?"

"He doesn't smoke. I don't, either."

"Did you happen to read anything, or see anything on television—or hear it on the radio, for that matter—about the *time* Michelle Cassidy was killed?"

"Sometime between seven and eight o'clock, wasn't it?"

"Then you know that?"

"I know that, yes."

"You read it, or saw it, or heard it someplace."

"Yes. I do *not* know the time from personal *experience*, if that's what you're hinting. I was *not* in Michelle's apartment at the time of her murder."

"Do you know where she lived?"

"No."

"Never been there?"

"Never."

"So you and Mr. Haynes were in each other's company from seven to ten P.M. on Tuesday night, the seventh of April."

"We were."

"And neither of you left the apartment during that time."

"We were both there from seven until ten."

"Did Mr. *Delacruz* leave the apartment?"

Kendall hesitated for a moment. Then he said, "I have no idea."

"Well, you said he began making ugly sounds around ten o'clock . . ."

"Yes, but . . ."

"So was he there all the time? Between seven and ten?"

"You would have to ask him."

"Well, you'd have known if he left the apartment, wouldn't you? For a sandwich? Or a smoke?"

"Joey doesn't smoke. Besides, he didn't even *know* Michelle. So if you're suggesting he *snuck* uptown to *kill* the lady . . ."

"Nothing of the sort," Carella said.

But he was thinking that Delacruz was the only person who could vouch for the whereabouts of Kendall and Haynes at the time of the murder. And both of them *did* know Michelle.

"Then *what*?" Kendall asked. "Oh, *I* see. It was Coop and *I* who did the deed in tandem, is that it? The real director and the make-believe director, running uptown to Diamondback to kill our star for reasons known only to God. By the way, before you even *ask*, Mr. Carella, I *know* she lived in Diamond-back because, as already noted, I *do* read the papers, *and* watch television, *and* listen to the radio. I don't know *where* in Diamondback, but do you really believe there's anyone in this city who does *not* now know that Michelle lived uptown with the man arrested for having stabbed her? And, I would have thought, *killed* her as well. But here you are, playing detective . . ."

"No, sir, not play . . ."

". . . in a cheap little *mystery* that has Coop and me . . ."

"No, sir, not a mystery . . ."

". . . stabbing Michelle . . ."

". . . cheap or otherwise."

"No? Then what is it when you suggest . . . ?"

"I've suggested nothing."

"When you wonder *aloud* then . . . would that be a fair statement? When you *wonder* if Coop and I caught a cab uptown, broke down Michelle's door, and brutally . . ."

"Murdered her," Carella supplied.

Kendall looked at him.

"That isn't a cheap little mystery," Carella said. "That is a woman getting murdered."

"The difference eludes me."

"The difference is she's really dead."

"Oh, I see."

"And someone caused her to be that way."

"Then it's a good thing Coop and I have such an airtight alibi, isn't it?" Kendall said.

"*If* Mr. Delacruz can vouch for it."

"He can *swear* to it, I promise you."

"Then you've got nothing at all to worry about."

"Nothing," Kendall said.

Carella knew that both Cooper Haynes and José Delacruz had to be talked to because they were Kendall's alibis, and all alibis had to be checked. Even then, the killer always turned out to be the good-looking, well-mannered, honor-student kid next door who always had a kind word for the neighbors and who wouldn't have touched a fly, unless it was open. So who the hell knew?

But whereas he would have adored talking to yet some more doubtlessly delightful theater personalities, his son Mark had to be driven to an away softball game at four that afternoon. He had already explained to Lieutenant Byrnes that he would appreciate leaving the office an hour earlier today because their housekeeper was on vacation and this was his daughter April's first day at ballet class and Teddy had to drive her there, which meant *he* had to drive Mark and four of his teammates to the Julian Pace Elementary School three miles from his own school.

Which was how, at six that evening, Carella was at the school's ball field patiently waiting for the game to end, and Kling was outside the apartment building at 827 Grover Park North, waiting for José Delacruz to get home, and Teddy was coming down the steps of the Priscilla Hawkins School of Ballet, April's sweaty little hand in her own, when she witnessed a red Buick station wagon backing into the grille of her own little red Geo.

The moment the doorman nodded that this was the person Kling was waiting for, he followed Delacruz into the building and caught up with him at the elevators.

"Mr. Delacruz?" he said.

Delacruz turned, startled. He was perhaps five feet four inches tall, thin and delicately boned, wearing a teal long-sleeved silk shirt buttoned at the cuffs, black pipestem trousers, and white Nike running shoes. His eyebrows were thick and black, matching exactly the straight black hair combed back from a pronounced widow's peak. He had intensely brown eyes, androgynous Mick Jagger lips, and a thin, slightly tip-tilted nose that looked as if he'd bought it from a plastic surgeon. Except for the Nikes, he resembled a matador more than he did a set designer. On the other hand, Kling had never met anyone in either of those exotic professions.

"Mr. Delacruz?" he repeated.

"Yes?"

Faint Spanish accent detectable even in that single word.

"Detective Kling, Eighty-seventh Squad," Kling said, and showed him his shield.

"Are you a cop?" the woman screamed.

Teddy was having trouble reading her lips. Ten-year-old April, who could have heard the woman from a block away, so loud were the decibels, looked up at her mother and signed *She wants to know if you're a cop.*

They had run over to the Geo just as the woman got out of the Buick to examine its rear end. Teddy couldn't imagine why the woman was looking for damage to *her* car when she was the one who'd just backed into *Teddy's* car.

No, I am not a cop, she signed.

"No, she is not a cop," April said.

"Then what's *this*?" the woman shouted, wildly flapping her hands at the DEA sticker plastered to the windshield on the passenger side. In this case, DEA stood not for *Drug Enforcement Agency* but rather for *Detectives Endowment Association.* If Carella had been Irish, there would have been an *Emerald Society* sticker on the windshield as well. And if he didn't devoutly believe that anyone born in America was simply an American and not an *Italian*-American or an *Any-thing*-American, there might have been a *Columbia Society* sticker there, too. As it was, the DEA sticker was on the windshield to indicate to any interested police officer that the car belonged either to a cop or a member of a cop's family.

April started to sign *She wants to know,* but Teddy had already caught the gist. She signed to her daughter to tell the woman that her daddy *was* a cop, yes, a *detective,* in fact, but what did that have to do with the fact that the woman had just backed into her car, smashing the headlight . . .

"Slow down, Mom," April said.

. . . and the grille and crumpling the hood?

"My father's a detective," April said calmly. "You smashed our headlight and grille and you wrinkled the hood, so what difference does it make *what* he is?"

Teddy was watching her daughter's lips. She nodded emphatically and began reaching into her handbag for her wallet with her driver's license in it. It occurred to her that her registration and insurance card were locked inside the car, in the glove compartment. She was unlocking the door on the passenger side when the woman yelled,"Where the hell do you think *you're* going?"

Teddy didn't hear her.

The woman grabbed her shoulder and spun her around, almost knocking her over.

"You hear me?" the woman shouted.

This time Teddy was reading her lips. She was also reading the spittle that spewed from the woman's angry mouth in a fine spray reeking of onions.

"You think you can get away with murder just cause your husband's a *cop*?"

The woman had both Teddy's shoulders now, and was shaking her violently.

"Is *that* what you think? Well, you got another think . . ."

Teddy kicked her in the left shin.

April ran to a phone booth.

Kling thought the apartment looked like a stage set for a play about a French king. But Joey Delacruz promptly informed him that he himself had designed and decorated the apartment "in an eclectic mix of Queen Anne, Regency, Windsor, and William and Mary," none of which sounded even remotely French to Kling, so much for that. Delacruz went on to say that he hoped his creation—the *apartment,* Kling guessed—would outlive his relationship with Kendall, which he sometimes felt was somewhat tenuous. Carella hadn't mentioned that Delacruz was gay. *Nor* Kendall, for that matter. Perhaps he hadn't felt it was important. Kling didn't think it was too terribly important now, either, unless one or the other of them—or *both* of them—had murdered Michelle Cassidy.

"Tell me about the night of April seventh," he said.

"Oh, my, but we *do* sound like a television cop, don't we?"

Kling didn't think he sounded like a television cop. He found the comparison annoying.

"Where were you that night, for example?" he asked.

"Right here," Delacruz said. "Excuse me, but am I supposed to know what this is all about?"

"Have you spoken to Ashley Kendall recently?"

"Not since this morning, when he kissed me goodbye and left for work."

Kling wondered if Delacruz meant *that* to be annoying, too. The image of a man kissing another man goodbye when he left for work. He thought about it for a second or two and decided it was less annoying than being told he sounded like a television cop.

Trying not to sound like anyone on *Hill Street Blues,* he said, "*Do* you remember where you were on the night Michelle Cassidy was murdered?"

"Am I supposed to know this woman?"

"Your friend says no."

"Ashley?"

"Mr. Kendall, yes."

"Does it bother you that we're gay?"

"Mr. Delacruz, I don't care what you are, or what you do, so long as you don't do it in the streets and frighten the horses."

"Bravo! Queen Victoria!"

"You're supposed to know *of* her, however."

"Queen Victoria?"

"Sure, Queen Victoria."

"I never *met* Michelle Cassidy, but I *do* know what happened to her, yes. I would have to be deaf, dumb and blind *not* to know."

"Good. So where were you on the night she got killed?"

"Right here."

"Anyone with you?"

"Are you corroborating something Ashley told you?"

"You said you hadn't spoken to him since . . ."

"That's right."

"Then what makes you think I'm trying to corroborate anything he said?"

"Oh, just a hunch, Detective Kling. Just a hunch."

"Where were you all day?"

"Today?"

"Yes. I've been waiting downstairs since . . ."

"Why didn't you simply ask *Ashley* where I was? He'd have told you in a . . ."

"I didn't talk to him."

"Well, *someone* must have . . ."

"Yes, my partner did."

"Couldn't *he* have asked? Or did you want to make sure Ashley wouldn't call ahead to warn me?"

"Warn you about what?"

"About what to say. In case you asked where I was on the night Michelle got killed."

"You've already told me you were here. And you've already told me you haven't spoken to Kendall since early this morning."

"How do you know it was early?"

"Because rehearsal started at nine."

"Elementary, my dear Watson."

"So what do you think, Mr. Delacruz?"

"Did Ashley tell your partner he was here with me on the night Michelle got killed?"

"Why don't *you* just tell me where he was?"

"He was here."

"All night long?"

"All night long."

"Anyone who can confirm that?"

"Oh dear," Delacruz said.

Kling waited.

"Don't you think I already *know* you know, Detective Kling?"

"Know what?"

"That Ashley had a meeting here with the man playing the Director in that idiotic play he's directing."

"From what time to what time?"

"Cooper Haynes got here at seven and left at ten," Delacruz said. "I know because that's *way* past my usual bedtime."

"Either of them leave the apartment at any time that night?"

"Not until ten o'clock. Mr. Haynes left at ten. Ashley stayed. Ashley *does* live here, you know."

"Did *you* happen to leave the apartment?"

"I was here all the while Mr. Haynes was here," Delacruz said, and smiled. "I know Ashley quite well, you see."

* * *

The doorman at Cooper Haynes's upper south side building told Kling that Mr. Haynes had left the building some ten minutes ago, to walk his dog. Kling caught up with him a good seven blocks uptown, following a leash to which a furry little dog was attached. The dog immediately began barking at Kling, the way all little dogs do in an attempt to convince people they're really fierce German shepherds or Great Danes in disguise. Haynes kept saying, "No, no, Francis," over and over again, but little Francis kept snapping at Kling, trying to bite him on the ankles. Kling wanted to *step* on the goddamn mutt, squash him flat into the pavement, dog lovers of the world, unite!

Haynes finally got Francis under control and they proceeded together up the avenue, the dog sniffing at each and every scrawny city tree they passed, occasionally peering up at Kling scornfully, as if it were *his* fault that none of the trees were compatible with his toilet habits. Haynes, dutiful citizen that he was, was wearing on his right hand a little plastic bag turned inside out. Once little Francis relieved himself, as they say, Haynes would pick up the leavings as required by law, and turn the plastic bag back upon itself so that nothing vile would have been touched by human hands.

Little Francis seemed particularly unwilling to oblige this evening. Haynes, like the patient master and good citizen he was, coaxed and cajoled but nothing seemed forthcoming. The dog merely kept turning up his nose in disdain at each and every spindly tree or stout fire hydrant they passed.

The dog's reluctance, coupled with Haynes's celebrity, caused a great many passersby to oooh and ahhh in amusement and appreciation. The recognition factor had nothing to do with the fact that Haynes was playing a director—in fact, *the* Director—in an awful little play uptown. Instead, it was due to his appearance five days a week on a soap opera called *The Catherine Wheel,* in which he portrayed a kind and friendly country physician named Dr. Jeremy Phipps. As they strolled up the avenue, incessantly stopping for the dog to sniff and dismiss, people greeted Haynes with a wave and a grin and a familiar, "Hey, Doc, how's it going?" or, "Hey, Doc, where's Annabelle?" which was the name of the duck who was the doctor's pet on the serial, and who had been recently kidnapped by a band of illegal Chinese aliens who were stealing waterfowl of that ilk and selling them to restaurants specializing in Peking cuisine. What with all the attention the dog gave to potential elimination sites, and all the attention Haynes gave to wheedling an offering out of little Francis, *plus* the further attention each and every citizen of this city, it seemed, lavished upon the good Dr. Phipps, Kling found it difficult to ask his questions with any sense of continuity or gathering force. But ask them he did.

"Were you, in fact, at the Kendall-Delacruz apartment on the night of April seventh between seven and ten P.M.?"

"Yes, I was," Haynes said. "I was looking for a mind-set, you see. Ordinary people think that all an actor does is jump into a role, the way children do when they're making believe. But, oh my, it isn't that simple, I wish it were. There's a great deal of craft involved, *and* skill, *and* research. Never mind talent, that goes without saying," he said modestly. "It's everything *else* that goes into a performance. I must say that Ashley gave me some valuable insights. I feel my interpretation of this enormously difficult role has improved a hundredfold since our discussion."

Somehow, Kling was beginning to feel that everyone in the theater lived in some kind of peculiarly egocentric wonderland. He was beginning to believe, in fact, that *none* of the people involved in putting *Romance* on the stage could possibly have killed Michelle Cassidy. Each and every one of them seemed too thoroughly involved in himself or herself alone, and such self-dedication excluded awareness of any other being in the universe. Kill *whom*?

Nonetheless—and doggedly, so to speak:

"Did either you or Mr. Kendall leave the apartment at any time that night?"

"I left at ten."

"But before then?"

"No. Neither of us."

"How about Mr. Delacruz?"

"I did not see him leaving at any time that night," Haynes said, and then, in triumph, "*Good* boy, Francis! Oh, what a *good* little boy you are!"

Alone in bed together later that night, they whispered in the dark.

"I'm afraid."

"No, don't be."

"I've always been afraid of cops."

"No, no."

Stroking, touching, comforting.

"Even when I was small. Cops always frightened me."

"There's nothing to be afraid of."

"Afraid they'd catch me *doing* something."

"No, no."

"Something *wrong*."

"I'm here, don't worry, darling."

"They make me feel guilty. Cops. I don't know why that should be."

"There, there."

Familiar flesh in the darkness, touching, stroking.

"They think we killed her."

"They think *everyone* killed her."

"Do you remember the Agatha Christie novel?"

"Which one?"

"Where everyone *does* kill her."

"Oh, yes. The film, too."

"Yes."

"A marvelous film."

"Yes."

"On a train."

"Yes. They all kill her."

"Clouseau. He was the inspector."

"No, that's not his name."

"What is it then?"

"Why did you have to say it?"

"I thought . . ."

"No, it isn't Clouseau."

"I realize that now."

"Now I won't be able to sleep all night."

"I'm sorry, darling."

"Between them and Clouseau, I won't sleep a wink."

"Just put it out of your mind."

"Clouseau and the goddamn police."

"I'm *so* sorry, really."

"Thinking we killed her."

"No, no, try to relax."

"Closing in on us."

"No, darling. Just relax."

Silence.

"There."

"Yes."

"Isn't that better?"

"Yes."

More silence.

"What *is* his fucking name?"

"Just put it out of your mind."

"The Belgian."

"Yes, but relax . . ."

"The inspector."

"Relax."

"I'm trying."

"Just let me . . ."

"I am."

". . . help you relax."

"Yes."

Kissing. Touching. Stroking the familiar flesh.

"Mmm."

"Better, darling?"

"Yes."

"Isn't that better?"

"Yes."

"Much better, isn't it?"

"Yes."

"Now give it to me."

"Yes."

"Give me that hot juice."

"Yes."

"Give it to me, *give* it!"

"Oh, Jesus!"

"Yes!"

"*Yes!*"

"Oh *yes,* my love."

Silence. The ticking of a clock somewhere in the apartment. The sound of even breathing.

"Joey?"

"Mmm?"

"It was Maigret. The inspector."

"Yes, thank you."

Silence. On the street outside, the sound of a wailing police siren. Silence again.

"Ashley?"

"Mmmm?"

"It was Poirot."

Alone in bed together that night, she told him she'd been charged with assault. Her eyes blazed, her fingers flew, she was still mad as hell. He watched her hands, troubled by the fact that she'd been given a summons here in their local precinct, charged with a misdemeanor, no less.

"What did you *do* to this woman?" he asked, saying the words, signing them at the same time.

What did I *do to* her? she signed. *Why don't you ask what she* did *to* me?, bobbing her head whenever she emphasized a word, underscoring it further with dark laser beams that flashed from her darker brown eyes.

He could not resist smiling, and made the mistake of signing and simultaneously saying, "You're beautiful when you're angry," which Teddy didn't find too terribly amusing at all.

Do you want to hear this, she shouted with her hands, *or do you want to bring me chocolates in jail?*

"I'm listening," he said.

The way she told it, before a patrol car could respond to the frantic call April made from a phone booth not five feet from where the irate woman was still screaming at Teddy, refusing to let go of the lapels of her suit jacket even though Teddy kept kicking at her repeatedly . . .

I was wearing French heels, she signed, *I had lunch downtown with Eileen . . .*

"How is she?" Carella said.

First, I came straight home to pick up April, drove her over to her ballet class. French heels with a little pointed toe, she signed. *Which is how she got the cut on her leg.*

Carella thought Uh-oh.

The woman, according to Teddy, was a behemoth weighing some two thousand pounds, shaking her till her teeth rattled, virtually lifting her off the ground while Teddy kept trying to kick her again. The woman's piercing shrieks finally attracted the attention of a police officer patrolling the parking lot on foot . . .

The dunce of the One-Five-Three, Teddy signed, naming their local Riverhead precinct, where six detectives had recently been arrested for stealing money and dope from various dealers.

The officer told them to break it up, calm down, relax, words to that effect, and then listened to the fat woman's account of how Teddy had smashed into the rear of her Buick, a total lie which Officer Stupid listened to gravely and solemnly, wagging his head in wonder and amazement. Little April kept trying to tell him that none of this was true, it was the *fat* lady who'd smashed into their car, which prompted Officer Fool to tell her to please let her mother speak for herself. April then had to explain that their mother was both hearing- and speech-impaired and could not convey her thoughts except through signing, which language perhaps Officer Incompetent comprehended. He admitted he did not. But he now looked at Teddy as if wondering whether or not it was legal for a deaf-and-dumb person to be driving in the first place.

By now, the fat lady had lifted her skirt to show her tree-trunk legs, one of which was bleeding from a small cut undoubtedly caused by Teddy's first kick to the shin. There were no visible signs of abuse or assault on Teddy *herself,* however, since all the woman had done was shake her till all her internal organs were hopelessly entangled. Officer Idiot was debating whether to just advise the ladies to exchange insurance information, and shake hands, and call it a day when the fat woman began screaming about her attacker being a police detective's wife, and all the cops in this city were the same, and how could she expect any justice from a cop protecting his own, and I want your name and your badge number, and I intend to take this to the Supreme Court, you hear? So Officer Imbecile, perhaps remembering the recent riot in Grover Park, and not wishing any kind of trouble at all on his hitherto peaceful little beat outside a shopping mall, decided in his Solomon-like street wisdom that it would be far easier to ask the dummy to come back to the precinct with him, where someone would write out a Desk Appearance summons for her. His exact words were *Let the court work this out,* the coward!

Seething, Teddy showed Carella the summons now:

YOU ARE HEREBY SUMMONED TO APPEAR IN THE CRIMINAL COURT OF THE DISTRICT OF RIVERHEAD TO ANSWER A CRIMINAL CHARGE AGAINST YOU.

OFFENSE CHARGED: Assault 3rd.

COURT: Riverhead Criminal Ct

PART: AR2

ADDRESS: 1142 Coolidge Boulevard, Riverhead

TIME: 9:30 AM

DATE 4/24

INSTRUCTIONS FOR DEFENDANT:

YOU MUST APPEAR AT THE TIME AND DATE INDI-
CATED ABOVE AND PRESENT THIS FORM TO THE
COURT CLERK.

Should you fail to appear for the offense charged
above, in addition to a warrant being issued for your
arrest, you may be charged with an additional viola-
tion of the Penal Law which upon conviction may
subject you to a fine, imprisonment, or both. Addi-
tionally, if you fail to comply with the directions of
this Desk Appearance ticket, any bail paid will be subject to forfeiture.

ADDITIONAL INSTRUCTIONS

CODEFENDANTS   **IF YES, NAMES:**
    Yes   √ NO

ACKNOWLEDGMENT OF DEFENDANT:

I, the undersigned, do hereby acknowledge receipt

of the above DESK APPEARANCE TICKET, personally
served upon me, and do agree to appear as indicated.

SIGNATURE OF DEFENDANT: *Theodora Franklin Carella*

"I see you signed it," Carella said.

Teddy nodded.

"What happened to the woman?"

*She came to the police station with us. Stood with her hands
on her hips, scowling, while a detective wrote the summons.*

"You say she was screaming at you . . ."

Yes.

"Shaking you . . ."

Yes.

"Was *she* charged with anything?"

No.

"Those jackasses just let her walk?"

Yes.

Carella looked at the detective's name in the space on the
summons. He did not recognize it.

"I see they fingerprinted you, too," he said.

She nodded.

"Took your picture . . ."

She nodded again. All her anger was gone now. She merely
looked terribly worried.

Shaking his head, he looked back to the due date on the
summons. "This is returnable in two weeks," he said. "Your
attorney'll want to . . ."

My attorney!

"Honey, this is a *misdemeanor* here," he said, "you can go
to jail for a year on it. We'll get somebody terrific, go for

outright dismissal, or dismissal in the interests of justice, or even adjournment in *contemplation* of dismissal. If the D.A. pursues, we'll file a cross-complaint against the woman, harassment for sure, maybe jazz it up to attempted assault. Don't worry, honey," he said, "really," and held her close, and kissed the top of her head.

She lay very still in his arms.

"This never should've got this far," he said. "The beat officer should have settled it on the spot, a goddamn traffic incident. They must be scared to death up there. All those detectives who got burned."

She said nothing. He could feel her tenseness through her thin nightgown.

"Don't worry about it," he said. "Any reasonable D.A.'ll dismiss this in a minute."

She nodded.

"This cop who took you in?" he said. "Was he white?"

Yes.

"And the detective who wrote the summons? Endicott? Was he white, too?"

Yes.

"How about the fat woman?"

Black.

Carella sighed heavily.

But I really don't see what difference that makes, Teddy signed.

"Well, it shouldn't," he said.

The bedside clock read a quarter past ten.

He reached over to turn off the lamp.

He brought her hand to his lips.

"Goodnight, honey," he said against her fingers.

* * *

Exactly one hour and ten minutes later, a naked man came hurtling through the open window of an apartment at 355 North River Street in downtown Isola, twisting and falling toward the sidewalk ten stories below.

His name was Chuck Madden.

11

MARVIN MORGENSTERN CALLED EARLY THE NEXT MORNING TO tell Carella his stage manager had jumped out a window the night before.

This was the first Carella had heard of it.

The incident had occurred downtown, in the Two-One Precinct, and none of the detectives there had made any immediate connection between the apparent suicide they'd caught, and the murder that had been all over everywhere for the past four days.

"How could they be so *dumb*?" Morgenstern asked on the phone, though in all fairness the detectives who'd caught the squeal downtown hadn't learned that the victim was stage-managing the same play the slain actress had been in until a thorough search of his apartment turned up a loose-leaf binder he'd kept listing the names, addresses, telephone numbers and schedules of anyone connected with the show. That was how they got Morgenstern's number.

"It's getting to be a regular epidemic here," Morgenstern told Carella.

Carella tended to agree.

A stabbing on the sixth.

A murder on the seventh.

A suicide—or what certainly looked like one—on the tenth.

The old hat trick.

The reason the detectives of the Two-One shrewdly suspected suicide was the fact that a note was in the roller of the typewriter on Chuck Madden's desk, and the note read:

DEAR GOD, PLEASE FORGIVE ME
FOR WHAT I DID TO MICHELLE

They did not know that Michelle was Michelle Cassidy until they found her name listed in the loose-leaf binder under ACTORS. From the naked broken parts on the sidewalk, the building's superintendent had identified "Mr. Madden in 10A," but until they leafed through that binder, they hadn't known that he was Mr. Charles Williams Madden, STAGE MANAGER of this play called *Romance*. That was when they called Marvin Morgenstern, PRODUCER.

Now Morgenstern was reporting all this to Steve Carella, DETECTIVE, even though Madden hadn't defenestrated himself anywhere *near* the confines of the Eight-Seven. Carella did not envy whoever in the department would have to determine jurisdiction on *this* one. Meanwhile, he told Morgenstern he would go talk to the detectives downtown.

They were still at the scene when Carella and Kling got there at nine-thirty that morning of the eleventh. So were Monoghan and Monroe from the Homicide Division.

"Well, well, well," Monoghan said, "look what the cat dragged in."

"Well, well, well," Monroe repeated.

The two were dressed in black, as befitted their station and calling. The weather being seasonally mild, each was wearing a tropical-weight black suit, a white pima cotton shirt, a black tie, black shoes and socks, and a rakishly tilted black fedora with a narrow snap brim. They thought they looked quite elegant. In fact, they resembled two portly morticians whose mutual bad habit was hooking thumbs into jacket pockets. They were both grinning as if pleased to see Carella and Kling.

"What brings the Eight-Seven to the scene of this morbidity?" Monoghan asked.

"This chamber of death and desolation," Monroe said, beaming and opening his arms wide to encompass the entire apartment. At the far end of what appeared to be the living room, a technician was dusting the sill of the window through which Madden had presumably leapt to his death. The window was still open. The curtains on either side of it rustled in a mild breeze. It was a spectacularly beautiful Saturday in April.

"Who's this?" a big, burly black man asked, and walked in from the other room. He was wearing a loud plaid sports jacket and brown slacks, and white cotton gloves. He was also in need of a shave, a sure sign that he was the cop who'd caught the squeal.

"You in charge here?" Carella asked.

"I'm in charge here," the man said.

"No, *we're* in charge here," Monoghan said.

Carella ignored him.

"Carella," he said, introducing himself. "Eighty-seventh Squad."

"Oh, yeah," the man said matter-of-factly. "I'm Biggs, the Two-One. My partner's in the bedroom." Neither of them offered his hand. Cops on the job rarely shook hands, perhaps because none of them was hiding a dagger up his sleeve. "I figured you'd be turning up sooner or later. The possible connection," he said.

"What connection?" Monroe asked.

"There's a connection?" Monoghan asked.

"To what?" Monroe said.

Both of them looked suddenly perturbed, as if this possible *connection*, whatever it turned out to be, might mean more work for them. In this city, the appearance of homicide cops was mandatory at the scene of any murder, but the precinct detective catching the squeal always followed the case to its conclusion. Most of the time, Homicide served in a purely supervisory—some skeptics might have said superficial— capacity. Quick to find fault, quicker to take credit, the cops from Homicide were not particularly adored by other members of the force, least of all those who were on the front lines of any investigation. Biggs's distaste showed on his round open face. Carella's expression ran a close second. Kling simply walked away.

"Michelle Cassidy," Carella said.

"The actress who's been all over television," Biggs said, figuring he'd shove a hot poker up their asses.

"*This* is connected to *that*?" Monroe said.

"*That* is connected to *this*?" Monoghan said.

"Just a *possible* connection," Biggs said. "You see this note, Carella?"

They all moved to where the typewriter sat on a desk facing the same window through which Madden had presumably jumped. Except for Kling—who was in the bedroom now, talking to Biggs's partner, another black man—they all leaned over the typewriter to look at the note:

DEAR GOD, PLEASE FORGIVE ME
FOR WHAT I DID TO MICHELLE

"Just what he said it said," Carella said.

"Just what *who* said?" Monroe asked.

"Morgenstern."

"Who the fuck is Morgenstern?" Monoghan asked.

"I read it to him on the phone," Biggs said.

"Who?"

"Morgenstern."

"Why?"

"He's the producer," Biggs said, and shrugged. "What do we do here, Carella?" he asked. "Whose case is this?"

"I think the chain goes back to us. But let's work it together till rank decides," Carella suggested.

"*We're* the ones decide here," Monroe said.

"I don't think so," Carella said.

"Me, neither," Biggs said.

"We're *Homicide,*" Monoghan said, looking offended.

Biggs ignored him.

"You shoulda seen what he looked like on the sidewalk," he told Carella.

"Am I the only one here just had breakfast?" Monoghan asked.

"Where's he now?" Carella asked.

"Parkside General. What's left of him. They had to scrape him off the sidewalk."

"Please," Monoghan said.

"This typewriter been dusted yet?" Monroe asked.

"No, the techs just got here a few minutes ago."

"How about the note?"

"That neither."

"You'll want to get both of those to the lab," Monoghan suggested.

"No shit," Biggs said.

"Henry? You want to come in here a minute?"

They all turned to where Biggs's partner was standing in the doorway with Kling. He was wearing jeans, loafers, a blue cotton turtleneck sweater and white cotton gloves. His name was Akir Jabeem. He introduced himself to Carella and the homicide dicks and then turned to Kling as if wondering who was going to break this to the others. Both men had obviously discussed this between them already. Kling nodded.

"We're not sure the guy was actually living here," Jabeem said.

"Then who was living here?" Monoghan asked. "If not him."

"What we're saying," Jabeem said, "is there doesn't seem much evidence of *habitation* here."

"I *still* don't know what the fuck you're saying," Monoghan said.

"Take a look in his clothes closet," Kling said.

They all walked over to the closet and looked inside. There were two pairs of pants hanging in the closet. One sports jacket. One pair of shoes on the floor. Loafers. Black.

"So?" Monroe said. "The guy didn't own too many clothes."

"Take a look in the dresser," Jabeem advised.

They all went over to the dresser. Kling and Jabeem had already opened the drawers. They looked in. The two bottom drawers were empty. In the top drawer, there were three pairs of undershorts, three pairs of socks, three handkerchiefs, and a blue denim shirt.

There was a night table on either side of the bed. An empty glass was on the table closest to the window. The one on the other table was half-full. Jabeem picked up the glass in one of his gloved hands, held it first under his nose, sniffing, and then under Carella's.

"Scotch?" Carella asked.

"Or something mighty like it."

Lying on the floor beside the bed was a heap of clothing that included a pair of undershorts, a pair of socks, a pair of workman's coveralls, a pair of high-topped workman's shoes, and a blue woolen watch cap. Presumably, these were the clothes Madden had been wearing before he'd stripped naked to jump out the window. The window in this room was sealed shut around an air-conditioning unit. Which may have been why he'd gone into the other room to do his high-diving act.

"Let's check the other room," Monroe said.

It was his smartest suggestion today.

The other room undoubtedly had served Madden as a sort of combined living room/work area. Not much larger than the bedroom, it was furnished only with a desk, a chair in front of it, a sofa upholstered in a black-and-white-check fabric, an easy chair done in the same fabric, and an open cabinet on top of which there was a shaded lamp. Sitting on the one shelf inside the cabinet were four tumblers and a bottle of Black & White Scotch that appeared to be about a quarter full.

"There she is," Jabeem said.

Inside the top drawer of the desk near the window, they found a stapler, a small box of staples, several pencils, a box of paper clips, and a sheaf of paper for a three-ringed loose-leaf binder of the sort Madden had used for his stage manager's records. Two of the drawers on the right side of the kneehole were empty. In the bottom drawer there was a boxed ream of typewriter paper. Biggs removed the lid. Inside the box, there were twenty typed pages of the manuscript for a play. The title page read:

THE WENCH IS DEAD

a play in two acts by

CHARLES WILLIAM MADDEN

and

GERALD GREENBAUM

The typescript seemed to match that on the note in the typewriter.

"This other name mean anything to you?" Biggs asked.

"He's in the play they've been rehearsing," Carella said.

"One of the bit players," Kling said.

"What play?" Monoghan asked.

"*Romance.*"

"The dead girl was starring in it."

"I don't know what the hell's going on here," Monoghan said.

"Let's check the kitchen," Monroe said.

This was his second smartest suggestion today.

The small refrigerator in the kitchen had nothing in it but a container of milk that had gone sour, a wilted head of lettuce, half a tomato growing mold, a partially full quart bottle of club soda, and an unopened package of sliced white bread. In the freezer compartment, there were three ice cube trays. Two of them were empty. The last contained ice cubes that were shrinking away from the sides of their separate compartments.

"Who's in charge here?" a voice from the entrance door bellowed, and Fat Ollie Weeks barged into the apartment.

"I am," Biggs said, and walked over to him, and glanced at the ID card clipped to his lapel. "What's the Eight-Eight doing all the way down here?" he asked.

"We caught the prior," Ollie said, smiling pleasantly.

"What prior?"

"Michelle Cassidy."

"You, *too*?" Biggs said.

"Oh, did somebody *else* catch that squeal?" Ollie asked innocently. "The girl's *murder*? Because if so, this is the first I'm hearing."

"Carella here caught the stabbing."

"Apples and oranges," Ollie said. "This is a clear case of FMU."

He was referring to Section 893.7 of the rules and regulations governing internal police matters in this city. The section was familiarly called the First Man Up rule since it dealt with conflicts involving priority and jurisdiction, detailing the circumstances and situations in which a police officer who'd been investigating a *prior* crime was mandated to investigate a seemingly related *subsequent* crime.

"Look, Ollie . . ." Carella started.

"I *already* dealt with you and the blond kid here," Ollie said, "I got nothing further to say to either one of you. In fact, I don't appreciate everybody I go talking to on this case, they tell me, 'Oh, *gee*, Detective Weeks, Carella's already been here, Kling's already been here.' You got no excuse investigating *my* homicide, so just . . ."

"Try Nellie's people going to the Chief of . . ."

"Try *this*," Ollie said, and held up the middle finger of his right hand. Nodding in dismissal, he turned immediately to Biggs and said, "You can go home, too."

"Oh, is that right?" Biggs said.

"Yes, Henry," Ollie said, reading his first name from the ID card clipped to his jacket pocket. "The guy who killed the girl is already in jail, so your services are no longer needed. Whatever this is here . . ."

"Did you see what's in the typewriter?" Biggs asked.

"No, what's in the typewriter?"

"Take a look."

Ollie looked:

> DEAR GOD, PLEASE FORGIVE ME
> FOR WHAT I DID TO MICHELLE

"Don't mean a shit," Ollie said.

"Sort of lets Milton off the hook, though, don't you think?" Carella said pleasantly.

"Who's Milton?" Monoghan asked.

"A poet," Monroe said.

"A what?"

"An English poet."

"I never heard of him."

"He wrote *Paradise Falls*."

"He's the fuckin agent who *killed* her," Ollie said, not so pleasantly.

"How about that note, Ollie?" Carella asked.

"How about it? It ain't even signed. How do *I* know who typed that note?"

"Milton sure as hell didn't. He's already in jail, remember?"

"*Anybody* coulda typed it. A *friend* of Milton's coulda typed it! A friend of his coulda shoved this guy out the window and then typed a phony suicide note. To get Milton off the hook. It don't mean a shit, that note."

"Nothing means anything . . ."

"That *note* doesn't!"

". . . just so you get the collar . . ."

"I know when somebody *did* something!"

". . . on the big case that's all over television!"

"I just want to make sure the guy who did it . . ."

"You just want to make sure you get famous."

"Come on," Biggs said. "We're working a homicide here."

"That's exactly why we're in charge here," Monoghan said.

"Exactly," Monroe said.

"*Because* it's a homicide," Monoghan said.

"*Two* homicides, if you count the broad got juked," Monroe said.

"No, that's why *I'm* in charge here," Ollie said. "Because the broad got juked *first*. You still here, Henry?" he asked, making the name sound like a racial slur. "Take your partner and go home. This *is* your partner, ain't it?" he said, jerking a thumb at Jabeem, who stood glowering at him now. "He sure *looks* like he might be your partner."

"You want to sort out whose case this is," Biggs said calmly, shooting Jabeem a glance that clearly said *Cool it*, "then go downtown and talk to the Chief of Detectives. Meanwhile, while you and him're debatin eight ninety-three seven, somebody jumped out a window right here in the Two-One, and that gives *us* a clear mandate to investigate the occur . . ."

"The note in that typewriter . . ."

"But like you said . . ."

". . . mentions the girl . . ."

"Yes, but . . ."

". . . who got killed in *my* precinct!"

"But the note don't mean a shit, remember?"

"We'll see what the *Chief* has to say about that," Ollie said.

"Good, go talk to him."

"That's just what I'm gonna do. Right this fuckin minute!"

"Good," Biggs said. "Go."

"We'll go with you," Monoghan said.

"Straighten out this mess," Monroe said.

"Good, go," Biggs said. "All three of you."

All three of them flapped out of the apartment.

"Shouldn't one of us talk to the super again?" Carella asked.

The superintendent was standing on the sidewalk outside the building, his hands on his hips, watching a pair of moving men struggling a huge sofa off a truck parked at the curb. He was a trim little man with graying hair, wearing blue polyester slacks and a long-sleeved blue sports shirt, the sleeves rolled up onto his forearms.

He had previously informed Biggs that his name was Siegfried Seifert, and that he had come to America from his native town of Stuttgart some twenty years ago. He still spoke with a marked German accent as he told the moving men to use the elevator on the left, which he advised them had been padded in anticipation of their arrival. Both moving men were black, Kling noticed. Mr. Seifert was white.

"I am standing here on the sidewalk," he told the four assembled detectives now, two of them white, two of them black, "when up from there he comes flying down," gesturing with his head to the ten stories above them. "He is almost falling on my *head*," he said, touching it in wonder and awe. His speech began sounding somewhat less accented— a phenomenon perhaps bred of familiarity—as he explained what a shock it was to see this nice young man splattered all over the sidewalk that way, "Naked, too," he added, as if Madden's state of undress had been more impressive than his plunge from the window above. Sounding more and more like a professor of English literature at Oxford (but such are the benefits of a second language, dollinks), he went on to say that he had recognized the man at once the moment he rushed over to the body. "His *face*," he added, not wishing the detectives to think he had checked out any *other* part of the poor fellow's anatomy, which he wouldn't have recognized in any case, never having seen him naked before.

What the detectives wanted to know was whether Madden lived in the apartment full-time.

"Because he don't seem to have too many clothes up there," Jabeem said, using the same head gesture Seifert had earlier used to indicate the ten floors above them. Or eleven if you counted ground level as ground zero. Some buildings in this city numbered apartments on the ground floor with only the letters A, B, C and so on, no numbers.

"What is it you mean?" Seifert asked.

"*Clothes,*" Jabeem explained, beginning to wonder all over again if this fuckin Nazi understood English. "In his closet, in his drawers."

"Not many *clothes,*" Biggs translated.

"I see him always wearing the same thing," Seifert said, shrugging. "Workman's overalls, tall shoes, a blue wool hat. No shirt."

"How about in the winter?" Carella asked.

"He is only living here since January," Seifert said.

"That's winter," Kling said.

"Well, a jacket sometimes. He sometimes wears a brown leather jacket."

"See anything like that up there?" Jabeem asked Kling.

Kling shook his head.

"What else have you seen him wearing?" Carella asked.

"I don't watch so much what he wears."

"Past four months, huh?" Biggs said.

"Three and a half," Seifert said.

"Some very cold weather during those months," Carella said. "Ever see him wearing an overcoat?"

"He was a healthy young fellow," Seifert said, shaking his head.

"Even healthy young fellas can catch pneumonia," Jabeem said.

The moving men kept going past with furniture. A woman living in the building came out to where they were standing in the sunshine and complained to Seifert that she'd had to wait ten minutes for the elevator. She told him that either people were always moving in or out or else one or another of the damn elevators was always out of order. She told him she was going to complain to the maintenance company. Seifert listened patiently, sympathetically clucking his tongue, explaining that this was an old building, and the elevators didn't always work proper how they should.

"Ever see him moving any of his stuff out?" Biggs asked. Carella was about to ask the same thing, all this activity.

"Well, even when he first moves in, there is not much furniture," Seifert said.

"I mean *clothes*," Biggs said. "Ever see him leaving with a suitcase? Or a trunk? Putting a trunk in a taxi? Anything like that?"

Carella was thinking along the same lines. Man comes through a bitter winter with nothing but the clothes on his back and a few things in his closet?

"I have never seen him moving things," Seifert said.

"Been any burglaries in the building recently?" Kling asked. He was thinking maybe somebody had *stolen* Madden's clothes.

"Not since before last September," Seifert said. "This is remarkable," he added, "a building without a doorman."

The detectives were inclined to agree with him.

"What kind of hours did he keep?" Jabeem asked.

"He is always coming and going," Seifert said. "He worked in the theater, you know, this is not like an honest job."

Carella smiled.

None of the other detectives did. Perhaps they agreed with Seifert's observation.

"Ever see any of the people he worked with?"

"Any of them ever come here?"

"The men or women he worked with? Ever see any of them?"

"I don't know who he worked with," Seifert said.

"If we showed you pictures, could you tell us whether any of them were here last night?"

"I wasn't here myself last night," Seifert said.

The detectives looked at him.

"I thought you said . . ."

"I was at a movie," Seifert said.

"You said you were standin here on the sidewalk . . ."

"Yes, *after*."

"After what?"

"The movie."

"Let me get this . . ."

"I came home from the movie, and I was on the sidewalk taking the air, when Mr. Madden comes down."

"What time was this?"

"Twenty-five minutes past eleven."

"How do you . . . ?"

"I looked at my watch."

"He came flying out the window . . ."

"Naked."

"Almost hit you . . ."

"Almost. But not."

"At twenty-five past eleven."

"Exact."

"You looked at your watch."

"Yes."

"What time did you leave for the movie?"

"It started at nine."

"So from nine till . . ."

"No, we left before nine. To get there. The movie house is just around the corner. We left here at about a quarter till nine. Me and my wife."

"What time did you get back here?"

"About a quarter past eleven."

"Just in time for him to almost hit you on the head."

"Well, a little before. Klara went inside, I stayed out to take some air."

"So from a quarter to nine till a quarter past eleven, you couldn't have seen anyone going in or coming out of the building."

"That's right."

So what the fuck good are you? Jabeem wondered.

"How about afterward?" Carella asked. "Did you see anyone coming out of the building *after* Mr. Madden's fall?"

"There was a lot of confusion. Police, ambulances . . ."

"*Before* the confusion," Carella said. "What'd you do right after the body came down?"

"I went inside to phone the police."

"Nine-one-one clocked the call at eleven-thirty," Biggs told Carella.

"Then what?"

"I came out again to wait for them."

"Blues responded at eleven thirty-seven," Biggs told Carella. "We got here ten minutes after that."

"So you weren't out here for a good seven, eight minutes," Carella said.

"That's right," Seifert said.

"So during that time, you couldn't have seen anyone leaving the building."

"That's right."

So what the fuck good are you? Jabeem wondered again.

"But there were *other* persons here," Seifert said. "When I came out again, there was already a big crowd."

All of them staring at the mess on the sidewalk here, Jabeem figured, none of them noticing anybody coming out of the building. All four detectives were silent for a moment.

Carella was wondering why Madden had taken off all his clothes before jumping out the window.

Biggs was wondering the same thing.

Kling was wondering if Madden had been *dragged* into the living room, and hoisted up onto the windowsill, and then shoved out the window.

Jabeem was wondering—just *supposing* now—if somebody *had* shoved Madden out that window, would whoever'd done it come marching out the front door of the building?

"Any other way out of the building?" he asked.

"Yes," Seifert said.

"Where?"

"There's a door in the basement. Near the laundry room."

"Where does it go?"

"To the backyard."

And clear into the big bad city, Jabeem thought.

Two technicians from the mobile crime unit were working the apartment when they got back upstairs. They had found dried stains on the sheets and one of them was taking sample cuttings which would be sent to the lab for analysis. Biggs asked if they might be semen stains.

"That's a possibility, who knows?" the tech said.

The other tech was on his hands and knees, going over every inch of the floor.

"You get lots of guys knock off a quickie before they do the Dutch," he said.

"Why's that?" his partner asked.

"Cause it's always nice to knock off a quickie."

"Those two glasses look like there *might've* been a girl in here with him," Biggs said.

"We'll be takin them with us, too," the first tech said.

The other tech was approaching the bed now, still on his hands and knees.

"Could be his *hand* was the girl," Jabeem said.

"They'll be testing those stains for her, too, won't they?" Biggs asked.

"If there *was* a her," Jabeem insisted.

"Yeah, the usual vaginal shit," the second tech said, and poked his head under the bed.

"Maybe that's why all his clothes were off," Kling suggested. "A girl."

"Sure would account for those glasses either side the bed," Biggs said.

"Could be a party happened last *week*," Jabeem said pessimistically.

"Hello, hello, hello," the second tech said from under the bed.

They all turned to him as he backed himself out.

He was holding in his gloved right hand a ruby-red earring that glowed like a werewolf's eye.

* * *

The assistant stage manager, a young black man who introduced himself as Kirby Rawlings, told them the only people here right now were him and the understudies, who he was running through the second act. In show business, apparently, everything was business as usual—even if your stage manager had thrown himself out a window the night before.

"We're all on a lunch break right now, though," Rawlings said.

"When's Josie Beales coming in?" Carella asked.

"Not till two o'clock."

"Know where we can find Mr. Greenbaum?"

"I think he went next door for a sandwich."

"Have I got time to make a call?" Kling asked.

"Sure, go ahead," Carella said.

He phoned Sharyn from the pay phone near the stage door entrance. The former boxer, Torey Andrews, sitting on his high stool, watched him as he dialed. This was one of Sharyn's days in the Diamondback office. The woman who answered the phone said she was in with a patient.

"This is Detective Kling," he told her, turning his back to Torey.

"Is this police business?" she asked.

"No, it's personal," he said.

He liked that. Saying it was personal.

"Just a minute, please."

Sharyn came on the line a moment later.

"Hi," she said.

"We've got to talk to a guy here," he said, "and then I can come uptown if you're free for lunch."

"It'll have to be a quick one," she said, "I'm really jammed today."

"I have to be back down here by two, anyway."

"I'll be waiting," she said.

They found Jerry Greenbaum sitting against the white-washed brick wall in the alley where Michelle had first been stabbed. He was eating a sandwich he'd bought at the deli opposite the theater, washing it down with Pepsi-Cola he sipped through a straw. He looked up when they approached, brown eyes alert in a narrow face, curly black hair giving him the look of a dark cherub. They told him they'd found a manuscript for a play titled . . .

"*Wench,* yeah," he said.

"Actually, *The Wench Is . . .*"

"*Dead,* yeah," he said. "It's from Marlowe."

"Philip?" Kling asked.

"Christopher," Jerry said, and quoted, " 'But that was in another country, and besides the wench is dead.' *The Jew of Malta,* 1589."

"We gather from the title page . . ."

"Yeah, Chuck and I were writing it together."

"How come?"

"We started tossing around ideas during rehearsal one day, and decided we ought to write a play," Jerry said, and shrugged. "We figured if Freddie can get *his* shit produced, then *anybody* can."

"When was this?"

"That we decided to do it? A few weeks ago."

"Wrote twenty pages since then, huh?"

"Oh, yeah. It's easy."

"Where'd you work?" Kling asked.

"Chuck's place mostly."

"The apartment on North River?"

"Yeah."

"Were you there last night?"

"No."

"When were you there last?"

"Wednesday night, I guess it was."

"This past Wednesday?"

"Yes."

"The eighth, is that right?"

"Whenever."

One of the few nights this past week when someone wasn't getting stabbed or shoved out a window, Kling thought.

"Did Madden live in that apartment?"

"I don't think so."

"Why do you say that?"

"I think he just kept it as a place to work."

"Did he tell you that?"

"No, it was just the impression I got."

"What gave you that impression?"

"Hardly anything in the fridge."

"You noticed that, huh?"

"Oh sure. I always wondered why he never *offered* me anything, you know? Then I realized he had practically nothing to offer. To eat *or* drink, I mean. It was Mother Hubbard's cupboard up there."

"Any idea where he was actually living?"

"With some woman, I think."

"What makes you say that?"

"He was going over there one night."

"Going over where?"

"Well, I don't know."

"Then how do you know he was . . . ?"

"He said we had to wrap early because his old lady was home waiting for him."

"Were those his exact words? Old lady?"

"Exact."

"You don't think he meant his *mother,* do you?"

"I really don't think so, fellas."

"And he said she was *home* waiting for him, right?"

"Home waiting, yes."

"He used the word 'home.'"

"Yes. Home."

"Did you ask him where *home* might be?"

"Nope. None of my business."

"Where else did you work? You said *mostly* his . . ."

"My place a couple of times."

"Did he ever make any phone calls? Either from his apartment or yours?"

"Couple of times, I guess."

"Any to this 'old lady' he mentioned?"

"Not that I know of."

"Who *did* he call, would you know?"

"Well, people in the cast mostly. About theater business, you know. Changes in rehearsal time, new pages, whatever. I wasn't really listening that hard."

"Did he ever call Josie Beales, would you know?"

"Yes, I'm sure he did."

"How'd he address her?"

"Address her?"

"Use any terms of endearment with her?"

"No, no. Just called her Josie, I guess."

"Just theater business, huh?"

"Yes, that's what it sounded like."

"Ever call *her* honey or darling or anything like that?"

"No, not that I heard."

"Was there a regular pattern to when you worked on the play?"

"Just whenever was convenient for both of us."

"No set pattern? Like Monday, Wednesday and Friday, or Tuesday, Thursday . . ."

"Nothing like that."

"Were you working with him on Tuesday night?"

Tuesday night. The night someone had stabbed Michelle Cassidy to death.

"This past Tuesday?" Jerry said. "No, I wasn't."

"Did you happen to *talk* to him that night?"

"No."

"Any idea where he might have been that night?"

"None at all."

"Where were you *last* night, Mr. Greenbaum?" Kling asked.

"At around eleven-thirty," Carella said.

"Home asleep," Jerry said.

"Alone?" Kling asked.

"More's the pity."

"Mr. Greenbaum, as soon as the lab finishes with that manuscript . . ."

"The lab?"

"Yes, sir, they'll be checking it for latents, bloodstains, any other kind of . . ."

"Jesus."

"Yes, sir. In any case, we'll be having copies made . . ."

"Why? You going to produce it?"

"We just want to see what's in it."

"*In* it?"

"Is there anything in it we *shouldn't* see?"

"Like what?"

"You tell us."

"Like a character planning to shove another character out a ten-story window?" Jerry asked.

"Any characters like that in it?"

"No," Jerry said. "The only person who gets killed is a woman. *The* Wench *Is Dead,* remember?"

"The guy is dead, too," Carella reminded him.

There was no such thing as a melting pot anymore, that was the tragedy. We were supposed to take them all in, welcome them all with a warm embrace, hold them close and dear, cherish them as our precious own, forge from a thousand tribes a single strong and vital tribe. That had been the idea. Not a bad one, actually. One people. One good and decent, brave and honorable tribe.

But somewhere along the way, the idea began to dissipate. It had lasted longer than most ideas in America, where everything is in a state of incessant change. In America, there's always a new president or a new war or a new television series or a new movie or a new talk show or a new hot writer. In view of the overwhelming *wealth* of ideas flooding America all the time, day and night, night and day, it wasn't too surprising that people began thinking maybe the idea of mixing all those separate colors and languages and cultures hadn't been such a hot one all along. That was probably when the flame burning bright and hot under the gigantic kettle that was this port-of-entry city began to dwindle until it burned too low for liquefaction.

The current hot idea was to keep sacred and separate the heritage of distant lands and foreign tongues. Not to *contribute* these treasures to the solitary tribe, not to *share* this wealth with the other members of this great tribe, but instead to protect this private hoard from all other hordes, to keep this fortune ever and always apart.

Where once "separate but equal" was a reviled notion, it was now viewed as something to which an entire people might actually aspire. Hey, *separate,* man, I can dig it! Long as it's *equal,* too. Where once the noble idea of a "rainbow coalition" conjured an image of bands of different colors riding the sky together in a bonded arch that led to a shared pot of gold, the impoverished expression "gorgeous mosaic" now conjured a restricted vision of tiny chips of colors separated by *boundaries,* each unit secure in its own brilliance and beauty, none contributing to the grander concept of a unique and remarkable whole.

Where once people pounded on the doors of opportunity and shouted, "*Forget* we're black, *forget* we're Hispanic, *forget* we're Asian," these same people were now shouting, "*Don't* forget we're black, *don't* forget we're Hispanic, *don't* forget we're Asian!" Where once there was pride and honor and dignity and hope in being American, now there was only despair at what America had become. Small wonder that immigrants remembered their native lands as being more serene and stable than they ever were. Small wonder that they chose to cling to an ethnic identity that seemed eternally unchanging to them, rather than to fall for the bullshit of one nation, indivisible, with liberty and justice for all.

The city for which Bert Kling worked was a city of tribal enclaves poised on the edge of ethnic warfare similar to that erupting all over the world. The riot in Grover Park last Saturday had been caused by a criminal intent on personal gain through planned mischief. But his scheme would not have succeeded if this city had not already been so divided along ethnic lines.

Ethnic.

The most obscene word in any language.

Sharyn Cooke's office was in Diamondback, where everyone in the entire world was black. Certainly everyone in her waiting room was black. That was when Kling realized he'd never seen a black doctor treating a white patient.

Sharyn's receptionist was black, too.

"Detective Kling," he told her, and from the corner of his eye caught heads turning, eyes swiveling. Everybody here was figuring the only business a honkie cop could have in a doctor's office was looking for some brother or sister got shot. "I have an appointment," he said. The appointment was for lunch, but he didn't mention that.

Sharyn came out a moment later.

She was wearing a white smock over a dark skirt. Stethoscope sticking out of a pocket. White Reeboks. He wanted to kiss her.

"I'll just be a second," she said. "Have a seat. Read a magazine."

He grinned like a schoolboy.

They had lunch in a diner off Colby. Everyone in the diner was black, too. This was the heart of Diamondback. He reminded her that he had to be downtown again at two, talk to a woman who might have had something to do with last night's excitement.

"Guy jumped out a window," he told her.

"Or was pushed," she said knowingly.

"Or was pushed," he agreed, nodding.

"Who's doing the autopsy?" she asked.

"He was taken to Parkside."

"That'd be Dwyer. Good man."

"How long have you been practicing up here?" he asked.

"Always," she said, and shrugged.

He hesitated a moment, and then asked, "Do you have any white patients?"

"No," she said. "Well, at Rankin, yeah, white cops come in all the time. But not here, no."

"Have you *ever* had a white patient?"

"In private practice? No. Why?"

"I just wondered."

"Have you ever gone to a black doctor?"

"No."

"Case closed," she said, and smiled.

"Who are you going out with tonight?" he asked.

"None of your business."

"Woman tells me she can't see me cause she's got other plans . . ."

"That's right."

". . . then it *becomes* my business."

"Nope."

"How about lunch tomorrow?"

"Busy then, too."

"Who with?"

"My mother."

"How come your *mother's* not none of my business?"

"That's a double negative."

"Busy twice in a *row* is a double negative. Why don't I join you and your mother?"

"I don't think that'd be such a good idea."

"Why not?"

"Cause Mama don't 'low no saxophone playin here."

"What does that mean?"

"Mama don't know you *white,* man."

"Time she found out, don't you think?"

"Three dates and we're getting married already?"

"Four counting today."

"Four, right."

"All of them wonderful."

"Not the first one."

"First one doesn't count. Who's this guy tonight?"

"I told you, that's none . . ."

"Is this your first date with him?"

"Nope."

"Is he black?"

"Sho nuff, honey chile."

"Does Mama know *him*?"

"She do."

"Does she allow you to play *his* saxophone?"

"Mama thinks I'm still a virgin. Mama don't 'low me to play *nobody's* saxophone *nohow*."

"Good for Mama," Kling said, and blinked in mock surprise. "You mean you're *not* a virgin?"

"Sullied through and through," she said.

"Well, when *can* we get together? Artie . . ."

"We're together now."

"Yes, but Artie wants to meet you."

"Who's Artie?"

"Brown. Who suggested Barney's, remem . . . ?"

"Right. Whose grandmother was a slave."

"Great-*great*-grandmother. He wants to have dinner with us and his wife."

"Good, I'd like to."

"Sure, but you're *busy* all the goddamn time."

"Not all the time."

"You're busy *tonight*, you're busy . . ."

"I made tonight's date a long time ago."

"How about *tomorrow* night?"

"I'd love to."

"Really?"

"Really."

"Good, I'll tell Artie. Chinese okay?"

"Chinese is fine."

"Who's this guy tonight?"

"None of your . . ."

"Sharyn?"

The voice was deep and mellow, originating at Kling's right elbow, and causing him to turn at once in surprise. The man standing there was tall and black and elegantly dressed in a suit several shades lighter than the color of his skin. Unless King was mistaken, the key hanging on a chain across his vest was a Phi Beta Kappa key, and unless he was further mistaken, the little plastic ID tag clipped to the lapel of the man's jacket had the words MOUNT PLEASANT HOSPITAL printed across its top.

"Jamie, hi," she said, and then immediately, "Bert, this is Jamie Hudson . . ."

"How do you . . . ?"

"Bert Kling," she concluded.

"Nice to meet you."

The men shook hands. Kling, big detective that he was, had already scanned the plastic identification tag and discovered that this handsome guy looming over the table was Dr. James Melvin Hudson, and that his department at Mount Pleasant Hospital was ONCOLOGY.

"Sit down a minute," Sharyn said.

Hudson—Dr. James *Melvin* Hudson, Oncology—immediately sat next to Sharyn, Kling noticed, and not him. The pair of them immediately fell into a lively conversation about a patient Sharyn had referred to Hudson—Dr. James *Melvin* Hudson—several months back, and who, as fate would have it, had got shot dead on the street last night.

"Bert's a detective," Sharyn said.

"Oh, really?" Hudson said.

Kling wondered why she had thought it necessary to mention that he was a detective, whereas she hadn't thought it necessary to mention that Hudson was a doctor. Perhaps she was informing Hudson that her relationship with Kling was a professional one, both of them being cops and all. In which case, why hadn't she informed Kling that the relationship with *Hudson* was a professional one, both of them being *doctors* and all. He suddenly wondered if Dr. James Melvin Hudson was the guy she was dating tonight. He suddenly felt like kicking him under the table.

"The irony is the man was dying of cancer, anyway," Hudson said. "I figure he had two, three months at most."

"Also, the man was such a square . . ."

"Letter carrier, wasn't he?"

"Straight as an arrow."

"Takes two in the head."

"Was it a drive-by?"

"No, he was at home in bed, that's the thing of it! These two guys came in and dusted him while he was asleep in bed."

"How do they know it was two guys?"

"Landlady saw them going out."

"Was it a mistake?"

"Looks that way. The building he lived in is full of dope dealers."

"What a break, huh?"

"Awful. I've got to run," Hudson said, and rose, and shook

hands with Kling again, and said, "Nice meeting you," and then turned to Sharyn and said, "See you at eight."

"Eight, Jamie," she said, and waggled her fingers at him as he rushed off.

They were both silent for several moments.

"A mutual patient," she said.

"Uh-huh," Kling said.

He was thinking he didn't stand a chance against Dr. James Melvin Hudson.

"*Another* thing I hate about doctors," he said.

He and Carella were standing under the theater marquee, waiting for Josie Beales to arrive. The clock in front of the hot-bed hotel across the street read ten minutes to two. Carella's watch read eight minutes to two. Either way, she wasn't here yet.

". . . is they think *their* time is more valuable than anyone else's," Kling said. "Have you ever noticed that if you're going to a hospital for the least little thing, they always get you there two hours beforehand? That's so the doctor won't waste any of *his* time, he can finish one lobotomy and rush next door to do another one. Meanwhile, *you're* waiting there since noon for a two o'clock removal of a cyst on your ass . . ."

"Did you ever have a cyst on your ass?" Carella asked.

"No. On my hand once. The point is, you haven't had anything to eat since the night before, even though this is going to be *local* anesthesia, and they drag you in two hours before to sit and wait for the *doctor's* convenience. It doesn't matter who you are, how important you may be, the minute you're in a doctor's office or a hospital, the doctor reigns supreme. You can be working a case where a homicidal maniac has killed fourteen people with an ice pick and he's working on number fifteen right that minute, but the doctor's time is more important than yours, and you can just sit there reading last year's magazines, pal, until he's damn good and ready to see you. I *hate* doctors."

"Boy," Carella said.

"I hate nurses, too. I go to a doctor's office, the nurse right away calls me Bert. I never met her in my life, we're all of a sudden on a first-name basis. President of the United States goes into a doctor's office, the nurse says, 'Have a seat, Bill, doctor will be with you shortly.' The only time *I* use anybody's first name is if I know him or if he's a thief. Nurses call anybody who walks in the office by his first name. Sit down, Jack. Sit down, Helen. Does she call the *doctor* by his first name? Does she buzz him and say, 'Mel, Bert is here.' No. It's '*Doctor* will see you shortly, Bert.' I hate doctors *and* nurses."

"But how do you *really* feel about them?"

"This guy doing the autopsy is supposed to be good, though," Kling said. "Dwyer."

"How do you know?"

"Sharyn told me."

"Who's . . . oh, Sharyn. How does *she* know?"

"She's a doctor."

"I thought you said she's a cop."

"She's a *doctor* cop."

"I thought you hated doctors."

"Not Sharyn."

"You're a very complicated person, Bert," Carella said. "If I may call you Bert."

A yellow cab was pulling into the curb. The way the sun was hitting the windows, they couldn't tell who was inside paying the driver. They watched, waited. The door opened, and Josie Beales swiveled on the seat, reaching with one leg for the sidewalk. She was wearing jeans, a tangerine-colored, cotton tank-top shirt with no bra, and brown sandals. Her strawberry-blond hair was pulled back in a ponytail, held with a brown ribbon that matched her eyes. A brown leather tote bag was slung over her shoulder, a blue-bound copy of *Romance* jutting up out of it. She glanced at her watch as she stepped out of the cab, looked up, and saw Carella and Kling approaching her. She appeared startled for a moment. Sunlight struck the single ruby-red earring in her left ear.

"Hi," she said, and smiled.

Something about the smile and the way she said that single word told them they had her.

"Few questions we'd like to ask," Carella said.

"Rehearsal starts at two," she said, and looked at her watch again.

"Won't take a minute."

"Is this about Chuck last night?"

"Yes. Few other things, too."

"Why would he have done such a thing?" she asked, and shook her head and sighed heavily. Carella had the feeling she'd done just that in a play sometime before. Maybe *several* plays.

"This is the note he left," he said, and took from his pocket a folded scrap of paper on which he'd copied the note in Madden's machine.

DEAR GOD, PLEASE FORGIVE ME FOR WHAT I DID TO MICHELLE

"I don't understand," she said. "I thought you already *had* the . . ."

"Yes, we thought so, too," Carella said.

Or at least *Ollie* thought so, and Nellie *Brand* thought so, and even Lieutenant *Byrnes* thought so. But they'd just found the twin to Josie's ruby-red earring under the bed in Madden's apartment.

"This would make it seem he'd . . . well . . . *done* something to her," Josie said.

Carella was thinking it sometimes worked if you opened the garden gate and led them down the path.

"It would make it seem he'd *killed* her, in fact," he said.

"Well . . . yes. But I thought . . ."

She looked at the note again.

"How do you know he wrote this?" she said. "It isn't signed."

"It was in his typewriter."

"This isn't even his handwriting," she said.

"That's right, it's mine," Carella said. "I copied it from . . ."

"How do you know what his handwriting looks like?" Kling asked.

"He was our stage manager. Stage managers write notes about rehearsal calls or costume fittings or whatever. Everybody on the show knows Chuck's handwriting. *Knew* it. Whatever. I think this is *awful,* him killing himself."

"How about him killing Michelle?" Kling asked. "If that's what he did."

"Well, he doesn't actually *say* that's what he . . ."

"No."

"In fact, the lines could be given any number of readings."

"Lines?"

"In his note. What he says in his note. If it *is* his note. You don't really know he wrote it for a fact, do you?"

"No, we don't," Carella admitted. "But *if* he did . . ."

"Then it would seem he killed Michelle," Josie said, and did the head-shaking, heavy-sighing bit again.

"How well did he know her?" Carella asked.

"I don't think he knew her at *all* well. I mean, she was living with her *agent*, I didn't think ... why would Chuck have killed her? What did *he* have to do with her?"

"It does seem odd, doesn't it?"

Gently down the garden, he thought.

"I mean, he only seemed to know her *casually*," Josie said. "I can't believe there was anything between ..."

"How well did he know *you*, Miss Beales?"

"Me?"

"Yes."

"Why?" she asked, and looked suddenly wary.

"You said he only knew Josie casually..."

"Yes?"

"So how well did he know you?"

"The only place I ever saw him was here in the theater," she said, and jerked her head toward the marquee.

"Do you know where he lived?" Kling asked.

"No."

"Never mentioned where he lived?" Carella said.

"Not to me."

"Ever been to his apartment?"

"Never. I just told you, the only place I ever saw him was in the goddamn *theater*," she said, and jerked her head toward the marquee again, sharply this time.

"How long have you known him?"

"Two months or so."

"When did you first meet him?"

"When I read for the part."

"When was that?"

"Beginning of March."

"Where?"

"Here."

"Where were you last night at eleven-thirty?"

"What?"

"Where were . . ."

"I heard you. Am I going to need a lawyer here?"

"Why would you need a lawyer? All we're doing is investigating a suicide."

"Why are you investigating a *suicide* to begin with? A man throws himself out the goddamn window . . ."

"We treat homicides and suicides in exactly the same way."

"But *homicide*'s the operative word here, isn't it? You show me a note you say Chuck left . . ."

"That's right . . ."

"And it says he *did* something to Michelle. Well, what somebody *did* to Michelle was murder her. That's *homicide*, isn't it? What you're trying to do here is implicate me in a goddamn *homicide*! Somebody writes a note, you don't even know if Chuck himself wrote it, so you automatically think Ah-*ha*, we've caught the Mad Stabber! *She's* the one who got Michelle's part, so *naturally* she's the one who put him up to killing her!"

"There's nothing in his note about that, Miss Beales."

"No, that's in your *heads*, is where it is," she said, and glanced furiously at her watch. "Are we done here?"

"Not yet. Where were you last night at eleven-thirty?"

"Asleep."

"Where?"

"Home."

"Alone?"

"Good title for a movie," she said.

"Miss Beales, we don't find anything comical about this."

"Neither do I!" she snapped.

"So where were you?"

"Home in bed. Alone."

"What time did you go to bed?"

"Around ten."

"Anyone with you before that time?"

"No."

"Talk to anyone on the phone before that time?"

"Yes."

"Who?"

"Ashley."

"Ashley Kendall?"

"Yes."

"What time was that?"

"Around eight-thirty."

"What'd you talk about?"

"What do you *think* we talked about? We've got a *play* opening in five days."

"Talk to anyone else before ten?"

"No."

"How about *after* ten?"

"I told you . . ."

"Yes, but did your phone ring at any time after you went to bed?"

"No."

"What time did you wake up this morning?"

"Eight-thirty. I had a voice lesson at ten."

"When did you learn Mr. Madden was dead?"

"I saw it on *Good Morning America*."

"Talk to anyone about it after that?"

"Yes."

"Who?"

"Freddie Corbin. He'd seen it on television, too."

"Miss Beales," Carella said, "the last time we talked to you . . ."

"I know. I said I was sorry for what happened to Michelle, but happy for myself. That doesn't mean . . ."

"Yes, you said that, too. But you *also* mentioned losing the mate to the earring you're wearing right this minute . . ."

"My good-luck earrings, yes."

"Recognize this?" he asked, and took from his jacket pocket a sealed plastic bag marked with the word EVIDENCE and containing the ruby-red earring they'd found in Madden's apartment.

"Is that *mine*?" she asked.

"Looks like it."

"I don't understand . . . where'd you . . . ?"

"Under Chuck Madden's bed," Carella said.

"Goodbye, fellas," she said at once, "I'm calling my lawyer."

12

LIEUTENANT BYRNES KNEW THAT CARELLA'S DEADLINE WAS Tuesday the fourteenth, and whereas he didn't wish to rain on Carella's parade, he simply could not see the *logic* in this thing. Which is why he gathered them all together in his office late that Saturday afternoon. Sometimes a great notion, he figured.

The detectives Byrnes had called in for his informal snow-balling session were Carella and Kling—the two actively working the case—and Brown, Meyer, Hawes and Parker, who'd seen enough about it on television and in the papers to believe they themselves were working the damn thing. This was now four-forty in the afternoon, and Parker wanted to go home. Truth be known, he *always* wanted to go home, even when it wasn't five minutes before the shift was about to be relieved.

"As I understand this," he said impatiently, "Nellie Brand's already *arraigned* Milton for the murder . . ."

"That's right," Byrnes said.

". . . and she's got to shit or get off the pot by Tuesday."

"In a manner of speaking," Carella said.

"In *another* manner of speaking," Byrnes said, "if we don't prove her wrong by Tuesday, she'll indict him."

"What do you mean *we*, Kemo Sabe?" Parker asked, and looked to the others for approval.

As usual, he looked like a bum. That was because he told himself he was on a perpetual stakeout where it was essential that he look like a bum. He had already detected that no one but Carella and Kling appreciated this fucked-up situation. He was right. None of the others wanted more heat from upstairs descending on the squad again. The case was solved, so let it rest. But their personal feelings for Carella and Kling outweighed such considerations.

"Does the Chief of Detectives know you're still working this thing?" Hawes asked.

He was leaning against Byrnes's bookcases, threatening to capsize them by sheer size and bulk, his wild red hair catching the afternoon sun, the wilder white streak in his left temple highlighted by the rays.

"Yes," Carella said. "The way Nellie spelled it out, if she indicts on Tuesday, Weeks gets credit for the kill. If we come up with anyone else, it's our collar."

"Weeks and the M&Ms went to see him this morning," Byrnes said.

"Who?" Meyer asked.

"Chief Fremont."

"What for?"

"To yell about FMU," Byrnes said. "From what he told me, he'd already agreed that our public face should be we've got the killer, but privately we're still looking cause nobody wants to prosecute an innocent man. So this morning, Weeks runs to him and says you're screwing up the case by looking under rocks for somebody doesn't exist. The M&Ms had their own axe to grind. They caught a whiff of headlines and they wanted Homicide to be handed the case on a platter."

"What'd the Chief tell them?"

"To cool it till Tuesday."

"So they're out of our hair for now."

"All of them."

"You want *my* private opinion," Parker said, "I think the agent's guilty."

"How about that note in the typewriter?" Carella asked.

"How about that earring under the bed?" Kling asked.

"Slow down," Brown said, "you're losing me."

"You're losing *all* of us," Parker said.

"Here's the note," Carella said, and placed it on Byrnes's desk. This time, it was a Xerox copy of the one the lab had already tested. All four of the other detectives leaned over the desk to look at it:

> DEAR GOD, PLEASE FORGIVE ME
> FOR WHAT I DID TO MICHELLE

"No signature," Parker observed.

"They don't always sign them," Meyer said.

"If we're about to step in shit here, we better at least have a signed note," Parker said.

"The girl's earring was under the bed," Kling said.

"What girl?"

"The actress who took over the dead girl's part."

"We call them *women* these days," Parker said.

They all turned to look at him.

"*Girls* are five years old and younger," he said.

"Were they lovers or what?" Hawes asked. "The actress and the vic."

"Not according to her."

"Then how'd her earring get under his bed?"

"That's what I'd like to ask her," Carella said. "That's why I'd like to bring her in."

"Did you talk to Nellie about this?"

"Not yet."

"About arresting her, I mean."

"No."

"Cause if we bring her in here . . ."

"I know."

"She'll be in custody . . ."

"We're already into Miranda," Parker said.

"We may even be jeopardizing the case Nellie already has."

"How?"

"I don't know how. Ask Nellie."

"Have we got an autopsy report yet?" Brown asked.

"Verbal," Carella said.

"Who examined him?" Hawes asked.

"Doctor named Ralph Dwyer."

"Parkside?"

"Yeah."

"Good man."

"What'd he say?"

"Said Madden did a great job on himself. All four extremities fractured, bones of the cranium and face comminuted, brain enucleated. He must've hit the sidewalk on his right side because that's where the ribs and pelvis were most severely broken. The fall also shattered his spine and burst his heart, a fine job all around."

"Did he think . . . ?"

"Did he say Madden was already . . . ?"

"No. He found fat embolism, inhaled blood, and hemorrhages around the injuries, all signs that they were intravital. The injuries."

"Meaning?" Parker asked.

"Meaning he was still alive when he hit the sidewalk."

"Blood work show anything?" Byrnes asked.

"Traces of Dalmane."

"Dalmane?"

"Enough for Dwyer to believe Madden was asleep when he went out that window."

"How do you jump out a window if you're asleep?"

"Somebody helps you," Carella said.

"She won't answer anything else unless we bring her in," Kling said.

"She's already got a lawyer," Carella said.

"Our guess is she's running scared."

"We get her in here, she may bleat."

"I doubt it," Parker said. "Her lawyer'll tell us to fuck off. He'll ask us to void the arrest."

"We've got plenty to charge her with. Conspiracy to murder . . ."

"Accessory before . . ."

"On what? A fuckin *earring*?"

"*And* a suicide note."

"The note doesn't implicate her."

"Have we got any latents?"

"Nothing wild. Almost everything in the apartment was wiped clean. The typewriter, the earring, the Scotch bottle, the club soda bottle . . ."

"Two glasses by the bed, huh?"

"Yeah."

"Must've been how he got the Dalmane in him, huh?"

"Must've been, yeah."

"You think she was wearing gloves?"

"While they fucked?"

"No, when she was cleaning up."

"Had to've done it before she tossed him out the window. Otherwise, there wouldn't've been time."

"Did she wipe the windowsill?"

"Yes."

"Couldn't've done *that* before."

"No, that had to be after."

"How about the sash?"

"Clean."

"The handles?"

"What handles?"

"The things you raise the window with, whatever the hell they're called. The little things you grab with your hands to pull the window up."

"Clean."

"Fuckin *cleaning* woman."

"The more I hear, the less I like it," Byrnes said. "I don't want to bring her in till we've got something better than this. We don't need a pointless exercise here."

"What if there's Dalmane in her medicine chest?"

"You know any judge who'll grant you a search warrant on the strength of an earring under a bed?"

"You'd never get a court order on such flimsy shit," Parker said.

"If we arrest her, we could . . ."

"How the hell can we arrest her, Steve?" Byrnes asked irritably. "All you've got is an *earring* at the scene. She could've left it there last *year,* for all we know. She told you she *lost* the damn thing . . ."

"She also told us she doesn't know where he lives," Carella said.

"Never been to his apartment," Kling said.

"So how'd the earring get there?"

"There's too much bothering me about this," Byrnes said.

"Me, too," Parker said.

"Let's say, just for the sake of argument," Meyer said, "she put him up to doing the Cassidy girl . . ."

"Woman," Parker corrected.

They all looked at him.

"It's what they're *called,*" he said apologetically.

"But let's say she did that, okay?"

"Which would be conspiracy."

"Sure. And let's say her motive was she wanted the other gir . . . the other woman's part in the play. So she gets this jackass to kill her, and she *does* get the part, it works *just* the way she planned it. Then why . . . ?"

"Right," Parker said. "Why the hell . . . ?"

". . . would she *kill* him?" Byrnes said.

"Cause he was the only link," Carella said.

"The only one who tied her to it," Kling said.

"They why'd she leave a phony suicide note?" Brown asked.

"To make it *look* like a suicide."

"Why?" Hawes asked.

"So we wouldn't carry it back to her."

"But we *are* carrying it back to her."

"Only because we found the *earring!*" Carella said, exasperated.

"You think she took off the earring, is that it?" Byrnes asked. "Before she shoved him out the window?"

"I think she took it off before they started making love."

"And forgot to put it on again?"

"Yes. If *you'd* just killed someone . . ."

"Come on, Steve," Hawes said. "She drugs the guy . . ."

"Yes."

"Drops Dalmane into the Scotch they're drinking . . ."

"Exactly."

"And then takes off her earrings before they make love? Didn't she have *other* things on her mind?"

"Like throwing him out the fuckin window?" Parker said.

"Wait a minute," Brown said, "I think Steve's right."

"No, he's not," Meyer said.

"Lots of women take off their earrings before they climb into bed," Brown said.

"Their watches, too," Kling said.

"Sometimes even their rings," Brown said. "So that's not unusual."

"*Both* earrings, right?" Hawes said. "She took off *both* earrings."

"Well . . . yeah."

"And then put on just *one* of them afterward?"

"Without noticing the other one was gone?"

"Without looking for the other one?"

"She's just thrown a guy out the window, and she realizes she's lost her earring, and she doesn't go *looking* for it?"

"When did *you* notice the earring was gone?" Byrnes asked.

"What?" Carella said.

"Your report says she was wearing only one earring . . ."

"That was Thursday, Steve," Kling said.

"When you noticed?"

"Yes."

"And she told you she'd lost it?"

"Right."

"This is two days after Michelle got murdered . . ."

"Yes."

". . . and Josie's running around with just the one earring in her ear. Who do you think killed Michelle, Steve?"

"Madden."

"You think Josie put him up to it, is that it?"

"Yes, sir."

"Then you must also think they were lovers."

"I do."

"And you think that by the ninth, when you noticed the missing earring, she already had a plan in place to murder him."

"I think that's entirely possible, yes."

"Possible, possible," Hawes said, shaking his head.

"You're saying she put Madden up to killing Michelle . . ."

"Yes."

". . . and then started planning *his* murder."

"Yes."

"Is that why she told you she'd lost her lucky earring?"

Carella looked at him.

"Steve?"

"Well . . ."

"Was she *planning* to leave that earring under Madden's bed?"

"Well . . ."

"Was she *planning* to implicate herself in his murder?"

The room went silent.

"She didn't do it, Steve," Byrnes said gently.

"You know who *did*?" Parker asked suddenly, grinning in his day-old whiskers. "Whoever *didn't* get the part."

It was now five-thirty P.M. that Saturday, the eleventh day of April. This was the day before Palm Sunday, and everyone was already thinking about Easter and Passover, which this year happened to fall on the same day, so much for religious diversity. But at nine o'clock on Tuesday morning, Nellie Brand would go to the grand jury.

Everybody, especially Parker, wanted to go home. However, they were the ones who'd been lucky enough to stumble upon a possible approach to this thing, so Byrnes insisted that they follow through on it, rather than dumping it on the night shift.

They broke up into three teams.

Carella and Kling, of course.

Meyer and Hawes.

Parker and Brown, lucky him.

They were looking for probable cause to go into Andrea Packer's apartment.

Since she knew Carella and Kling by sight, and since they didn't want her dumping evidence before they even had a court order to look for it, it was thought provident to send two of the other detectives to her building.

The doorman at 714 South Hedley had been working at the building for twenty-five years, and he was due to retire in June. His plan was to move back to the house he'd owned in Puerto Rico for the past ten years now. Do some fishing. Walk the beach. Smell the tropical flowers. He did not want trouble here. That was the first thing he told Parker and Brown.

He didn't want trouble two months before he was supposed to retire.

Parker felt real sorry for this little spic here who could hardly speak English, going back where coconuts would fall on his head while he sipped *piña coladas*. Twenty-five years standing in a doorway with his finger up his ass, now he was afraid of getting involved, didn't want trouble on his watch.

"This is a homicide we're investigating here," Parker said.

The magic word.

Homicide.

Supposed to cause them to wet their pants.

The little spic just blinked at him.

"You know a tenant named Andrea Parker?" Brown asked.

"I juss worr here," the doorman said.

"Cómo se llama?" Parker asked, showing off the Spanish he'd been picking up from this girl named Catalina Herrera he'd been seeing. Called herself Cathy, listen, who cared *what* she called herself? She wanted to think she was really American, that was fine with him, even if she did speak with a Spanish accent you could cut with a machete, but on her it sounded cute.

"You hear me?" he asked.

"Sí ya lo oí, no soy sordo," the doorman answered in Spanish, apparently figuring Parker was more fluent than he actually was, most of his exchanges before now having taken place in Cathy Herrera's bed—*Catalina's,* who was kidding who?

"Huh?" Parker said.

"Luis Rivera," the doorman said.

"Listen, Luis," Parker said, "nobody's tryin'a get you in any trouble here. All we want to know is does Andrea Packer live alone here or does somebody live with her? If so, who is it? That's all we want to know. You stand here at the door all the time, protectin the tenants here in this building, ready to defend them with your life day and night, twenty-five years you been here, that's a brave thing you done, Luis, that takes real *cojones*. But now we're dealin with a homicide here, Luis, which is murder, as you know, *homicidio,* we call it in Spanish, a very serious crime, Luis. So just tell us yes or no, she was living with somebody or she wasn't, and we'll take it from there, what do you say, *amigo?*" Parker said, and winked.

"I call dee super," Luis said.

There were four pharmacies within a six-block radius of Andrea Packer's building. Meyer and Hawes entered the first one at ten minutes past six that Saturday evening. By now, all of the detectives were very conscious of the time. Tuesday at nine seemed very close, and tomorrow was not only Sunday, it was *Palm* Sunday. In this city, things had a habit of slowing down on holidays even when the holiday was merely a prelude to a bigger holiday—like the Passover and Easter celebrations *next* Sunday.

"They're both spring festivals, anyway," Meyer said, apropos of nothing. "Joyous celebrations of life."

Hawes didn't know what he was talking about.

The pharmacy was one in a chain of big impersonal discount stores that on television advertised courtesy, friendliness and personal attention. There were six pharmacists in white coats scurrying around behind the counter, all of them women. There were twice that many people standing in line in front of the counter. Hovering over everything was an air of absolute panic. Meyer was happy he wasn't here to have a prescription filled. The people on line gave both detectives dirty looks as they stepped up directly to the counter. A man wearing sweats and running shoes seemed about to say something to Hawes, but Hawes merely glared at him and he changed his mind.

"Police," Meyer said, and showed his shield. "May we speak to your head pharmacist, please?"

The head pharmacist—or *chief* pharmacist, as she introduced herself—was an exceedingly tall woman named Felicia Moss, her eyes a piercing brown, her hair pulled back into a severe bun that emphasized startlingly beautiful features in a face as chiseled as a Roman marble.

"I'm sorry," she said when they told her what they wanted. "That would be completely contrary to policy."

"What policy?" Meyer asked.

"Company policy."

"Why?" Hawes asked flatly.

"Pharmacist-patient confidentiality," she said.

"There's no such thing," Hawes said.

"All we want to know is whether or not you've filled any prescriptions recently for a woman named . . ."

"Yes, I . . ."

"Andrea Packer, and whether one of those . . ."

"I quite understand what you're looking for. The answer . . ."

"Miss Moss, let's not be ridiculous, okay?" Hawes said. "We're investigating a homicide here . . ."

"And *I* have prescriptions to fill," she said. "Good day, gentlemen."

It was going to be one of those days.

The superintendent of Andrea Packer's building was a burly white man not quite as bald as some people Parker knew, but plenty bald enough. His scalp was red and flaking. It looked

as if he'd spent a lot of time up on the roof taking the sun.
His eyes were blue and piercing and suspicious.

Brown asked him if there was a tenant named Andrea
Packer in the building.

"I'm not required to give out information on my tenants,"
he said. He had not yet given them his name or offered them
his hand. He had simply materialized from the bowels of the
building when the doorman picked up a handset at the entrance
desk and punched out a mysterious number.

"What's your name, sir?" Parker asked.

He had found over the years that using the word "sir" very
often caused them to wet their pants.

"Howard Rank," the super said.

"Mr. Rank," Parker said, "I don't know what you mean by
required or not required, who's saying you're *required* to do
anything here? We're asking a simple question we can get
the answer to just by looking at the mailboxes in your hallway
there, for which we don't need any authority but the shield
in our pocket. We did you the courtesy of asking *you* the
question instead of walking over there to the mailboxes, so
why don't you do *us* the courtesy of giving a simple answer
instead of required or not required?"

"She lives in the building, yes," Rank said.

"Good, now can you tell us what apartment she lives in,
or do we have to go look at the mailbox for that, too?"

"She lives in apartment 4C."

"Thank you," Parker said. "Now can you tell us whether
she lives alone up there, or whether there's somebody living
with her?"

"I can't tell you that," Rank said.

"Why not?" Brown asked sharply, glowering.

"Super-tenant confidentiality," Rank said.

* * *

The drugstore on the corner of Easton and Hedley had been at this same location for fifty years; it said so in gold-leaf lettering on the front plate-glass window. Stepping into the shop, Carella had the feeling he was walking into an apothecary somewhere in London, though he'd never been to London and didn't really know whether or not they were called apothecaries there. But there was something reminiscent of Charles Dickens here, something about the little bell tinkling over the paned-and-paneled front door, in itself a rarity in this city of instant break-ins. The heavy glass-fronted cabinets, the thick wooden shelves, the bell jars and decanters all seemed to contain rare oils, ointments, and unguents transported from the farthest reaches of the world. There was something ineffably timeworn and musty about this shop and the creaky old man behind the counter. This was a shop to enter on a rainy day.

"Yes, gentlemen?" the man asked. "How may I help you?"

Like the Dickens character he most surely was, he wore a long-sleeved lavender-colored shirt and a little purple bow tie, and a plaid vest over which a watch chain ran from pocket to buttonhole. He squinted at them through narrow little glasses, dark eyes bright behind them. His skin was the color and texture of thin parchment paper.

"We're police officers," Carella said at once, though the man seemed not at all afraid of imminent robbery.

"How do you do," he said, "I'm Graham Quested."

Dickens for sure, Carella thought.

"We're trying to track a prescription," Kling said.

"Ah yes," Quested said.

He told them he'd had many such requests from the police over the years, usually in cases where overdoses of prescription drugs seemed indicated during autopsy. He also told them he'd been held up sixty-two times at this location since he opened the store fifty-one years ago come August.

"All sixty-two of the robberies took place during the past twenty years," he said. "I guess that says something about the way this city is changing, doesn't it?"

Carella guessed it did.

"What we're looking for," he said, "is a prescription you might have filled for a woman named Andrea Packer."

"Not a name that's familiar to me," Quested said. "Which doesn't mean anything, of course. She could have been someone who just walked in off the street, rather than one of my regular customers. When would this have been, would you know?"

"I'm sorry, we don't."

"A prescription for what?"

"Dalmane."

"Very popular sleeping pill. Its generic name is flurazepam, one of the benzodiazepines. More than fifteen, sixteen million prescriptions written for it each year. Do you know her doctor's name?"

"No."

"Andrea Packer, did you say?"

"P-A-C-K-E-R."

"Do you have an address for her?"

"714 South Hedley."

"Right around the corner. Was she a suicide?"

"No, sir," Carella said.

"Because benzodiazepines are rarely used in suicides," Quested said. "Have to take ten to twenty times the normal dose to do yourself in that way. Dalmane's got the longest half-life of any of the ben . . ."

"Half-life?"

"That's the time it takes to eliminate *half* the drug the person ingested. If you took a ten-milligram capsule of something, for example, and its half-life is two hours, then an hour after ingestion there'd still be five mils in the bloodstream."

"What's the half-life of Dalmane?"

"Forty-seven to a hundred hours," Quested said.

Kling whistled.

"You said it. A person using Dalmane can sometimes have as much of the stuff in his blood during the day as he has at night. Let's have a look at the files, shall we?"

And then, surprisingly for a fellow out of *Great Expectations* or *Oliver Twist*, he led them to a computer in a back room brimming with mortars and pestles, and searched first for Andrea Packer's name, and then her address, and then the brand name Dalmane and next the generic name flurazepam and lastly the chemical group benzodiazepine and came up with nothing each and every time.

"Oh, gentlemen," he said, looking truly regretful, "I'm so terribly, terribly sorry."

The door to apartment 4D was opened by a young black man wearing blue jeans, a gray T-shirt with a maroon Ramsey University seal on its front, and horn-rimmed glasses that gave him a peering, suspicious look. He had asked them to hold their badges up to the peephole in the door before he'd opened it for them, and now he studied their shields and ID cards at greater leisure and with closer scrutiny. Satisfied at last, he said, "What's the trouble?"

"No trouble," Brown said.

"What's your name, son?" Parker asked pleasantly.

He had determined over the years that using the word "son"

also caused them to wet their pants, especially when they were nineteen years old and black, the way this kid seemed to be.

"Daryll Hinks," the kid said.

"Do you know the lady who lives in 4C next door?"

"Only by sight."

"Andrea Packer, that her name?" Brown asked.

"I don't know her name. Long blond hair, nineteen, twenty years old, good-looking girl. What'd she do?"

"Nothing. Ever see her going in or out of that apartment?"

"Sure."

"Apartment 4C, right?"

"Yeah. Next door."

"Ever seen anybody *else* going in or out?"

"Sure."

"A man, for example?"

"What is she, a hooker?"

"What makes you say that?"

"You're asking about men going in and out . . ."

"No, no, we're just thinking of a *specific* man."

"Did this man do something?"

"Yeah, he threw himself out a window," Parker said.

"Oh."

"Yeah."

"Gee."

"So would you have seen a guy maybe six feet tall, husky white guy, twenty-six years old, brown hair, brown . . ."

"Yeah," Hinks said.

"Liked to wear painter's coveralls, high-topped work-man's . . ."

"Yeah, I've seen him. Talked to him in the elevator, in fact."

"Ever see him going in or coming out of apartment 4C?"

"Yeah."

"When?"

"Well, I leave for school early in the morning . . ."

"Ever see him coming out of there early in the morning?"

"Oh sure."

"What time in the morning?"

"I leave at seven."

"Thanks," Brown said.

"What'd she do?" Hinks asked again.

The pharmacist at G&R Drugs on Hedley and Commerce knew Andrea Packer by name and by sight. She was, in fact, a regular customer at the store. He described her as a "lissome" blonde, maybe twenty years old or so, with dark brown eyes and a kind of "flamboyant" manner.

"I think she's an actress or something," he said. "Or a model. One or the other. We had some interesting talks about movies. Did you see the movie *Orlando*? We had some interesting talks about that movie. It's about gender exchange, I guess you'd call it. It was very interesting. You should try to get it from your video store. We also talked about *Speed*, which is a different sort of film, but also very interesting. Either of the two are well worth . . ."

"When was she in here last?" Hawes asked.

"Oh, I don't know, she's in and out all the time. Toothpaste, lipstick, deodorant . . ."

"How about prescription drugs?" Meyer asked.

"I'd have to look that up. She had a cold recently, I know, and was taking an antibiotic . . ."

"How about sleeping pills?" Hawes asked.

"Oh, yes, she had a running prescription for those."

"Running?"

"Refilled it every month or so."

"When's the last time she refilled it?"

"Couple of weeks ago, I guess. I'd have to check the computer."

"What drug?"

"Dalmane."

AFFIDAVIT FOR SEARCH WARRANT

BEFORE ME, A JUDGE of the entitled **COURT,** personally came: Detective/Second Grade Stephen Louis Carella, **a POLICE DEPARTMENT** officer to me well known, and who being by me first duly **SWORN,** made **APPLICATION** for **SEARCH WARRANT,** and in support of this **APPLICATION** on **OATH** says:

That he has **REASON TO BELIEVE,** and **DOES BELIEVE** that the **LAWS OF THIS STATE,** particularly:

Penal Law §125.25

to wit: Murder in the second degree

have been violated by: Andrea Packer

and it is the **AFFIANT'S BELIEF** that **EVIDENCE** or **FRUITS OF THE CRIME** are presently to be found in the following described location **to wit:**   714 South Hedley Avenue

Apartment 4C

Isola

Affiant specifically requests warrant to search for:

A container of prescription drugs with a label from G&R Drugs at 1123 Commerce Street, dated this past 27th day of March, and bearing the following information:

Rx#   445 358
PAT: PACKER, ANDREA
ADD: HEDLEY AVENUE
MED: DALMANE 30 MG CAP
       TAKE ONE CAPSULE AT
       BEDTIME AS NEEDED
QTY: 30
REF: 1

THAT THE REASON FOR THE AFFIANT'S BELIEF IS AS FOLLOWS:

1.   At 11:30 P.M. on this past eleventh day of April, Charles William Madden leaped or was pushed to his death from a ten-story window at 355 North River Street, Isola.

2.   A report from the Toxicology Section of the Police Department Laboratory states that traces of the sleeping pill Dalmane found in the victim's bloodstream indicate ingestion of amounts of the drug sufficient to have caused a state of sleep.

3.   Victim could not possibly have thrown himself from the window while in a state of Dalmane-induced sleep.

4.   Two glasses found beside victim's bed indicate the presence of alcohol and suggest that one of the drinks may have been laced with Dalmane.

5.   Anthony Givens, a pharmacist at G&R Drugs, recalls filling the above cited Dalmane prescription for Ms. Packer on this past twenty-seventh day of March.

6.   Daryll Hinks, a neighbor living next door to Andrea Packer, in apartment 4D at 714 South Hedley

Avenue, states that he saw Charles William Madden entering or leaving Ms. Packer's apartment at hours that would indicate he was living with her at the time of his death.

7.   Based upon the foregoing information and upon affiant's personal knowledge, there is probable cause to believe that a container of Dalmane capsules in possession of Andrea Packer may constitute evidence in the crime of murder.

Wherefore AFFIANT PRAYS that a SEARCH WARRANT be issued, according to LAW, commanding all and singular acting within their jurisdictions, either in the day time or the night time, or on Sunday, as the CIRCUMSTANCES of the occasion may demand or require, with the proper and necessary assistance, to SEARCH the previously described location, and SEIZE AS EVIDENCE any of the following:

Container and contents of G&R Drugs prescription numbered 445 358, made out to Andrea Packer, for 30 capsules of 30 MG Dalmane capsules. And any and all evidence that may relate to the murder of Charles William Madden.

The judge struck out the last sentence of Carella's affidavit as being too broad in its scope, something Carella knew, anyway.

Otherwise, the petition was granted.

They were waiting in the hallway outside her door when she got back from rehearsal that night at nine. Their court order for a search warrant had not included a No-Knock provision, which they'd have been foolish to ask for in the first place. This wasn't an armed and dangerous desperado living in apartment 4C. This was merely a woman some five feet nine inches tall and weighing a possible hundred and twenty-five pounds, who'd first dragged a sedated man across the floor of his apartment, and hoisted him up onto the sill of an open window, and then shoved him out to the street ten stories below.

She was taking her keys out of her handbag as she stepped out of the elevator. She saw them at once, hesitated a moment, and then walked directly toward them.

She looked tired tonight.

It must have been a grueling rehearsal.

"Hello," she said, "what a surprise," and smiled faintly.

"Miss Packer," Carella said, "I have here a court order authorizing the search of your apar . . ."

"A *what*?" she said.

"A search warrant," Kling said. "Could you please unlock the door?"

"No, I will *not* unlock the door," she said, backing away from them. "A *search* warrant? What in the hell *for*?"

"Maybe you ought to read it," Carella said, and handed it to her.

She read it silently.

"I want to call my lawyer," she said.

"Fine, you can call him while we conduct our search."

"No, I want to call him *now*. Before I let you in the apartment."

"Miss Packer," Carella said, "I'm not sure you understand. This is a court order. If you refuse to . . ."

"I'm not refusing anything. I simply want my lawyer here while you . . ."

"Miss Packer," Kling said, "I suggest . . ."

"Oh, stop with the Mutt and Jeff routine, will you please?"

"Either open the door or we'll be forced to arrest you for obstructing governmental administration," Carella said.

"What kind of double talk is that?"

"It means you're preventing a search ordered by a court," he said. "And if you persist, we'll have to arrest you."

"Is he telling me the truth?" she asked Kling.

"He's telling you the truth."

"What is this, Nazi Germany?"

"No, it's America," Carella said.

"Jesus," she said, and angrily rammed her key into the keyway. She unlocked the door, threw it open, and stamped immediately to the phone on the kitchen wall. The detectives followed her into the apartment, pulling on white cotton gloves as she dialed.

"Where's your bathroom?" Kling asked.

"Don't you *dare* use my bathroom!" she shouted.

"Nobody's going to use your bathroom," Carella said. "You've already read the warrant, you know what we're looking for."

"You just keep out of my personal . . . Mr. Foley, please. This is Andrea Packer, tell him it's urgent. Don't you go anywhere in this apartment without me!" she warned.

"Miss Packer . . ."

"You can damn well wait till my lawyer . . ."

"No, we can't," Carella said.

"Holly?" she said into the phone. "This is Andrea. I've got two detectives here . . . where are you *going*?" she shouted to their backs. "Holly, you'd better get here right away," she said into the phone again. "They're searching my apartment, they've got something signed by a judge, just *get* here!" she shouted, and slammed down the phone and went flying through the apartment after them.

They had passed through the bedroom already, where they'd glanced toward an open closet door revealing what were clearly men's clothes. If the judge hadn't specifically deleted the "And any and all evidence" phrase from Carella's petition, they might have risked taking the stuff as proof that Madden had been living here. After all, they hadn't been *searching* for the clothing, but had merely happened to spot it hanging there "in plain view," a favorite expression of confiscating cops the world over. But with Andrea Packer in hot pursuit, they were unwilling to jeopardize finding what they had come here for, so they barged straight into a bathroom done in pale blue tile and decorated with midnight-blue towels and went directly to the sink where they also happened to notice a man's razor sitting on the rim in plain view. Carella yanked open the mirrored door of the cabinet with his gloved right hand, and he and Kling leaned in over the sink, their eyes riffling the labels on the various little brownish-orange, white-lidded plastic bottles on the shelves. Several of the drugs had been prescribed for Charles Madden, another pretty good sign that he'd been living here. Most of them were prescriptions in Andrea's name, though, the 250-milligram capsules of amoxicillin, and the A.P.C. with codeine, and the 400-milligram tablets of meprobamate, and the Nasalcrom 4% spray, and the Donnatal, and the 500-milligram capsules of tetracycline, and the AVC cream and . . .

"There it is," Kling said, and reached into the cabinet.

He rattled the container to see if there were any pills still in it, and then pried off the lid with his thumb. They were looking at possibly a dozen capsules of Dalmane.

"All right," Andrea said, appearing behind them in the bathroom doorway, "my lawyer's . . ."

"You're under arrest," Carella said.

13

SHE CALLED HER LAWYER AGAIN FROM THE SQUADROOM, TO LET him know she was now in a police station, and he promised to get there immediately. It was now almost ten P.M. and he still wasn't there. They asked Andrea if she'd like a cup of coffee or something, and she told them to go to hell. They had already recited Miranda to her and presumably she now understood her rights, which is why she refused to say anything but "Go to hell" until her lawyer got here. She'd already told them his name was Hollis Foley, and that he'd be bringing with him a criminal lawyer whose name she didn't know, so they should be expecting *two* attorneys to show up at any moment.

"Meanwhile, just leave me the hell alone," she said, which was a rough equivalent of "Go to hell" again.

Kling went to his desk to call Sharyn. He was still on the phone when Andrea's attorneys arrived at ten twenty-five, both of them brusque and businesslike, her personal attorney

immediately asking Andrea if she was all right. The criminal
lawyer introduced himself to the detectives—his name was
Felix Bertinotti—and then asked why his client had been
arrested. Carella explained that they planned to charge Miss
Packer with second-degree murder, and the lawyer at once
advised Andrea not to answer any questions. Andrea wanted
to know if that wouldn't look bad for her, and Bertinotti
counseled that her silence could in no way be considered
prejudicial if or when this specious case ever came to trial.
He was already spouting "Innocent Client" talk even though
there wasn't a television camera in sight. Andrea insisted that
she hadn't done anything and therefore had nothing to fear
from the police, so why *couldn't* she answer whatever questions they had? The cops stood by, saying nothing. The deci-
sion was for Andrea and her attorney to make. As Carella had
mentioned earlier, this *was* America, after all.

"May we please talk to Miss Packer privately?" Bertinotti
asked, at which point Carella and Kling and Lieutenant
Byrnes—who had come in when he'd learned of the arrest—
debated whether or not they should get the D.A.'s Office in
on this right now, or wait until they were sure they had real
meat here. They decided to wait. Andrea and her lawyers did
not finish deliberating till a quarter past eleven.

"Miss Packer has decided to answer your questions," Bertinotti announced, which came as a surprise to Carella. He
could never understand why it was always the hardened crimi-
nals who took full advantage of Miranda and refused to give
you even the right time, whereas the amateurs always figured
they could beat you at your own game. Or maybe Andrea
figured this was the role of a lifetime and was now relishing
the opportunity to give an Academy Award performance that
would prove she was something more than just another pretty

face. Besides, she had two attorneys here with her to call off all bets if the going got rough, so maybe she figured she had nothing to lose. Though her personal attorney clearly knew nothing about criminal law and would be as useful to her as an onstage telephone that didn't ring when it was supposed to.

They read Andrea her rights yet another time and ascertained that she understood them and was willing to answer their questions. She was still in the clothes she had worn to rehearsal, blue jeans, loafers, and a lemon-colored T-shirt. Her long blond hair was pulled back into a ponytail and she was wearing no makeup. Carella wondered if they should offer her a lollipop.

"Miss Packer," he said, "I wonder if you can tell us where you were last night at about this time?"

The clock on the wall of the interrogation room now read eleven-eighteen P.M. Andrea sat at the head of the long narrow table, her attorneys flanking her right and left. A police stenographer was sitting alongside Bertinotti, taking notes. Kling was sitting beside him and across the table from Byrnes. Carella was standing. He worked best on his feet.

"I was home," Andrea said.

"Home is where?" Carella asked.

"Home is where you barged in earlier tonight," she said angrily, and snapped a look first at him and then at Kling.

"There was a search warrant," Carella told Bertinotti, and smiled. "No doors broken down, Counselor."

Bertinotti did not return the smile. Instead, he shrugged as if he didn't believe Carella. He was wearing a dark blue suit, as was Andrea's other attorney, and it looked as if he had freshly shaved before coming over here. Carella guessed he was expecting TV cameras outside, though at two hundred pounds and some five feet eight inches, one would have thought he'd try to avoid such exposure.

"What I was asking for was your address," Carella said pleasantly. "For the record."

"You *have* my address."

"Would it be . . . ?"

He picked up the arrest form.

". . . 714 South Hedley Avenue, apartment 4C?"

"Yes."

"Thank you. And you were there last night between what time and what time?"

"I got home from rehearsal at eight. I didn't go out again after that."

"Was Charles Madden at that rehearsal?"

"He was. He's our stage manager."

"*Was* your stage manager," Carella corrected, just to keep this thing in perspective.

"Yes."

"Did he go home with you from the theater?"

"No."

"But you *were* living together, weren't you?"

"Yes."

"How long had he been living in your apartment, Miss Packer?"

"Since the beginning of March."

"Since the first of March?"

"No, the sixth, the seventh, around then."

"Where did he live before then?"

"He had an apartment on River Street. *Still* had it until . . . well."

"Until the time of his death?"

Again, to keep it all in perspective.

"Yes," Andrea said.

"Which was last night at eleven-thirty."

"That's when I understand it happened," Andrea said, and looked down at her hands in her lap.

This was something actresses did, Carella noticed. Lowered their eyes like nuns when they wished to appear virtuous or innocent. It was highly effective. He would have to watch movies more closely from now on, see whether the good actresses ever did it.

"You didn't happen to be in his apartment at that time, did you?" he asked.

"No, I . . ."

"Really, Detective," Bertinotti said. "She just told you . . ."

"Yes, but I was wondering if she might be able to clear up something that's puzzling me."

"What's that?" Andrea asked.

"Miss Packer," Bertinotti said, "you're not required to help Detective Carella with his befuddlement."

Andrea's other lawyer, apparently excited by all this cops-and-robbers shit, actually chuckled at his colleague's remark. Bertinotti seemed pleased. Andrea seemed pleased, too. All three of them were very pleased all at once, as if they'd already been to trial and won an acquittal.

"Well, I hate to see him *puzzled,* really," Andrea said, smiling. "What is it you'd like to know, Mr. Carella?"

"Do you use the prescription drug Dalmane?" Carella asked.

"You know I do," she said, still smiling. "You found a bottle of it in my medicine chest."

"Did Mr. *Madden* ever use Dalmane?"

"I have no idea."

"Because, you see, we found Dalmane in his bloodstream."

This was clearly news to Andrea. Maybe she didn't know

you could take blood samples from a blob on the sidewalk, or maybe she didn't think the police would have bothered testing a man's blood when he'd obviously *fallen* to his death.

"Who's *we*?" she asked.

"Toxicology Department at the lab."

Andrea gave a slight shrug as if to indicate she didn't know how this information was in any way pertinent to why she was here in a police station.

"I'm assuming," Bertinotti said, "that you have this . . ."

"Yes, Counselor, we have the report."

"May I see it?"

"Sure," Carella said, and gave his own little shrug as if to indicate that surely the learned attorney didn't think he was *inventing* a goddamn toxicology report. Handing him the sheet of paper, he turned to Andrea and casually asked, "Did Mr. Madden ever use any of your Dalmane?"

"Yes, I think he may have," Andrea said, recovering quickly. She now knew they had Dalmane in Madden's blood and Dalmane in her medicine chest. Carella figured the trick she had to perform in midair was getting the Dalmane *out* of her bathroom and *into* Madden's blood without making it seem she'd put it there.

"When you say you *think* he may have . . ."

"I seem to remember him asking me . . . I don't even remember when this was . . . but I think he once asked me if I had anything that could help him sleep."

"But you don't remember when?"

"No, I don't. I'm telling you the God's honest truth," she said.

Sure, Carella thought.

"Do you think he may have helped himself to some Dalmane last night?" he asked. "To take to his apartment?"

"He may have, I can't say for sure. He knew I *had* Dalmane, you see . . ."

"Then again, you say he didn't go back to your apartment from the theater."

"That's right, he didn't."

"So if he *did* take any from the bottle in your bathroom, he must have done that before he left the apartment for the day."

"I would guess so. I really don't know what he did."

"Because we didn't find any Dalmane in *his* apartment, you see. Or any empty bottles that might have *contained* Dalmane. Which is odd, don't you think?"

"I don't know if it's odd or not. I don't know what he took or didn't take last night. Or anytime yesterday, for that matter."

"Well, he took *Dalmane,* that's for sure. It showed in his blood work this morning."

"I don't know anything about blood work."

"Neither do I, actually," Carella lied. "What I'm wondering—out loud really—is how that Dalmane could possibly have . . ."

"If you've got anything to ask my client," Bertinotti said, "please ask it. No wondering, please. Wonder is for sliced bread. Stick to the questions."

"Certainly, Counselor. Question, Miss Packer. Did you go to Mr. Madden's apartment at any time last night?"

"No, I did not."

"You didn't go there with him directly from the theater, did you?"

"No."

"Or at any time later?"

"I didn't go there at *all*. I was *home* last night. *All* night."

"Did you know where Mr. Madden was?"

"Of course I did. He told me he was going to the apartment to work on his play."

"Told you that when?"

"When we were leaving the theater."

"After rehearsal."

"Yes."

"At which time you went home, and he went to the apartment on River Street."

"Yes. He used it as a sort of office."

"I see."

"After he moved in with me. He would go there periodically to work on the play. He was writing a play with Jerry Greenbaum."

"So I understand."

"*The Wench Is Dead.*"

"Christopher Marlowe," Carella said.

Andrea looked surprised.

"Do you think Mr. Greenbaum was there with him last night?" Carella asked.

"You would have to ask Mr. Greenbaum."

"We already have."

"Was he?"

"No."

"Then *he* couldn't have pushed Chuck out that window, could he?" Andrea said, and smiled.

"I guess not," Carella said. "But *someone* did. Because a sleeping man can't drag himself out of the bedroom and into the next room, you see."

"He could if he was only *half* asleep," Andrea said. "Maybe he took a Dalmane, as you say . . ."

"Which he may have got from your medicine chest that morning . . ."

"Well, I don't know whether he did or not . . ."

"But *if* he did."

"I only said he *might* have. I didn't follow him around to see if he was snitching sleeping pills from the medicine chest."

"Of course not."

"Miss Packer, I feel I should warn you," Bertinotti said.

"I'm only saying *if* he did," Andrea said, "as you seem to *think* he did."

"Well, it was in his blood," Carella said. "I was simply repeating what's in the toxicology report. But what you're suggesting is he may have been wandering around in this drugged state, and just *accidentally* . . ."

"Exactly."

"That's something I hadn't thought of," Carella said. "He could have taken the Dalmane . . ."

"Sure."

". . . and then was . . . well . . . walking around the apartment before he went to bed, and all of a sudden he got drowsy and just fell out the window."

"As an actress, I can see that happening," Andrea said.

"Pardon?" Carella said.

"A scene like that."

"Oh."

"It would play."

"Him falling out the window in a half-stupor, you mean?"

"Yes."

"Miss Packer," Bertinotti said, trying to warn her again that this smart-ass detective was closing in and she'd better watch her onions, "I think . . ."

"We know there was a woman in that apartment with him last night," Carella said.

"It wasn't me," Andrea said. "Anyway, how do you . . . ?"

"Miss Packer," Bertinotti said again, more sharply this time. "I think we . . ."

"We have vaginal stains," Carella said. "From the sheets on the bed."

Andrea looked at him.

"What I'd like to do," he said, "even though I'm certain we can do this under Miranda *without* a court order . . ."

"Do what?" Bertinotti asked at once.

"Have a vaginal smear taken, Counselor."

"You'd damn well *better* get a court order before you invade her privacy that way!"

"I intend to do that, sir."

"Good, go do it. Meanwhile, the questions are finished."

"Counselor," Carella said, "if Miss Packer wasn't in that bed with Mr. Madden last night, she's got nothing to worry about. But if we come up with a DNA match, then we've got her there with him before he went out that window. You might want to discuss this with her in private."

Bertinotti looked at her.

"Give us fifteen minutes alone," he said.

He was back in ten.

"Is there a D.A. on this case?" he asked.

Nellie Brand got uptown at two minutes past midnight. Officially it was Palm Sunday, but she wasn't dressed for church. They had caught her at a dinner party, and she was wearing her basic black and pearls with high-heeled black patent pumps. She apologized for her improbable appearance, talked to Carella to find out what they had, and then went in to talk to Andrea's lawyers.

Foley just sat there with his finger up his ass.

Bertinotti did all the bargaining for their client.

Nellie knew her evidence wasn't overwhelming, but she wasn't ready to let Bertinotti plead her down to a stroll in the park. The very fact that he was willing to bargain at all told her that Packer had been in Madden's apartment on the night he'd taken the plunge. But she knew she had nothing that really tied Packer to the Cassidy murder. Even so, she told Bertinotti she was going for Murder Two on *both* cases, under the theory that Packer had acted in concert with Madden on the Cassidy murder. Murder Two was an A felony that carried a lifetime sentence. Bertinotti knew she was being ridiculous, otherwise why were they here talking?

He told her he'd agree to Man One on the Madden case, if she forgot the Cassidy case entirely. She told him that was out of the question, the two cases were irrevocably linked, and if she couldn't wrap both, she wasn't going to deal at all. He reminded her that she already *had* somebody in jail for the Cassidy murder . . .

"Please, Counselor," she said. "You're not suggesting I send an innocent man to prison, are you?"

"Perish the thought," Bertinotti said.

Foley, the jackass, actually chuckled.

"I was merely positing the notion that perhaps the voracious appetite of the public for mystery, intrigue and revenge would be sated if you dropped the A felony on the earlier murder . . ."

"No way."

". . . and substituted for it a *B* felony, to wit Conspiracy to Commit."

"Eight and a third to twenty-five on each," Nellie said.

"I was thinking two to six on the conspiracy."

"No way. The max on both."

"Concurrently."

"Consecutively," Nellie said.

"I can't accept that."

"Then get your client ready for the stirrups."

"Mrs. Brand, she's twenty-one years old . . ."

"Right. She killed two people and you want her out when she's twenty-nine? Forget it. Let's roll the dice, and let a jury decide. Maybe you'll win. Maybe she *won't* have to spend the rest of her life in hell on a pair of A felony convictions. But take my deal, and she'll be out before she's forty."

Bertinotti thought about this for a moment.

"All right," he said at last. "I'll take the Bs. Eight and a third to twenty-five on each. Consecutively."

"We've got a deal."

"Let me talk to her."

"Then it's my turn," Nellie said.

The idea came to me right after Michelle got stabbed in the alley that night. First I thought it was too bad someone hadn't done the job properly because then the leading role in *Romance* would have been open, and who better to fill it than the *second* lead, right? Who better than me? Chuck and I were joking about it in bed that night, how unfortunate it had been, you know, that the stabber hadn't actually *killed* that bitch.

We'd been living together, Chuck and I . . .

Well, gee, it must've been more than a month by then. Was it that long? I think so, yes. Since before we even started rehearsals. We fell in love the minute we laid eyes on each other. I met him when I read for the part, stage managers do that all the time, read opposite whoever's trying out. It was so romantic. I couldn't take my eyes off him. I went to bed with him that same night, it was that kind of thing, a real *coup de foudre,* amazing. So romantic and sexy and *immediate,* do you know?

This was even before they called to say I had the part. I thought at first they meant the leading role, the starring role, because that's what I'd read for, but instead it was the *second* lead, what Freddie calls the Understudy in his play. Listen, I was happy to get *anything* at all, believe me, I would have taken one of the bit parts, moving furniture, whatever, playing a waitress or a reporter, one of the bit parts. It galled that someone like *Michelle* got the part, of course, but listen, that's the way it goes, sometimes a not very good actress gets lucky, she wasn't a terribly good actress, you know, I mean anyone can tell you that. Even *Josie* is better than she was. Josie Beales, I mean, who finally . . .

Boy, *that* was amazing, I have to tell you.

I never expected *that.*

I think it started out as just kidding around, Chuck and me. In bed. We'd just made love, I think, it was the night she'd got stabbed, we already knew she was all right and would be back at rehearsal the next day. Chuck was telling me how much better I was . . . as an *actress,* that is. He'd never been to *bed* with her, I'd have killed him, that's not what I'm saying, he wasn't comparing us as *lovers* or anything. Solely as actresses. He told me, in fact, that there'd been some kind of debate about who they should offer the part to, the leading role, the Actress, the three of them had talked it over, Morgenstern and Freddie and Ashley. And they decided to offer the part to Michelle, "Probably because she had bigger tits," Chuck said, and I said, "Oh *yeah,* you mean you noticed?" and we were clowning around like that when he said, "The part should really have gone to you, Andy," and we sort of got quiet for a while, and then he said, "It *would've* gone to you if that guy had succeeded tonight."

Well we talked about that for a while.

About whether I'd *really* have gotten the part if Michelle had actually got killed that night.

We decided I would have.

We decided I would have been the logical choice.

Decided, in fact, that I would *still* be the logical choice if anything happened to Michelle. If, for example, whoever had tried to kill her tonight came back and *really* did the job. We had no idea who'd stabbed her, we didn't *care* who'd stabbed her, we were just saying suppose he came back and stabbed her again, only this time it took.

Then I would get her part.

We were convinced I would get her part.

Which, of course, would make me a star.

Because of all the publicity already surrounding the play, you see. And all the publicity that would come if she actually *got* killed.

So . . .

We decided to do it.

And . . .

Well . . .

He went over there and did it.

Stabbed her.

Went over there with a knife under his jacket, and threw the knife down a sewer afterward. Nowhere near her building. She lived up in Diamondback, can you believe it? I'd be scared to death going home up there at night after rehearsal. I don't know where the knife is now. Where do sewers go? I know they don't empty into the river because that would be polluting the water, wouldn't it? But where *do* they go?

Wherever they go, that's where the knife is. It was a knife from my kitchen. A bread knife. He wrapped it in a towel and carried it under his jacket, this brown leather jacket he has. Stabbed her when she opened the door.

P.S., I didn't get the part.

They gave the part to Josie instead.

Listen, she's a very capable actress, I'm the first to admit that. But that's like comparing apples and oranges, isn't it? Josie hasn't had the *training* I had, she doesn't have the *experience* I have, she simply isn't in my *league*.

How the hell can you *figure* something like that?

Chuck said maybe she was sleeping with Morgenstern. Otherwise, why would they have passed *me* over . . .

And remember, they were considering giving the part to me in the first place, when they decided on Michelle instead . . .

Pass *me* over and give the part to her fucking *understudy*?

This was a B movie, am I right?

Giving the part to someone as inexperienced as Josie?

I *still* can't believe it.

Well . . .

I started worrying about a few things. And I started thinking about a few things, too. I probably wouldn't have *done* anything further . . . I mean, what the hell, a part is a part, you lose out on one part, there's always another part. So, honestly, I don't think I'd have done anything further, in *spite* of worrying about Chuck maybe cracking, maybe feeling remorse for what he'd done, maybe going to the police and confessing, who the hell knew *what* he might do? I mean, he kept telling me he loved me, would he have killed Michelle if he *didn't* love me? But romance is one thing and guilt is another, and I could tell this was beginning to eat at him, especially since it hadn't had the desired *effect*, we'd killed *one* bitch only to have *another* one take her place. So I was worried about him, yes, worried about whether he'd have the strength to see this thing through. Men can be so weak sometimes, even the strongest of them, physically strong, I mean, he was so big.

And I started thinking maybe we should go after *Josie* next, do to her what we'd done to Michelle because then they'd *have* to give me the part, wouldn't they? If Josie was out of the way? Wouldn't they *have* to give it to me? Who *else* could they give it to? The fucking cleaning lady at the theater?

And then I found the earring.

Josie's earring.

Do you believe in fate?

I absolutely believe in fate.

I found it on the sink counter in the ladies' room. At the theater. I almost gave it back to her. I knew it was hers, of course, I'd seen her wearing them before. Almost gave it back. Almost missed the clear *signal* that earring was sending me. That earring was telling me what I had to do next, you see. It was telling me how to get the part I should have had to begin with, and it was *also* telling me how I could quit worrying about Chuck maybe cracking and involving me in a murder that was his idea, after all, he was the one who first suggested it, you can believe that or not, I don't care.

I figured if I could . . .

If I could make it look like someone had committed suicide, you see . . .

Well, make it look as if *Chuck* had committed suicide, actually . . .

Leave a suicide note and all.

Type up a suicide note.

Make it seem as if he was remorseful for having killed Michelle, but then . . .

And this was the good part.

Make it look as if the suicide had been *faked,* the suicide was really a *murder,* do you see? Someone had *killed* him and tried to make it *look* like a suicide, I'm sure you see a lot of that, I've been in a dozen plays where that happened. In fact, I was *counting* on your looking for something like that, a fake suicide. I was *counting* on you finding the earring I left under the bed, *Josie's* earring. I was *counting* on you figuring she was the one who'd been there, she was the one who'd made love to him.

We made such good love that night.

I surprised him there.

Knocked on the door. Hi, Chuck.

He looked so handsome.

We made such good love.

I'd like a drink, I told him afterwards. No, don't get up, I'll make them. I mixed them in the kitchen, dropped two Dalmanes into his. Here's to us, darling, here's to our future. He was out like a light ten minutes later. I rolled him off the bed and dragged him to the bedroom window, but the damn thing was sealed shut around the air conditioner, so I had to drag him all the way into the living room, he was so big, so heavy. I left him on the floor under the window while I did what I had to do. I was still naked. I left the glasses where they were. A woman there, right? Put away the bottle of Scotch. Typed up the note. Still naked. Tried not to make it too *specific* because I wanted you to figure out some things for yourself. If it looked *too* phony, you'd begin to think it was *supposed* to look phony, that someone was trying to *make* it look phony. I wiped off everything I'd touched, even the earring. I was going to leave the earring in plain sight, but then I thought *that* might seem too obvious, too, so I put it

under the bed. Not too *far* under it. I wanted it to be found.
I wanted you to think she'd dropped it on the floor, Josie,
and it had just rolled under the bed, and there it was. While
I was getting dressed, I couldn't find my panties, he'd tossed
them across the room someplace. I almost panicked. I found
them hanging on one of the dresser knobs. I'd been searching
all over the floor, and there they were hanging on this knob.
Can you imagine the hundred-to-one shot that was? Chuck
throwing them across the room and them landing on a knob?
The things that happen.

Getting him out the window was the hard part.

He was so heavy. Such a big man.

I propped him up and sort of draped his arms over the sill,
and then I tried hoisting him up over it. I was already dressed
and beginning to sweat, struggling to lift him. I wanted to
leave the apartment the minute I got him out the window, run
down the back stairs, get away from the building in what I
hoped would be a lot of confusion outside. But I was beginning
to panic again because I wasn't sure I could manage it, it was
taking all my strength just to get his *chest* up onto the sill.
And then all at once I . . . I don't know what it was . . . I
suddenly seemed so much stronger, maybe it was an adrena-
line rush or something, I don't know, but all at once I was
lifting him and . . . and he was suddenly weightless . . . falling
away from my hands . . . out and . . . and gone. Just gone.

All the way home, I kept praying you'd find the earring
and think Josie was the one who'd killed him.

Because then you'd go get her.

And I'd get the part.

You didn't see any palm trees growing in this city except
in the tropical-bird buildings of the Grover Park and Riverhead

zoos, and in several of the indoor buildings at the Calm's Point Botanical Gardens. This city was no garden spot. But on Palm Sunday, you'd think the plant was indigenous to the area.

Half the Christians who carried leaves of the stuff to church that Sunday didn't know that the day celebrated Jesus' triumphal entry into Jerusalem. All they knew was that the priest would bless the frond and then they would carry it home and fashion it into a little cross which could be pinned to a lapel or a collar. Some of the palm crosses were quite elegant with fancy little serrated tips on the post and transverse pieces.

Mark Carella wanted to know why his father hadn't made a little cross for *him,* the way all the other kids' fathers had made for *their* sons. Carella explained that he was no longer a practicing Catholic. April, overhearing the conversation Carella was having with her twin brother, announced that she wanted to become a rabbi when she grew up. Carella said that was fine with him.

Mark wanted to know why they had to go to Grandma's house two weeks in a row. They were going there next Sunday for Easter, so why'd they have to go today, too?

"Grandma's always so gloomy nowadays," he said.

This was a true observation.

Carella took him aside and told him he had to be a little more patient with Grandma until she was able to adjust to Grandpa being dead. Mark wanted to know when that would be. Mark was ten years old. How did you explain to a ten-year-old that it took time for a woman to adjust to the traumatic death of her husband?

"I miss the way Grandma used to be," Mark said.

Which was another true observation.

Carella suddenly wondered if the man who'd shot and killed his father realized that he'd effectively killed his mother, too.

"Why don't you tell her?" he said. "That you miss her?"

"She'll cry," Mark said.

"Maybe not."

"She always cries now."

"I cry, too, honey," Carella said.

Mark looked at him.

"I do," Carella said.

"Why'd that son of a bitch have to kill him?" Mark said.

When Rosa Lee Cooke was coming along in Alabama, there weren't any white restaurants colored folk could go eat in. The restaurant Sharyn took her to today was thronged with white people. Crane her neck hard as she could, Rosa Lee could see only one other black family there. Black man and his lighter-colored wife, three children all dressed in their Palm Sunday best. Rosa Lee herself was wearing a tailored suit the color of her own walnut complexion; Sharyn had taken her shopping for it as a birthday gift. She was also wearing a bonnet she'd bought for herself, trimmed with tiny yellow flowers. Wouldn't be Easter till *next* Sunday, but she couldn't resist previewing it today.

She wasn't a drinking woman, a little sip of sweet wine every now and again. But today was the day Jesus had marched into Jerusalem with his head held high, and she felt a little drink in celebration might not be remiss. So when Sharyn asked if she'd like a cocktail before lunch, she said she wouldn't mind a Bloody Mary.

Rosa Lee had been thirteen when Sharyn was born, and now—at the age of fifty-three—the women truly looked more like sisters than they did mother and daughter, a compliment both had heard so often they were now sick to death of it. Same color eyes, same color skin, same smooth complexion, but Sharyn's hair was trimmed close to her head whereas her mother's was shiny with tight little curls springing from below the brim of her fancy hat.

They clinked glasses and drank.

A white man at a nearby table was openly admiring them. Rosa Lee noticed this, and turned her eyes away, just like she'd done in the South when she was a little girl. No sense inviting rape, she'd been taught back then, and it had stuck with her all her life. Wasn't a white man on earth could be trusted. Black man sees Rodney King getting beat by white cops on television, the black man says, "So what's new? This's been going on all along, only difference is we finally got *pictures* of it." *White* man sees Rodney King getting beat on television, he says, "Oh, how terrible, those cops are *beating* that poor black man," as if this was something didn't happen every day of the week in every city in America, white cops beating on a black man. Or messing with a black woman. Putting their hands inside a black woman's blouse. Doing even worse things to a black woman, touching her where they had no right touching, just because she was in their custody.

"I called last night, y'know," she said. "Wanted to make sure you said ten o'clock for church."

"Yes, I got the message," Sharyn said.

"So why didn't you call back?"

"I got in late. I called this morning, soon as I . . ."

"Where were you?"

"Out."

"Who with?"

"You don't know him."

"Where'd you go?"

"Dinner."

"Where?"

"In the Quarter."

"Dangerous down there. You shouldn't be going down there at night."

"The *Quarter*? It's mostly gay, Mom."

"Not all of it's gay. There're places in the Quarter a person could get hurt."

"Well, not where we were."

"Where were you?"

"A restaurant called Petruccio's."

"Italian?"

"Yes."

"Too much garlic in Italian food," Rosa Lee said. "Why'd you pick an Italian place?"

"*He* picked it."

"Who's he?"

"Man named Jamie Hudson."

"I don't know him. Do I know him?"

"No, Mom."

"How'd you meet him?"

"At the hospital."

"He a doctor?"

"Yes."

"That's good. You staying home tonight?"

"Actually, I've got another date."

"Tomorrow's a workday, you should stay home tonight, get your rest. How you gonna help sick people, you runnin aroun all the time?"

"It'll be an early night," Sharyn said.

"Where you going?"

"For Chinese food."

"I like Chinese," her mother said. "Who with? This doctor again?"

"No, another man."

"What's *his* name?"

Sharyn hesitated.

"Bert Kling," she said.

"Bert *what*?"

"Kling."

"What kind of name is that?" her mother said.

"It's just a name," Sharyn said.

"That's some kind of name, all right. How do you spell that name?"

"With a K."

"K-L-I-N-G?"

"Yes."

"That's some kind of name."

"Good afternoon, ladies," the waiter said, materializing suddenly at their table. "May I bring you some menus?"

"Yes, thank you, please," Rosa Lee said. "I'm so *hungry* all at once, aren't you, Shaar?"

Shaar.

She had the sudden impulse to tell her mother that Bert Kling was a white man.

She squashed it like a bug.

Thieves knew all about coincidence.

They knew that if they were holding up a mom-and-pop grocery store at the same time a blue-and-white rolled by, that was coincidence and they were looking at twenty in the slammer.

Cops knew about coincidence, too.

They knew the dictionary definitions of coincidence by heart: "To occupy the same position simultaneously."

Or: "To happen at the same time or during the same period."

Cops knew that ninety-four percent of the people who got killed in this fair nation of ours got killed because they *happened* to be occupying the same position simultaneously as a person with a gun or a knife or a baseball bat. To put it yet another way, they *happened* to be at the same time or during the same period where something terrible was about to occur, like having their brains bashed out or their livers surgically removed.

Cops believed that every encounter on the face of the earth was coincidental.

Take it or leave it.

Bert Kling happened to be sitting in a booth with two beautiful black women in a restaurant called Pagoda Palace at nine-fifteen that night, coincidentally alone with them because Arthur Brown had excused himself not a minute earlier to go to the men's room.

It was coincidental that two white men were sitting in the booth opposite theirs.

It was further coincidental that two black men walked into the restaurant at that moment in time and began following the headwaiter to a booth just beyond theirs.

All coincidence.

Then again, Kling wouldn't have been sitting here with Sharyn Cooke if a hostage cop named Georgia Mowbry hadn't got shot in the eye on the twenty-ninth of March, an event that had caused him and Sharyn to meet coincidentally the very next morning. Georgia getting shot had been a coincidence in itself; she'd just been standing there in the hallway, talking to the assigned hostage cop, when the door to the apartment opened and the guy inside started shooting.

Cops didn't want to hear from coincidence.

Cops knew that shit happened.

Nothing happened for a minute or so.

The headwaiter seated the two black men, and asked if they'd care for something to drink, and the two men respectively ordered a Scotch on the rocks and a Corona and lime, and the headwaiter padded away. The man facing the front door—and coincidentally the table at which Kling sat across from two black women—glanced in their direction, and then said something to his friend, and then stood up immediately and walked to where Kling was sitting with his elbows on the table, smiling, in the middle of a sentence.

What he was saying was that he'd had the feeling all through the Packer Q&A that the actress thought she was playing a role on television.

"I had the feeling . . ."

"This dude bothering you?" the man said.

Last Saturday's race riots were still on everyone's mind. Lots of people had died in Grover Park last Saturday. Blacks and whites. The memory of this was part of the equation. The memory was part of this coincidental happening that was about to evolve at a frighteningly fast pace.

"Everything's cool, man," Caroline said.

She'd been married to Arthur Brown for a good long time now, and she was used to his size and his authority, used to feeling protected when he was around, not only because he was a cop but also because he was a loving, caring husband. But she didn't for a moment feel threatened in any way when the black man appeared at their table. In fact, she figured the man thought he was being a Good Samaritan, two black women sitting alone here at a table, honkie sits down across from them, intruding on their space, the brother was making sure everything was all right.

But he wasn't going away.

"It's cool, really," she said, and smiled in dismissal.

"Ain't enough white women in here for you?" the man asked Kling.

"These are friends of mine," Kling said.

"You hear whut I ast you?" the man said.

"It's okay, we're . . ."

"*Hey!*" one of the white men in the booth across from them yelled. "He told you he *knows* them. Fuck off."

The black man turned. His friend was already coming out of the booth up the aisle. It was starting.

Kling didn't know who threw the first punch. It didn't really matter. He knew only that suddenly the two white guys and the two black guys were tangling, and he saw a gun in somebody's hand—too damn many *guns* in this city, in this country, in this world—and he shouted "Police! Drop the gun!" and that was when he spotted Brown coming out of the men's room at the far end of the restaurant and breaking into a run the moment he realized what was happening.

Sharyn was a cop, and she knew what to do when cops were in a situation where there was a wild gun on the scene, *two* wild guns as she now saw, one in the hand of a black man, the other in the hand of a white man, this was going to be last Saturday all over again! She scrambled over the low green-lacquered wall that divided their booth from the one adjoining it, long legs flashing, over and into the other booth where a white couple was digging into a steaming bowl of moo goo gai pan, "Sorry," she mumbled, "sorry," and ran right over them and through them, her high heels digging into the green Naugahyde seat, and dropped into the aisle on the other side, and sprinted to the front of the restaurant and called in a 10-13 from a phone hanging on the wall alongside the cigarette machine.

When Brown reached the booth, he saw Caroline standing there with one of her high-heeled shoes in her hand, holding it like a hammer, ready to hit anyone who came anywhere near her, white *or* black. Brown had drawn his pistol even before he saw the pair of wild guns on the scene, but that was because he'd seen Kling's gun already in his hand, and he knew he wouldn't have unholstered it without first considering the guidelines. Both detectives were mindful of the fact that the place was packed and that an exchange of gunfire was inadvisable, but the white man and the black man facing off with guns bigger than they were didn't have any guidelines to worry about, and they sure as hell looked as if they were intent on shooting to kill at any moment now. Brown was bigger than Kling or any of the other men, and he could yell louder than anybody in this city. He shouted at the top of his lungs that he was a police officer and that if everybody didn't drop all those goddamn guns in the next ten seconds he was going to break some mighty hard heads here.

It was over as soon as it started.

Everybody had calmed down and everything was under control by the time the six radio cars squealed into the curb outside in response to Sharyn's call.

Coincidentally, the white man who'd told the brother to fuck off was wanted for armed robbery in the state of Arizona.

In bed that night, he asked her what she'd thought of the evening.

"The food or the floor show?" she asked.

"The company," he said.

"I've always liked Bert," she said. "And I liked her a lot, too."

"You think it'll work?" Brown asked.

"I hope so," Caroline said.

They undressed each other in the dark.

They could have been white and white, or black and black, or anything and anything for that matter, because they could not see each other in the dark. Kissing in the dark, standing inches apart from each other, they undid buttons and lowered zippers until at last they were naked in the dark, pressed against each other in the dark, hard against her, soft against him, touching, feeling, blind in the dark. In the dark, her skin was silken smooth, it felt like polished alabaster. In the dark, his skin was silken smooth, it felt like polished ebony in the dark.

They moved to the bed at last, and lay side by side in the dark together, kissing, touching, exploring in the dark, lips against lips, flesh against flesh, their ardor heightened by what had happened earlier tonight, their desire fueled by a desperate need to demonstrate that it could be otherwise, it did not have to be *that* way, it could be *this* way, hearts beating together in the dark.

He entered her in the dark and felt her enfolding him and enclosing him, murmuring softly against his lips as he thrust more deeply into her, gently in the dark, withdrawing again and moving into her again, hips rising to meet each thrust, wet and warm in the dark, his measured steady rhythm drawing from her a measured steady response until together they learned a wilder beat, found together a greater freedom, discovered together a riff that joined them in the dark, and rushed them thunderously toward a farther shore where they shattered against each other in the dark and clung to each other like children.

Later, in the light, they looked at each other.

He was still white.

She was still black.

"Let's give it an honest shot," she said.

"Let's," he said.

By the year 2000, 2 out of 3 Americans could be illiterate.

It's true.

Today, 75 million adults… about one American in three, can't read adequately. And by the year 2000, U.S. News & World Report envisions an America with a literacy rate of only 30%.

Before that America comes to be, you can stop it… by joining the fight against illiteracy today.

Call the Coalition for Literacy at toll-free **1-800-228-8813** and volunteer.

Volunteer Against Illiteracy. The only degree you need is a degree of caring.

Ad Council Coalition for Literacy

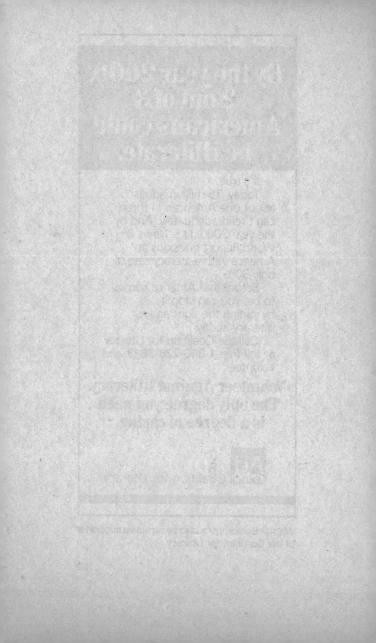